Etched in Starlight

Hannah's Heirloom ~ Prequel

Rosie Chapel

First printing 2016
ISBN: 978-0-9954303-1-0

Ulfire Pty. Ltd.
P.O. Box 1481
South Perth
WA 6951
Australia

www.rosiechapel.com

Cover artwork by H.E. Rodgers

This book is dedicated to
my amazing family ~ with all my love

Acknowledgements
To Helen ~ my heartfelt thanks for your tireless work on
my book covers.
Your ability to create an image that captures the essence of
a story is nothing short of remarkable.

To Janet, Mark, Marie and Jess ~
my profound gratitude for your invaluable assistance during
the editing process.
Your patience and support is greatly appreciated

Author's Note

While researching this book, a couple of things occurred, which caused that whole 'shiver down the spine' sensation. The first was when I was trying to come up with a name for Maxentius' love interest in Armenia. The woman's name needed to be traditionally Armenian and I spent a long time searching for one that I felt suited the character, small though her part is. I came upon 'Narineh' by accident and loved the way it sounded; to me it hinted at beauty and mystery. When I discovered that it meant pomegranate or fire, I knew I had to use it!

The second happened while at a recent archaeology lecture. One of the slides was of a tablet relating to treatment being dispensed to soldiers on Masada. The tablet read thus; -

Doc. Masada 723

List of hospital supplies
... bandage ...
For [...]us, bandage
For ...]elius, laundered (fine?) bandage
The sick
Date? For the sick (in care) of (?) Nicostratus
For ...]lius, sick, eating oil, 1 ounce (?)
For Valerius, sick, eating oil, 1 ounce
For ..., sick
For ..., sick, eating oil, 2 ounces

As you can see, the name of one of the soldier's listed is Valerius. Coincidence? I think not.

Etched in Starlight

Hannah's Heirloom ~ Prequel

Prologue

The pain was unbearable, Lucius Maxentius Valerius could hardly breathe and his head was pounding. He tried to move but his limbs refused to respond. Where was he? As he lay on the cold floor, memories flooded into his mind. An ambush; the sound of clashing weapons; the screams of his men; the smell of blood. He recalled being set upon by several bandits who, intent on cutting him down, had backed him along a corridor. He had thought that they would kill him, for he had no chance of escape. How on earth had they come upon this citadel unawares? What had happened to the men on the watchtowers? How had they missed this horde of unruly insurgents?

Accepting that he would die in this savage wilderness, Maxentius had experienced a fleeting moment of sadness knowing that he would never see his mother and sister again. That all they would have to remember him by would be a formal missive stating that he died defending Masada.

Then relief as a familiar voice, bawling curses, distracted the bandits. Screaming that they'd better get off his commander or they'd be sorry, the voice belonged to Quintus Sergius Crispus; a young man who had only been on the outpost for a few months. Yet even in so short a time Sergius had proven himself a loyal and competent soldier. Far more so than many of the other men under Maxentius' charge, most of whom were insubordinate and fractious; disillusioned with the army and fed up with guarding an outpost in the middle of a desert, miles from what they considered to be civilisation.

Sergius was slashing at everyone who moved and slowly, very slowly, was beating them back. Metal against metal, metal against flesh, these sounds would haunt the exhausted man for days. As a soldier, of a little more than twenty and six years, Maxentius had already seen countless battles. He felt that he was too young to be in charge of a garrison, but his actions in Armenia and Parthia had been commended and his superiors deemed him a solid and reliable leader. Now his soldiers were under attack, he was unable to defend himself, never mind the garrison and he had no clue how many had been injured or worse.

This brief respite had given Maxentius and his second in command, Gnaeus Marcus Aelianus — who had followed Sergius into the corridor — the break required to beat back their assailants. Sergius, despite his berserker strike, was wounded and leaning against a wall, a vicious gash across his abdomen. He dropped his gladius, the sword clattering onto the tiles and blood from the blade splattering dark red across the pristine floor. While Marcus ensured that the last of their attackers would not be ambushing anyone ever again, Maxentius rushed over to Sergius, catching his subordinate as he slithered down the wall.

All around them an eerie silence descended. It was as though they were the only three left alive on this citadel. Marcus came to help his commander with Sergius, the two of them virtually carrying their injured comrade along the corridor, into the first room they came to. It was sparsely furnished — one of the rooms they had rarely used.

A rug lay over the geometric black and white tiles; a large wooden cupboard stood against one wall with an empty shelf above it, and against the opposite wall stood two ornately designed chairs. A few large baskets were stacked near the doorway, but that was all. The room was airy and quite spacious; it was also quiet and away from the main entrance to the palace. Maxentius hoped that if they managed to remain undiscovered, they might have a slim chance of escape, once Sergius had rested.

He heard an odd sound and glanced towards the doorway. A strange woman stood in the shadows, half-hidden against the frame. She was wearing the most peculiar attire, nothing he'd seen before. Absently, he wondered whether it was a new fashion for Hebrew women. He held her gaze — she had the most startlingly green eyes — and tried to convey his desperation without words. He fancied that she nodded and then she was gone. It happened so quickly, he wasn't sure whether he'd really seen her or she was a figment of his fevered imagination.

Shaking his head to dismiss such nonsense, Maxentius had turned his attention back to Sergius. The soldier was failing rapidly, his breathing coming in sharp bursts, his jaw clenched in agony. Maxentius muttered that they had to try to stem the bleeding. Wrenching open the doors of the cupboard, he noticed a pile of what appeared to be clean cloths stored inside. Grabbing a handful, he pressed them against the gash, holding them firmly in place. Gently lying Sergius on one of the rugs, he motioned Marcus to fetch some more cloths, which he bundled together to form a pillow of sorts, keeping Sergius' head slightly raised.

That was all of which Maxentius had been capable. He collapsed against the wall, gasping for breath, his own injuries sapping what little strength he had left. Marcus had not fared much better; he was bleeding from several wounds all over his upper torso. Unless their attackers had taken what they'd come for and fled; or by some miracle Marcus and he could carry Sergius unnoticed, to the side gate in the western wall just beyond the administration building, they were doomed.

The two men chatted desultorily for a little while, listening for the footfalls, which would herald an approach, but all remained quiet. The only sounds were their own breathing and Sergius' occasional moans. Their comrade was deeply unconscious and neither man had enough knowledge of healing to help him. Maxentius had never felt so impotent — so much for being capable enough to command a garrison.

The next little while was a blur, all three men slipped in and out of varying degrees of consciousness and Maxentius was astonished that Sergius had survived that first night. On a shelf in the adjacent room, he had found a flagon of water and a few small bowls, but knew that any food was stored in the kitchens, across the courtyard, and he did not dare risk trying to get there and back unobserved.

Occasionally they heard footsteps and muted chatter from distant voices, but for some reason, no one came into the room where they lay. The days merged into one, Maxentius did what he could to keep Sergius' wound clean. Rinsing a piece of cloth in the small amount of water they had left, he wiped away any pus or blood that had congealed and then covered the gash with clean cloths. Beyond that, he could do nothing. Eventually, owing to loss of blood, lack of any decent sustenance and utter exhaustion, all three fell into a stupor.

Unbeknownst to them, a young woman had decided that she would quite like to use a couple of the rooms off the courtyard as her own quarters. They were away from those that the rebels had commandeered yet conveniently close to the laundry and kitchens. She thought to use one to store all her medicines and the other as a bedchamber.

She was busy caring for a large number of Zealots, wounded when they attacked the garrison. Appalled at how many had died before she could help them and frustrated at such a shocking waste of life for the sake of a few Roman swords, the young woman was determined that none of those she was treating would die also. She had spent hours mixing salves, balms and ointments, which she applied to a whole host of injuries. She hoped that her remedies would prevent any infection, concealed deep within, from all the dust and dirt that had been kicked up in the melee.

As she was checking the rooms surrounding the courtyard, she noticed a large pool of what she immediately recognised to be dried blood marring the tiled walkway, as well as a sword lying against the wall. Wary now, for she was certain that all the Zealots were accounted for and had been assured that no Roman remained on the plateau, she continued her search, unsure about who or what had bled so profusely, suddenly coming across the room where the three men lay. Stifling a scream and with complete disregard for her own safety, she fell on her knees and began to examine the one closest to the door. Hastily checking over all three, she then flew along to the makeshift office where her brother was ensconced.

"Aharon, please come, there are three badly wounded men. I need you to help me get them into proper cots." Her brother gaped at her in shock.

"Who are they?"

"I have no idea, just three soldiers." She shrugged. To her it did not matter who they were, she just knew they needed her skills or they would die. Although dubious as to whether any of them had a chance, she wasn't letting them go without a fight.

"If they are Romans, sister, I will call Simeon and Malachi and we will finish them."

"No!" Her reply was sharper than she intended and she softened her tone, pleading, "Aharon, it is three days since our men ambushed this rock. I know what damage the Romans inflicted upon our people. I have spent hours trying to heal them and yet I refuse to stand aside and let you kill three unarmed men in cold blood. That is murder and against our laws." She took a breath "You cannot."

Her brother stared at her for long moments, debating whether it was worth arguing. She would never forgive him if he followed through with his threat and he really wasn't up to dealing with her ire. His sister watched his face; desperately hoping her brother would acquiesce to her demand. She knew the second he'd decided and flung her arms around him.

"Thank you, Aharon! Oh thank you so much."

"Do not make me regret this; even wounded, these men are dangerous."

"Trust me, my brother, this is one of the best decisions you have ever made." She kissed him on the cheek and shot off in the direction from which she had come, yelling out for help to move three pallets into the room.

Although perturbed, Aharon grinned to himself, his sister was utterly irrepressible. Persuading Hannah to accompany them to Masada was a responsibility that he had not taken lightly, but there was no one left in Jerusalem to watch over her and the unrest within the city was enough of a concern that he could not countenance leaving Hannah there on her own. Shaking his head he followed slowly after her, wanting to see these men for himself.

Entering the room, Aharon could tell, even with no medical experience, that all three were seriously ill and one was much worse than the other two. He bit his lip, uncertain whether he should share his opinion with Hannah; however she spun around as he walked through the door, telling him very quietly that one of them was unlikely to survive, but that she wanted to do everything she could for him, for all three of them.

"If nothing else, Aharon, I can ease his pain, so if we do lose him, his death will be less agonising." Hannah's riotous chestnut curls were falling out of her tidy plait and her elfin face — usually so bright — was marred by a frown as she concentrated on what she needed to do. Simeon and Malachi had brought in three cots and she was covering them with soft blankets and double folding a sheet over a lump of straw that she had fashioned into a pillow.

"Just have a care, my sister. Please have a care." Aharon pressed her arm and she nodded abstractedly, her mind focused on the task in front of her. Aharon left her to it, making a mental note to tell his wife what her friend was doing.

Hannah bustled about, tucking clean fresh sheets over the blankets. Then, carefully, her two assistants lifted each man onto a cot. Covering all three with yet another sheet and one more blanket, she began to prepare her remedies. Salt dissolved in a bowl of water, a few drops of myrrh and frankincense added, to help fight the infection. A batch of the salve she had been using on the other injured men would be suitable too. Then she poured a small measure of the poppy juice into a flagon of diluted wine and honey, to help dull their pain.

Trembling a little, she lifted the tunic of the man closest to the door and nearly vomited. The gash was horrendous. She could not understand how he still lived; the wound was stinking, oozing with a greenish, yellow pus and blood. She gritted her teeth, swallowed and taking short shallow breaths began to clean it. It took some time, for it was long and deep and some of the skin had to be cut away as it was too shredded ever to heal. The man never stirred, he was barely breathing and his heartbeat was little more than the fluttering of a bird's wing.

Eventually, satisfied that she had cleaned the wound thoroughly, she pushed the salve in as far as possible and then covered it with a piece of cloth soaked in the same mixture. Spying several other injuries, she cleaned them all, adding more salve, making sure the bindings were not too tight, just enough to stop the salve soaked cloths from slipping off.

Washing her hands, Hannah moved onto the next man, repeating her actions, checking every cut, nick and slash. The young man was riddled with them, some deep, some superficial. The woman coated all with salve, bandaging everything neatly. Finally, only one man remained; he looked to be older than the other two, although not by much.

His tunic was smeared with blood, but Hannah surmised that some of it might well be that of his comrade's. He had a considerable number of nasty lacerations, but it was his chest that bothered her. His breathing seemed laboured and the colour of his skin wasn't normal. Unsure exactly what was going on, she cleaned his cuts, bandaging those that required it and decided to try massaging some arnica into his chest. It could do no harm and if there was bruising, this particular ointment should reduce it somewhat. As she completed her ministrations, he regained consciousness, his eyes locking with hers. For a moment their dark emerald depths mesmerised her. His face registered confusion and fear and he made to sit up, but she pushed him back with a gentle hand.

The pain was unbearable, Maxentius could hardly breathe and his head was pounding. He tried to move but his limbs refused to respond. He stared at the woman, who took his hand and spoke in gentle tones —

"I do not know whether you can understand me, but I am here to help you." He looked at her steadily and inclined his head slightly. She smiled and pointed to herself.

"My name is Hannah."

Chapter One

Eight years earlier ~ Rome

A young man strode along the street, head held high, arms swinging by his sides. He was tall with a muscular build, dark haired and, unusually for a Roman, green eyed. It was a sunny day, but not too warm and a gentle breeze kept the air fresh. He was feeling particularly satisfied with himself as he had just been to swear his oath of allegiance to the Roman Army. He was no longer answerable to anyone else save his general.

The young man's name was Lucius Maxentius Valerius and he was ten and eight years old.

Maxentius had been ordered to present himself at the docks on the Tiber, three days hence at the first hour. From there, a vessel would ferry him and his fellow recruits to the port at Ostia where they would board a troop carrier destined for Antioch. From Antioch, their journey would take them overland into the Roman client kingdom of Armenia, where they would combine with forces led by a formidable general named Gnaeus Domitius Corbulo.

Armenia acted as a buffer state between the two mighty empires of Rome and Parthia with territory constantly being won and lost by both sides and, recently, Parthia had installed their own candidate on the Armenian throne. Occurring at the same time that Nero became Emperor, the young ruler had reacted immediately sending in Corbulo. Protracted negotiations had proved fruitless and, never one to sit back and be walked all over, Corbulo had successfully ousted the Parthians. This was only a temporary fix however, as the threat remained. Roman troops had continued to protect the frontier until Tiridates, current king of Armenia, saw reason and renounced Parthia, pledging allegiance to Nero and Rome.

Parthia had long been a thorn in Rome's side. A little over a century previously, Rome had sought to conquer the kingdom and plunder its riches. Unusually for Rome, they had underestimated their enemy. Incompetence, unheeded advice and traitorous informants led to the worst Roman defeat since their catastrophic loss to Hannibal. There was absolutely no way that Nero was going to allow history to repeat itself.

Maxentius knew all of this and had no idea what lay ahead, but he was happy with his choice. The first member of his family to enter the military, he was conscious that his father did not approve, preferring that his son follow him into what he considered to be, the less perilous life of politics. This career path held no interest for Maxentius and he recognised that danger could come from anywhere, often the most unexpected of places.

His training had lasted for several months and he was accomplished in all the disciplines required of a Roman soldier, including marching, combat preparation, battlefield tactics, equipment care and horse riding. He was fitter than he had ever been and, his superiors felt him more than ready for a life in the military.

Arriving home, Maxentius called for his mother as he strolled through the atrium. He found her relaxing in the garden with a group of her friends, no doubt enjoying a good gossip. He went over to her, kissing her on the cheek, in complete disregard of Roman etiquette. Claudia Valeria ginned up at her handsome son and asked how everything had gone.

"It is done, I leave in three days." She looked rather shocked, not expecting their separation to be so sudden, but made no comment other than to congratulate him. He nodded to the women and took his leave, remarking that he was going to say goodbye to a couple of his own friends who lived nearby.

"Don't be late, Maxentius," his mother warned. "I intend to have a private family meal tonight; it may be the last chance we get." He smiled at her and promised, farewelling his mother's coterie and making good his getaway before they all started asking him awkward questions about girls and marriage. One in particular, had made it quite clear that she would be delighted if he were to wed her elder daughter. While, the girl was perfectly lovely, Maxentius had no such intentions and, was thankful that soldiers were not permitted to marry, providing him with a legitimate excuse and without hurting anyone unnecessarily.

Breathing a sigh of relief, he strolled the short distance along the street to the house where lived Servius Arrius Calvus, one of his closest friends. Invited to wait by the impluvium, Maxentius glanced around, contemplating how much of his life had been spent in this house. The two had known each other since childhood, their parents being great friends. In fact, it was a badly kept secret that Arrius' older brother Julius and Maxentius' younger sister Antonia had been spending more than a little time together. It would be a favourable union if all parties agreed, but Antonia was only sixteen and although many of her friends had married, Claudia did not feel her youngest child quite ready.

While Maxentius was ruminating on this, Arrius loped in. The same height as Maxentius, but rake thin and his scruffy tunic covered in paint, hung off him. Arrius hadn't quite decided what he wanted to do with his life, so he spent his days painting frescoes for whoever would pay him. At the moment, he was refreshing some of the rooms in his own home as a way of thanking his parents for putting up with him. The two men greeted each other and Arrius asked whether it was now official; Maxentius nodded and the two fell into lively discussion about the journey and what to expect as a soldier.

Shortly thereafter, the third member of their group, Aulus Livius Maro arrived. These three, who had been inseparable for years suddenly realised their friendship would never be the same and that in all likelihood Arrius and Livius would never see Maxentius again. Tacitly agreeing not to mention this, they spent the next couple of hours talking about how exciting a life in the army would be, imagining all the things Maxentius might get to see and do. Of course, being young and therefore invincible, they ignored the realities of injury, captivity or death.

Too soon, Maxentius had to say goodbye. They did not drag it out, simply clasped arms and nodded, each going off in their own direction. Maxentius did not look back, but found the farewell to be harder than he had expected. Arriving home, he hurried into his bedroom to freshen up and change his clothes, before going along to the triclinium for dinner.

True to Claudia's word, only his family were present. As they ate, the four of them chattered about what Maxentius would need to take with him — very little — and what to do with the things he left behind — throw them out — something his mother refused to sanction. At the end of the meal, Claudia slipped away, returning with a small cloth bag, which she handed to her son.

"In honour of your acceptance into the Roman Army, I would like you to have this token." Maxentius dug into the bag and pulled out a strange clasp. It was a large ruby, not quite a teardrop, not quite an oval, something in between, nestled in a setting of burnished gold, with a sturdy pin at the back. The setting itself was most unusual and, although rather intricate, was too solidly made ever to be mistaken for a woman's gem.

Claudia watched her son's face as he rolled it around in his hand, the clasp was quite heavy and would hold a cloak securely.

"Your father gifted me the stone on his return from Hispania. I had the setting fashioned after a soldier's helmet. One of the major flamines blessed it; I hope it will bring you good fortune and keep you safe."

Maxentius stared at the clasp, its ruby depths seemed to glow, so rich was the colour. He put his hand on his heart.

"Thank you, my mother, I will treasure it." Silence fell across the room, each lost in thought until his father, clearing his throat, rather gruffly called for more wine and the moment was gone. They moved onto lighter topics, the rest of the evening passing in a flurry of chatter and laughter and it was late before they retired to bed.

Maxentius stood at his window for a long time, staring up at the night sky. The stars were out in abundance; he pondered the enormity of the world and how far across it he would be travelling. Then, brushing aside such whimsy, he closed the shutters and got into bed, asleep within minutes.

The next two days went by in a flash; Claudia expected him to say goodbye to every last one of their friends — a considerable number — and everything he was taking had to be washed and packed. In addition to the clothes he travelled in, he could include a few extra items. Then there was the plethora of equipment, along with miscellaneous bits and pieces — all essentials, but when put together weighed about sixty librae — or pounds. Taking more clothes only added to this weight and, despite his mother's protestations to the contrary, was unnecessary.

Fortunately, all soldiers were provided with a wooden cross frame on which everything could be tied. Although the pack was heavy, the soldiers slung their shields across their backs when marching and were able to balance the frame on top thus distributing the load. It was a minimal existence but Maxentius felt it rather freeing, if not a tad heavy. At least while on board the troop ship, his pack would be stored away until they disembarked at Antioch.

The third day dawned with a slight chill in the air and a damp mist clung to the ground, which seemed to fit the mood of parting. His family stood at the doorway and waved him off, their goodbyes already said. His mother and sister were biting their lips not to cry and his father's jaw was clamped tightly shut. He turned once, raising his hand in farewell and then hurried along the street, breathing a small sigh of relief when he was out of sight. He hated upsetting his family, but he wanted this life, he knew he could be a good soldier; he just needed a chance to prove it.

Striding down to the docks, he met the other recruits and they all boarded a small riverboat that transported them down the winding Tiber to Ostia. Transferring onto the huge troop carrier, they were ordered to place their packs in a holding area and then to assist the officers if required.

The oarsmen were already in position and it seemed to Maxentius that they had only just embarked when the ship began to move. A huge sail, ready to be unfurled once clear of the harbour and into the sea lanes, hung from the central mast. Maxentius had never been on a ship before and had heard about men being sick with the roll of the waves; he hoped he wasn't going to embarrass himself. Standing at the rail for a few moments, he watched as the port disappeared, but was soon helping the other crew with their duties.

The sea voyage was mostly uneventful, the weather was kind and they only had one or two days of blustery gales. The ship put in at Lechaeum in Corinth and they had a few days shore leave while the ship was re-stocked with supplies and water. Maxentius found the place fascinating and spent hours exploring the port town. He saw all manner of interesting wares for sale at the markets, curious foods and odd-looking utensils. One afternoon, while strolling along the harbour, he even witnessed something called an octopus being hauled ashore. Watching the fishermen deal with all those tentacles, he was moved to wonder how on earth the creature managed to move through the water without getting completely tangled up. His sister could barely manage that feat with only two legs and on solid ground. He found it strange that the locals were rather partial to a taste of this eight- legged sea creature; he was happy to let them, his stomach not quite ready for so foreign a culinary experience!

Setting sail again on the last leg of their sea voyage, the ship passed Cyprus before docking, finally, at Antioch a little less than a month after their departure from Rome. The soldiers had barely got their land legs back before they began the long march towards Tigranocerta — the newer of Armenia's two main cities — before continuing on to Rhandeia, situated in the north west. From here, some would be sent onwards to join up with Corbulo and his troops, who were currently involved in skirmishes further along the frontier.

If the weather held, the journey should take them just over four weeks across unfamiliar and harsh terrain. This would definitely test the mettle of the new recruits.

Chapter Two

Hundreds of miles away, in a city struggling with turmoil and mounting chaos, a shout went up along a narrow street.

"Physician, we need the physician." The anguished cry echoed off the walls. A door, above which a shingle hung announcing that a physician indeed worked there, was thrown open and a burly man with brown hair and tired features, peered out. He noticed two youths hobbling along. Between them, his arms hooked over their shoulders, they carried another. The older man waved them into the building.

"Are you the physician?" asked one of the men, exhaustion from the weight of his burden clear in his voice. Their host nodded.

"I am Gideon," he replied. "What has happened?"

"We were coming home from Temple and were set upon by a gang." Such things were becoming more than just an occasional occurrence. Political and religious upheaval permeated the city and it was hard to know whom to trust. Young men were being beaten up, for no apparent reason, by thugs who roamed the streets, intent on fighting someone, anyone, without care as to who they were. Many had ended up in Gideon's rooms some had not left alive.

As the wounded man was carried into the room, Gideon turned to his assistant asking for a bowl of clean water and a cloth. The young boy scurried to do his master's bidding, carrying a large bowl over to the table, going through another room and returning with a huge flagon, almost half the size of the lad. He tipped a small amount of the flagon's contents into the bowl, before heaving it up onto the table. The diminutive assistant then wrapped a sheet around his waist and washed his hands, thoroughly, in the bowl of water. Gideon followed suit, throwing the dirty water out, rinsing then refilling the bowl, adding salt and frankincense.

Gideon helped the two young men lift their friend onto the table. He was barely conscious and bleeding from several nasty cuts. A split lip, a bloody nose and bruising to his face and body added to his woes. Collecting a pile of cloths cut into small squares, Gideon placed a few into the bowl. While they soaked up the salt and frankincense mixture, he removed the man's tunic, covered him with a sheet and began to clean his wounds.

The physician talked through what he was doing while he worked and his small assistant seemed to anticipate what his master would require; handing over more cloths or pots of ointment before being asked. The room was quiet; the only sound the muttered comments from the physician. The two friends of the injured man were also hurt, although not as badly and the physician's assistant calmly took over their care. Meticulously checking both men, the boy cleaned and treated each injury. It was a couple of hours before Gideon and his assistant were satisfied that they had checked every wound, however small, ensuring that all were clean, had been covered in salve and, if necessary, bound.

The man on the table, whose name they discovered was Malachi, lost consciousness while Gideon had been treating him but his heartbeat was steady and he looked to be a sturdy youth. The physician did not have any serious concerns about him. He would just need to rest and avoid fights for a while. The young assistant took the other two, Simeon and Binyamin, into the main room of the house, offering them a warm drink while they waited for their friend to wake up.

The two men chatted with Gideon who followed them through and the boy, while seemingly occupied with other things, listened in on their conversation. He often picked up interesting titbits of information; no one really noticed him, he was like Gideon's shadow, so small and quiet, useful attributes in a time of uncertainty.

It wasn't very long before Malachi came to and the three men slipped away, thanking their healers and pressing coin into Gideon's hand. Despite knowing that free medical treatment was not approved, the physician acting on his own discretion, tried to refuse it. The men insisted, so he accepted the payment with good grace; besides his supplies always needed replenishing. It was now late afternoon and although Gideon was available any time of the day or night, his official working day was drawing to a close.

The young lad was cleaning the treatment room, scrubbing the table and piling the dirty cloths and sheets into a basket to be laundered. Opening the shutters, Gideon let the cool breeze waft through the room, pushing out any stale air. The sounds of the street permeated the space, laughter and chatter, children playing, their giggles reverberating off the warm stones. The boy sighed, it had been a long day and he was looking forward to a hot meal and a good sleep.

"Thank you for your assistance today, you are becoming invaluable to me." Smiling down at the youngster, Gideon brushed his hand over the child's head and the boy looked up at him.

"Thank you, my Uncle. I love helping you, I am learning so much. I hope to be as knowledgeable as you some day."

"Well, if you continue to learn as quickly as you are now and are always this enthusiastic, I am sure you will." The boy grinned at such praise, while removing his makeshift apron, which was splattered in blood and dirt, adding it to the basket of items to be washed. Then he took off the triangle of cloth both he and his uncle wore over their heads to keep their hair out of their eyes, and anyone watching would have been shocked to see that the young boy's hair fell to his waist in rich chestnut curls.

"I am not sure how much longer your parents will allow you to assist me though. Your mother prefers that you learn to weave and cook." Gideon continued. The child shrugged carelessly.

"I do not care for such things. Every time I attempt to cook, the food tastes terrible and they all complain. I can weave and sew, but it is boring. I like to be here, learning about healing. It fascinates me and I think I could be good at it." Gideon smiled indulgently.

"I think you could too, my dear, let's hope your mother agrees."

The child's name was Hannah and she was ten and one years old.

Living with her mother, father and brother, just along the street from her uncle's home, Hannah was an unusual child. Somewhat of a hoyden, she was happiest playing with her brother and his friends — who were content to let her tag along — rather than with other girls. Along with her dark curly hair, Hannah had green eyes, a rare trait, and her features were elfin-like, as was her stature; the complete opposite of her strapping brother, Aharon, who at ten and five years old, towered over her.

Hannah's father, Efraim, was a merchant and they lived in a decent neighbourhood. Although not a family of high status, they were considered relatively wealthy by some standards. Blessed with a comfortable home, cheerful healthy children and good food on the table, they were part of a close-knit community where families supported one another and no one in need was ever turned away.

Despite a tendency for tomboyish activities, Hannah loved her parents and did try to behave in a manner expected of a young girl. Her quest for knowledge however, far outweighed her desire to please her family and she spent every spare minute with her uncle. Gideon, son of Yaakov, was a clever man who had studied the art of healing for many years. Determined to be the best physician he could be, Gideon had travelled to the medical schools in Smyrna and Corinth as well the School of Medicine in Alexandria, honing his skills. He became a *rofe* or skilled physician at quite a young age, returning to Jerusalem to put his hard-earned expertise into practice in his own neighbourhood.

Gideon, a solitary man, had never thought to marry and found children difficult to relate to. His brother's daughter however, had wormed her way into his affections from a young age. As a child, she had loved to potter about his rooms, tidying his jars, stacking his bowls and baskets, happily folding cloths and bandages. He had indulged the girl assuming she would tire of her games and leave him alone. Hannah had no such intentions, the more time she spent with her uncle the more interested she became with his work.

A precocious child, Hannah had been taught to read and write almost as soon as she could talk, and once Gideon thought her old enough and careful enough, he had allowed her to study his medical manuscripts. Hannah was a voracious reader and absorbed everything he gave her like the proverbial sponge. Gideon had made prodigious notes on everything he had learned and had added copies of manuscripts by other medical luminaries to his vast collection.

Hannah had long wanted to assist her uncle but, initially, Gideon felt that a surgery was no place for a young girl, tactfully suggesting that she should be spending more time with her mother, learning the skills a wife would need. Hannah had no desire to be married. The thought of looking after a man, to wait on him hand and foot — something that she perceived her mother did for her father — was not in Hannah's plans. She was determined to be a physician and nobody was going to stop her. Headstrong and tempestuous, Hannah somehow persuaded her parents that there was no harm in her spending time with her uncle.

She learned about cleanliness and how to care for the skin, about dietary habits, that fresh air was better than closed rooms, that it was vital to wash your hands before and after treating someone as well as before and after meals. She learned to sew — making up cloths, sheets and bandages and fashioning aprons and headscarves that protected their own clothing and their hair.

After a day helping Gideon, she would spend the evenings reading one of his manuscripts or notebooks. Much as Hannah's parents preferred that she undertook more ladylike activities, they realised that their daughter was supremely happy and for a time they humoured her, both believing that she would grow bored and return to the arts and crafts that the rest of her contemporaries were mastering.

Hannah knew she wasn't like the other girls who thought her strange for choosing to spend time with a grumpy physician, but it never bothered her. She played with her brother and his friends, and helped her uncle. The only girl with whom she spent any time was Raizel, the daughter of family friends who lived in the same district and was a year older than Hannah. A gentle child, Raizel was a steadying hand on Hannah's more outrageous exploits and Hannah protected her friend if ever the need arose.

Chapter Three

Armenia ~ AD58

The soldiers had been marching for what seemed like forever, their shoulders were sore and aching from the constant chafing of the wooden frame, which held their packs. It was days since they had skirted Tigranocerta, following the River Tigris north west and, some were starting to think that Rhandeia — their destination — was a figment of the general's imagination. The weather had been atrocious; lashing rain, even hail, along with howling winds and so cold it felt as though their limbs might snap off. That this was unseasonable was of no comfort to those new recruits who feared they would never be warm or dry again. Even campaign weary veterans were heard to mutter that this was like nothing they'd ever experienced.

Maxentius was determined not to let it break him, he was stronger than this; he would not be brought to his knees by the weather. He knew that a number of his comrades had fallen seriously ill and one or two had died from complications after contracting chills that the sufferer had ignored. Thankfully, he also knew that they must be close to their journey's end, as after days and days of barren landscape with minimal signs of life — just the occasional farm where they had been able to beg, or in actual fact commandeer, clean water or fresh food — they had begun to pass small hamlets.

Ahead, through the gloom, he could just about make out what appeared to be a town, it was certainly larger than a farmstead. They would set up camp there tonight he was sure of it. If it was a town, there might be somewhere they could buy decent food, instead of the basic rations they'd been living, nay existing, on for the last three weeks.

Around two hours later, the column was called to a halt and the soldiers set about pitching camp. With admirable efficiency all the tents, which — except for the centurions and the general who each had individual tents — housed eight men, along with everything else that would be required, were set up within an hour. Most soldiers opted for their beds, going straight to sleep. It had been a long and arduous day and exhaustion was a constant companion. Maxentius made sure his tent was as it should be, then, went in search of hot food. So close to their destination and with a dearth of supplies remaining, it was barely edible slop but it was hot and filling and he went back for seconds, accepting that he was a glutton for punishment.

He spent an hour or so chatting with some of the others who had also braved the food. Maxentius was finding his station amongst these men, plenty of whom were hardened warriors, having seen numerous battles. They seemed to respect him, if for nothing else than his resilience and refusal to let anything get him down. He asked whether any of them had been to Armenia or Parthia before. Most had not, but a few were returning to their legion after being seconded elsewhere for a short period.

Listening to the soldiers talk, Maxentius surmised that any battles fought here would not be the easy victory the Romans had come to believe was theirs, almost by right. The Parthians were fierce warriors who burned with a passionate hatred of the Romans, plus there was always the risk of border skirmishes with Armenians sympathetic to Parthia. While Maxentius conceded that it was important to retain control of Armenia as a buffer kingdom, he wasn't so sure that the horrendous loss of lives was worth it. He had no intention of voicing this, however and kept his counsel, knowing that it was likely he would be executed immediately for such an opinion; he was a mere recruit — what did he know.

He retired to his tent, mulling over the discussions. An intelligent young man, Maxentius wanted to understand the whats, whys and wherefores of the campaign he was now a part of, believing that the more information you have, the better able you are to make strategically effective decisions. To his mind, campaigns were more than just face-to-face combat; they involved understanding the enemy, how they thought, what their motives were, whether it was purely about territory, or whether there was something else? Little did Maxentius realise that he was already thinking like an accomplished soldier.

He slept well, rising with the dawn, helping his bunkmates — their group of eight was known as a contubernium and had been together since landing at Antioch — to pack up their tent, as all around them soldiers did the same. Once done, Maxentius assisted others in striking the rest of the camp and within a short time the contingent were on their way — a ditch, several post holes and a few areas of turned earth, the only evidence of their overnight stay.

The weather had improved, finally. The sky was clear and the sun was shining. That in itself was enough to make the soldiers, especially the recruits, feel less pessimistic. The land was changing, becoming more fertile and crops flourished. They marched for another four days and at last a city rose up in the near distance. They had arrived at Rhandeia.

The fortress was outside the city walls and the long train marched in, marshalling themselves into rows for inspection. Auxiliaries appeared to take charge of the horses and supply wagons and, with military efficiency, everything was organised and stored away within a very short time.

The legatus or commander, a veritable giant of a soldier dressed in full armour, exited the headquarters building — known as the principia — and, striding towards the quadrangle, reviewed the newly arrived troops. Weary after their interminable march, many soldiers looked unkempt and rather the worse for wear, having somehow avoided the daily checks for tidiness. This was unacceptable and more than should have been were reprimanded for slovenliness. It was expected that each soldier maintain fastidious cleaning habits and as all carried shaving and bathing paraphernalia, there was no excuse for looking scruffy. Maxentius silently praised all the gods that he hated the feeling of stubble on his chin and had shaved that morning. Inspection over, they were dismissed to their quarters and advised that the meal would be served in one hour.

Each row marched off; the only sound was the crunch of their footsteps in the dust and the clinking of swords. Maxentius followed the man in front of him and they were directed into the fourth barrack. As with every military encampment throughout the Empire the layout of these buildings were all exactly the same. Each barrack housed a centuria, or eighty men, the long wooden block being divided up into ten smaller rooms which slept up to eight — the same contubernia who had been sharing tents on the march. A tiny anteroom which housed a small kitchenette and somewhere for the soldiers to store their belongings, opened off each bedroom. Centurions had their own, more spacious, quarters at the end of each barrack.

As a general rule there was no central dining area for the soldiers, each was expected to cook for himself. At this fortress things were organised differently and twice a day a meal was available in a huge hall situated at the end of one of the lines of barracks. Each week, on a rotation basis, one barrack was in charge of cooking for the rest of the fort. The commanders had decided that this was the only way to ensure that their soldiers were getting enough sustenance to fortify them on the arduous campaigns they were involved in. The food was simple yet filling; grains, beans, some meat, dried fruit and bread.

Maxentius and his contubernium found their quarters and unpacked. Orders would be given the next day as to who would remain at Rhandeia and who would march on to meet Corbulo. As soon as they were sorted, the eight soldiers joined the rest of their centuria for the meal. It was a relaxed occasion, the men glad to be in a proper fortress and not sleeping under canvas. The food was far better than the swill they'd been surviving on for the last week and there was plenty of wine. It did get somewhat rowdy, but the centurions were content to let their subordinates have their heads for once and didn't interfere.

It was very late before they retired to their bunks and Maxentius lay awake for quite some time, ruminating over everything that had happened since he had taken his oath. Even though it was barely two months, it felt like a lifetime and he had already changed. He knew that as a soldier of Rome he was at the whim of his commanders, that whatever he was instructed to do, he would do without question. He understood that he was merely an instrument, to act without mercy, but also without cruelty. In battle, he would be expected to kill, simply because he had been ordered to do so, but should never relish or exult in the act of killing; emotions must be removed from the equation, almost as though he and his fellow soldiers were soulless machines. This aspect did worry Maxentius, but he tried not to dwell on it.

In some respects, to confront an army with this attitude was probably far more daunting than facing an indiscriminate swarm of bandits, who attacked with reckless abandon, thrilling to the chase and thirsty for blood, but with no particular strategy. The strength of the Roman legionary lay in his ability not to let his feelings towards his enemy cloud his judgement, creating a soldier who was detached, ruthlessly efficient and never to be underestimated.

Eventually, Maxentius fell into a restless slumber, despite his fatigue, thoughts of what was to come playing on his mind. Too soon, it was time to get up and he felt groggy from lack of a decent rest. Washing quickly, he tidied his bunk, which looked as though he'd been using it as a wrestling ring, before queuing with his bunkmates for the first meal. After the morning inspection, duties were handed out. Life in a fortress was never dull, every day there would be training and drill, on top of that there were regular patrols and sentry duty.

Each soldier was taught how to use every weapon — practicing archery, spear throwing and swordsmanship; they also learned the proper care of horses and how to ride, much of which Maxentius was already skilled at. Some of the recruits would assist in the workshops; for maintaining weapons and other equipment was as vital as making sure their surroundings were secure. Not just soldiers training for warfare, these men were also clerks, engineers, stonemasons, carpenters and craftsmen.

As there was a valetudinarium or hospital within the fortress, there was also a duty roster detailing those men who would assist the qualified physicians, for although there was a regular medical corps, orderlies were a necessity.

At this fortress, the current commander's policy was that, without exception, his soldiers should become proficient in as many disciplines as possible and the men were rotated through jobs on a regular basis. Anyone who excelled in a particular skill however, could be made a supervisor for that trade, craft or activity. In this way it was unlikely that any soldier could ever complain that he was bored; their days were full and it was rare for any man to be unoccupied.

Today, besides the two hours of regular training, most of the newly arrived soldiers would accompany the patrols in order to become familiar with the locale. Half of the contingent from Rome would be leaving in three days, to meet up with Corbulo and his legions. Other than those returning to their own units, no one yet knew who would be dispatched.

Maxentius didn't really mind either way. He would enjoy staying within the comparative safety of the fortress, but this wasn't the reason he'd joined the army. While he had no desire to kill a fellow human being — even if he was an enemy — he wanted to understand how the army worked at every level; from manning a garrison, to deciding that warfare was the only option, how the generals planned their strategies, how to recognise that negotiations had failed and who to trust.

Believing that this could only be achieved in the field, so to speak, Maxentius rather hoped he might be chosen, but as there was nothing he could do about it, he knuckled down to his duties for the day.

Chapter Four

Hannah worked quietly in one corner of the room, her slender body enveloped in an apron, her hair caught back under a scarf and her hands washed. Gideon was examining a man on the table, talking through the injuries while he did so. Listening intently, Hannah also watched her uncle's fingers as, methodically, they checked the damaged body lying in front of him making sure he did not miss anything.

The young man whose name was Daniel, was known to Hannah. In fact, Hannah knew nearly all the people who came through Gideon's door. She had grown up with them, most she had played with at one time or another and more than a few were her brother's friends. Daniel was one such person; he had been a friend of Aharon for so long he was virtually part of the family.

His injuries seemed severe to Hannah's relatively inexperienced eyes. She had dealt with cuts and bruises, broken bones and had even helped with a birth where the baby had to be cut free from its mother's womb owing to serious complications. Nothing had prepared her for this. Daniel looked as though he had been run over by a wagon and then attacked by a wild beast. He was bleeding from an alarming number of slashes, his nose was crooked, his left cheek and upper lip were badly split and it appeared as though both of his legs had been broken.

Determined to help Gideon and by extension Daniel, Hannah squared her jaw and continued to lay out everything her uncle would require — cloths, bandages, bowls, a diverse array of instruments, thread and plenty of water, both hot and cold. Gideon finished his examination; Daniel was unconscious, so they did not need to worry about managing his pain at the moment, but there was the added concern about shock. No one knew who had brought the young man to Gideon's rooms. It was early evening and there had been a loud knocking followed by a shouted demand, but when the physician opened his door there was only Daniel, lying broken and bleeding on the street.

He had sent a child to fetch Hannah, for much as he knew her mother would prefer that she pursued more decorous activities, he would need her help this night. She had learned a lot over the past year or so; she was quiet, unobtrusive and seemed to anticipate his requirements. Gideon was dreading the day she would be persuaded to abandon his practice for marriage.

Hannah carried over the large bowl of warmed water, having added salt and frankincense. Gideon dipped a cloth into the mixture, soaking it thoroughly before beginning to wash the wounds, motioning for Hannah to do the same from the other side of the table. Working together, they discussed the injuries in undertones; Gideon letting Hannah tell him what she thought had happened and what treatment to use, correcting her occasionally, but gratified to observe how much she had learned.

With consummate patience, Hannah helped to clean Daniel's damaged body, rinsing out the cloth constantly, so as not to cause cross-contamination. Then she covered each wound with a salve, one that Gideon had created, using a blend of oil, myrrh, frankincense and honey. Well known for its healing properties, honey also helped thicken the mixture, making it easier to apply. The broken limbs needed setting and they would need another man to assist; Hannah simply wasn't strong enough yet to hold the bones steady. While Gideon worked on those cuts that required stitching, Hannah rushed along the street to her home, hoping that Aharon was there. To her relief he was and although not particularly comfortable with anything medical, readily agreed to help.

Pulling a cloak over his shoulders, he hurried back along the path; Hannah following behind, running to keep up with her brother's long strides. Night had fallen and the streets were almost empty. In the distance there was the sound of revelry or maybe another riot, but it was too far away to worry the siblings.

Pushing open the door to Gideon's rooms, Aharon brought up sharply when he saw his injured friend, blood pooling across the table from where the damaged bones had sliced through the flesh on Daniel's legs.

"Who did this?" he muttered in shocked tones. Gideon shrugged.

"We have no idea, he was dumped outside of my door, his wounds are grievous and he may not make it through the night." Hannah gaped at her uncle, she knew that Daniel was hurt, but she didn't think he was that badly hurt. Shaken, she paled but refusing to let it affect her, drew a steadying breath. If she wanted to be a physician, these were the things that she must be able to deal with. Dragging her attention back to the job in hand, she listened while Gideon explained what they needed to do.

"Both of the finer, or thinner of the two bones in the lower half of each of his legs have been broken, we need to straighten them, allowing them to realign, otherwise it is unlikely he will walk again, whether he survives at all. He is losing blood at a dangerous rate and I fear for him." Aharon looked markedly queasy at this, but straightened his shoulders and stood where Gideon instructed. Hannah held the ankle of Daniel's right leg steady and the two men pulled and twisted until the bone was eased back into place. They repeated their actions on the left leg, during which, Daniel came round, screaming in agony as his bones sort of slotted back against each other.

Hannah took the young man's hand and, brushing the hair off his face, spoke in soft tones, telling Daniel what had happened to him. She explained his injuries and how they had been treated. Aharon was astonished; he had no idea that his sister was so knowledgeable. Her green eyes held Daniel's dark brown ones and she kept up a flow of chatter, distracting him from Gideon's ministrations.

The blood had slowed and Gideon checked to make sure that there were no stray fragments of bone in the wounds, before cleaning both legs again and covering the whole of each limb in a thick coating of salve. Over the first layer of bandages, a wooden splint was bound gently to each leg, ensuring that they remained straight and then Gideon added several more layers of bandages to protect the damaged limbs.

As they finished their task, Daniel was very sick, but Hannah expected this and had a bowl ready. Once she was sure Daniel was over his bout of nausea, she went over to the sink and washed the bowl thoroughly, coming back to the patient with a cup of water for him to rinse his mouth. Then she wiped his face and neck with a cool cloth, still talking to him, noting that he was clammy, but that so far his temperature was only slightly higher than normal; only to be expected given what he'd just been through.

"Do you know who did this to you, Daniel?" she asked quietly.

"It was a gang, I was walking home and they just came at me from nowhere. I didn't recognise any of them. I was just walking home. I don't…" he trailed off, shaking his head unable to believe that this had happened to him in broad daylight in his own neighbourhood. "Nobody came to help me either, they must have heard me yelling, but no one came. What is our city coming to?" His face already etched with pain, took on a sadness that was palpable.

They all looked at each other. These attacks were now far too common. The political unrest within Jerusalem was creating a volatile environment. Splinter groups and religious factions were causing mayhem throughout the city and what once had been confined to a few random attacks by bored ruffians had escalated out of all proportion into gangs who roamed the streets looking for the slightest excuse to brawl. The tension between the Romans and the Jews was close to boiling point.

For long enough there had been discontent over the behaviour of the Roman governors and the ongoing ideological differences between the polytheistic Greco-Roman world and the monotheistic Jewish belief system. As if this wasn't enough and adding to the already strained political stability, now there was the further provocation of an increase in taxes and one which the Jews were determined not to pay.

Concerned for their own futures, many complained loudly and bitterly about what they considered to be the coercive rule of the Romans, while others felt that it would be more preferable to aim for some kind of a peaceful coexistence with their occupiers. Religion and politics — there was no middle ground, the gap was too wide and, as has been the same throughout the history of the world, impressionable young men tired of feeling impotent are an easy target for those who appear to offer freedom from oppression.

Aharon and his friends were no different, often disappearing for hours on end to take part in covert meetings or becoming involved in skirmishes with the authorities. They were still young and thankfully, so far, none had been caught up in anything serious, but the potential for violent conflict simmered just under the surface. Hannah was worried about repercussions on their family, begging her brother not to be caught up in such madness, but he had assured her that he was careful and that he would never put their family at risk. She did not have his confidence; she helped her uncle every day with the aftermath of these confrontations — Daniel being the latest case in point.

She drew her brother aside,

"Aharon, look at Daniel! This cannot be a random attack, someone knows that you all are part of some group or other and those who oppose it are sending a message. Who else has to be hurt for you all to realise how dangerous this city is? Please, think of our parents, if anything happened to you, it would be the death of them." Aharon stared at his sister. How did she know so much about what was going on? She was just his little sister, she was barely ten and three years old, surely too young for such concerns. Then he recalled how she helped Gideon and the way she talked to Daniel, realising with a jolt that, yes she was his little sister, but she was also highly intelligent, all that knowledge about healing learned at their uncle's side.

Her ability to fade into the background meant that often, people failed to notice her presence and she was obviously absorbing snippets of information, not much getting passed her. He would need to be more discreet; he knew she wouldn't say anything to their parents, but she would definitely give him a piece of her mind if she thought he was behaving in a way that might jeopardise their family.

Hannah gripped his hand in her earnestness and held his gaze for long moments. Aharon inclined his head, tacit acknowledgement of her entreaty. Her fingers relaxed their hold and her lips curved in a gentle smile as she turned back to the patient. Wise beyond her years, Hannah said no more, simply carried on talking to Daniel.

"Daniel, I will be here with you through the night and if the pain becomes too much to bear, please tell me…" waiting until she knew he understood her request. Daniel muttered an acknowledgement. Lifting the man's head she continued, "…here, sip a little of this. It will give you an untroubled rest," encouraging him to take a small draft of poppy juice, while Gideon asked Aharon to go and tell Daniel's family what had happened. Aharon had a quick word with his friend and then slipped quietly out of the door.

Hannah and Gideon tidied the room, gathering up blood soaked pieces of cloth, the worst of which would be burned. Hannah cleaned all the instruments, dropping them first into a bowl of boiling hot water, then emptying that out and washing them again, this time, adding vinegar to the water, scrubbing everything to ensure not a trace of blood or tissue remained.

Daniel could not be moved from the table he was lying on — not yet — his injuries were too critical, but Hannah deftly eased out the soiled sheets from underneath him, replacing them with clean ones, covering the young man with yet another sheet and drawing a warm blanket around him. Then she spent some time wiping his face and rinsing his hair, removing any dirt, dust or blood that still clung to him, talking all the while, distracting the youth with her gentle conversation.

Daniel's eyelids drooped as the opiate took effect; he started to say something but was asleep before the words left his lips. Hannah stood for a few moments, watching to make sure his breathing was regular and his heart rate steady. Satisfied that they had done all they could for now, she tucked his hand under the blanket and let him sleep.

Joining her uncle in the adjoining room, Hannah sank into one of the chairs, utterly exhausted, enjoying a brief respite aware that she would not get much rest this night. The two of them would take turns to keep watch over their patient; he needed constant monitoring to have any chance of survival. Infection was still a huge concern and although Daniel was young, strong and healthy, it might not be enough.

Shortly thereafter Aharon reappeared with Daniel's father, Yosef, the two men filling the small room while they listened to Gideon's prognosis. Yosef was pale as he processed Gideon's words, although the physician assured the worried man that he would do everything in his power to save his son. Gideon then took Yosef through to the surgery where the man's son lay unconscious but alive. The two older men stood shoulder to shoulder surveying Daniel's broken body and Yosef was astounded that his son had survived this long. Silent tears coursed down his cheeks and Gideon rested his hand on his friend's arm in sympathy.

"If he lives through this night, we may have hope," the physician said quietly. "I think however you must be prepared. I cannot give you any guarantees for his injuries are very bad. Elisheva may wish to see him, just in case." Yosef nodded, not trusting himself to speak and Aharon, sensing that Yosef was loath to leave his son, said he would fetch Daniel's mother.

Hannah brought through a chair for Yosef, ushering him into it while handing him a cup of warmed milk, to which she'd added a sprinkle of cinnamon. She handed another cup to Gideon and placed a tray of hot fresh bread and olive oil on the bench. Barely aware of the child, they accepted her offerings almost absently, their attention focused on the injured man. Hannah was used to this, in fact she rather liked that she could go about her duties with no one really seeing her. Being small did have its advantages. Making sure that all was as it should be, she left the two men to their vigil and returned to the back room. She curled up in the chair, warming her hands on her own hot drink, breathing in the aroma of the spice and letting it soothe her mind.

It was a long night. Elisheva arrived, joining her husband, holding Daniel's hand and talking to her son while he slept. Hannah and Gideon checked him periodically and so far there was no sign of infection. The young man's temperature, although rather higher than normal, was not indicative of fever and his breathing was not erratic. His skin was still clammy, but during the night his colour seemed better. As the dawn broke, the soft pink light lifting the gloom, they dared to believe that Daniel might just make it. He had woken occasionally, enough to speak and his words were lucid. His eyes, while pained, were not over bright and when Hannah had last checked, his wounds showed no evidence of poison.

Finally, by mid-morning when Gideon felt that the danger had passed, he sent his niece home. Despite having managed a few hours of sleep, Hannah was so tired that she could scarcely put one foot in front of the other, finding she did not even have the strength to open the door to her home. Unable to lift the latch she gave up and simply leaned on it, surprising Aharon who happened to be leaving just as she arrived. Catching his sister as she fell through, he lifted her, carrying her to her bed, pulling the blanket up and dropping the shutter. Watching her for a few moments, making sure she was sleeping, Aharon ruminated over everything this small girl had done for his friend and hoping that it was the worst she would witness.

Chapter Five

Armenia ~ AD59

If it wasn't the merciless heat it was the mud. Maxentius wished that just once they could fight on a dry surface in the cool of autumn. It seemed to him that every skirmish they had been involved in happened during extremes of weather. While accepting that their enemy wasn't disposed to sit around waiting for the perfect weather to attack the Romans, the young soldier had the impression that the worse the elements, the more likelihood there was of facing down a band of rebellious locals, who appeared to relish the challenge. Why anyone imagined it would be a good idea to have a battle in such atrocious conditions was beyond him, or maybe that was precisely the point.

It was almost two years since his arrival in Armenia and Maxentius had seen much action. Chosen to go with the contingent that would meet up with Corbulo, who had been repelling attacks in the northwest, Maxentius had rarely been in one place for more than two nights. The long Roman-Armenian border meant that the soldiers were moving constantly and the battle lines changed like the wind. Unlike others of Rome's adversaries, the Parthians and by extension their supporters, were well organised and, apparently, had an endless supply of soldiers.

Of late, however, Tiridates, the Parthian vassal, had avoided becoming involved in any major battles, settling for lightening raids in an attempt to disrupt the communication and supply channels used by the Romans to support the now divided legions. A seasoned warrior, Corbulo was familiar with such tactics, ordering a network of forts to be constructed, protecting not only the supply routes but also any settlements whose inhabitants championed the Roman occupation.

Although the forces were well spread out, the Roman army was bolstered by neighbouring client kings, who sent out rapid strikes from their own territories, keeping Tiridates and his allies stretched to their limits and hopefully weakening them. In addition, the rulers of Lesser Armenia and Pontus supplied auxiliaries and allied forces from their kingdoms.

Rome was aided further by the fact that Vologases I — the Parthian king and Tiridates' brother — was himself trying to quash numerous insurrections within his own country, leaving him unable to provide his sibling with any assistance. Thus the campaign had been relatively successful and Corbulo's next objective was Tigranocerta. He turned his legions south, leaving garrisons stationed along the frontier. Occasionally disenfranchised locals confronted the soldiers, so the odd skirmish still required subduing. Corbulo, however, had lost patience with any who resisted and was lenient only to those who surrendered.

As it had been on their march to Rhandeia, the terrain on the way to Tigranocerta was unforgiving; leaving their supplies, especially water, dangerously low. Up until a few days ago, the weather had been unbearably hot, the desert air sucking up every last drop of moisture. Then the rain had started, a light mist at first, becoming torrential, turning the vast expanse of hard packed earth into a sea of mud. The only consolation was that at last they could fill their canteens. Determination and the thought that when they reached their destination they might be afforded a dry bed, was about the only thing that kept the soldiers putting one foot in front of the other. Well, that and the threat of death should they show any sign of dissension.

The soldiers had been marching through a deluge for the better part of two hours and knew that they were passing territory that had, until recently, changed hands as often as night follows day. The legion that had come to relieve them at Rhandeia had forced the Parthian sympathisers back across the frontier; killing thousands and they believed the area to be subjugated. This land, however, was not yet pacified and pockets of resistance were still to be suppressed.

Aware that the churning sludge underfoot meant any combat would be more than a tad strenuous, the soldiers maintained strict vigilance. The gloomy sky and ceaseless rain made visibility difficult and the centurions had sent out scouts who were patrolling to the limits of their range. Suddenly a shout went up from the front of the column and with immediate understanding, the soldiers moved into formation. Turning, they saw an immense corps of men bearing down on them across the black mud; their leader bellowing orders in a strange tongue.

Over such open land, the Romans had been marching contubernium, or eight abreast. Following a barked command every other soldier stood back two paces making it appear as though there were sixteen ranks of men rather than just eight. This tactic offered far greater flexibility of movement and was very easily coordinated, especially in difficult terrain or when faced with a sudden attack. Soldiers on horseback manoeuvred their mounts to either end of the columns, with a few spread out behind the lines in support of the men at the rear. Although much more loosely organised than the tightly packed configuration used in a pitched battle, this formation was a formidable sight. More than enough to make a less determined foe retreat with alacrity, but desperation makes fools of even the most rational of men.

In silence, thousands of soldiers, in full armour, shields and swords gleaming dully in the half-light, waited for the order to charge. Infantry on the front line held their pila — a sort of javelin — ready and, although the heavy rain made their use questionable, the archers cocked their bows. At a signal from Corbulo, the horn sounded, galvanising the soldiers into action. They bore down on their attackers who, although from a distance appeared to be well organised, on closer examination lacked cohesion. A flaw, which would be exploited by the Romans with devastating efficiency.

Arrows flew, scattering the oncoming throng, followed by a wave of pila, many slamming into their opponents' shields rendering them useless. The two sides met in a clash of swords and shields that to the untrained eye would have a resembled utter chaos, but the Roman Army had faced worse than this barbarian horde. Even the latest recruits, who had joined this legion less than two moons ago, had already experienced skirmishes along the border and knew what to expect. Combat such as this was as instinctual as breathing, the arduous training undertaken by the Roman soldiers created a force whose sole objective was to annihilate anyone who challenged their authority.

In the atrocious conditions, Maxentius fought alongside his men, making sure he knew where they all were. As with his fellow centurions, he led by example and would never send the men under his command into a situation he himself would not be prepared to enter. Having spent the better part of two years with the soldiers he now led; Maxentius knew every last one by name, quite a bit about each of them and, with most, something of their families. His reasoning being that if they believed he cared about them as a person not just a soldier, they would likely bring to him any grievances they might have, rather than allow them to fester until blown out of all proportion, to the detriment of the unit.

This attitude had created a very tight-knit, loyal group and although Maxentius knew that there were those amongst his peers who considered him somewhat unconventional — soldiers did as they were told or they faced severe disciplinary action — he didn't care. In his opinion, respect was earned not enforced and he would go to great lengths to protect his soldiers — a sentiment that was reciprocated.

The skirmish raged on interminably. The endless rain had made the plain they were fighting on a quagmire and every step required herculean effort. The archers, their bowstrings soaked and useless, had now joined the other infantry, wielding swords with ruthless accuracy. Maxentius had assumed that the clamour of battle would be cacophonous, but was always surprised at how muted it actually was — as, strangely, other than the clash of metal against metal or against flesh and the bitten off grunts and cries of the men as they fought — there was little sound. Maybe it was because everything was concentrated on not allowing your enemy to gain ground. As Maxentius struggled to stay upright in the slippery mud, the world around him faded into white noise, his attention concentrated on killing before being killed, and ensuring none of his immediate comrades became encircled by their adversaries.

Eventually, as though there was ever really any doubt, Roman military discipline gained the upper hand. Those of the rebels who hadn't been injured fled as the rear echelon came through clearing the field — they left none alive.

That night the rain stopped, finally, and the soldiers managed to pitch camp on slightly higher ground that was somewhat less of a bog than they had been used to recently. As he was lying on his cot, trying to snatch some sleep, Maxentius ruminated over the day.

During the last two years, he had killed more men than he cared to count and was rather worried that he was losing his humanity. The first few times his sword had hit its mark had left him drained and saddened, prompting him to question his calling. Regardless of your opponent's ideals, to be looking into the eye of a man whose death you are inflicting was not something he could have trained for, or took lightly. Since then however, it had become almost routine, and he found it troubled him.

Maxentius had risen through the ranks more quickly than he anticipated and, following the deaths of several officers — and as there were only a limited number of experienced soldiers — had been made a centurion. A rare promotion for one as young as Maxentius, but he had proven himself to be an efficient solider, seemingly able to predict the actions of the enemy almost as though he could divine their thoughts.

Taking the time to listen, both to his commanders and the other soldiers, especially those who had been in — what they considered to be — this god-forsaken country for several years, Maxentius gleaned everything he could about the tactics of their enemy. He made the effort to meet with locals whenever possible in an attempt to understand their grievances, encouraging cooperation and an open dialogue between the Romans and those who felt the occupation of their lands had rendered them powerless.

He had gained the respect not only of his comrades but also the other centurions, many of whom had been in the army for well over a decade and his perspective on any given strategy was always requested. Maxentius had even come to the attention of Corbulo in a favourable way. This wasn't necessarily a good thing, but it meant that he had a reasonable chance of being transferred to somewhere less remote for his next posting.

The long march was nearly over, for which everyone was truly thankful, the scouts advising that they had seen Tigranocerta looming on the horizon, maybe only two or three days away. Maxentius pushed his thoughts aside and tried to sleep.

The next morning, Maxentius was awoken by a loud hubbub, voices raised in anger. Dragging himself out of bed and dressing with haste, he exited his tent to see whether they were under attack again. He came across a group of soldiers who were shouting something about conspiracies and assassinations. It took Maxentius a good fifteen minutes to get them to calm down enough to explain with some form of coherence what on earth was going on. One of them, Secundus Tullius Rufinus, a gruff career soldier nearing retirement, was a man with whom Maxentius had become good friends over the last two years. A most reliable officer, Tullius was always good to have by your side in the heat of battle. Maxentius called his friend over —

"Tullius! Finally, someone with some sense. What is all this racket about? Who has been assassinated?"

"It appears there was a plot on Corbulo's life. No, no…" Tullius raised his hand to placate his superior, as Maxentius started to interrupt, "…he isn't harmed! During the night, someone found out what was afoot. I have no idea who it was or how they discovered what was going on, but as you heard it's created a bit of a ruckus. Apparently it was those, supposedly, loyal…" this was growled in sarcastic tones, "…Armenian nobles; you know the ones who joined us at Rhandeia, that were involved. Once he heard what was going on, Corbulo had them brought to his tent and after interrogating them, ordered that they be executed." There was silence when Tullius finished his account. Others who had gathered around to listen just stood; stunned by the news.

Maxentius was horrified that it had come to this.

"I cannot believe that they managed to trick us into believing they are loyal. We have protected them throughout this miserable march. Kept them safely away from any skirmish we have fought and this is how they repay us?" Maxentius shook his head in disbelief and disgust. "Every time we think we have made progress by negotiation or when that fails outright warfare, we lose it again owing to the greed of these duplicitous nobles." He punched his fist into the palm of his other hand, pacing the ground in agitation.

"What did they think? That if they assassinated Corbulo, it would end Rome's commitment to subduing this land? They are fools! It would have changed nothing. Another general would be in place before they could blink and, although Corbulo has a reputation for harsh treatment, sometimes the devil you know is better than the one you have yet to meet."

The others agreed and fell to debating whether Corbulo really intended to kill the traitors. Maxentius thanked Tullius and then strode off to join his fellow centurions, who were also discussing the conspiracy. All were dumfounded.

The nobles were executed in front of the whole legion, their bodies left for the carrion birds; Corbulo ordering that the head of one of them be kept. In a sombre mood, the soldiers struck camp and began the last leg of their march into Tigranocerta. Two days later the vast column of men approached the city walls. Corbulo indicated that he wanted the severed head of the nobleman catapulted into the town. Once this had been carried out and without waiting for an invite, the general clicked the reins of his huge stallion and led his soldiers — all clad in full battle armour — into the city.

Coincidentally, the severed head landed almost at the feet of the city council, who had gathered to discuss whether it was worth defending their city against the oncoming Romans. The sight of this simple, yet ghoulish warning of what they might expect, should they resist the advancing army, was enough to make them capitulate unconditionally.

In reward, Corbulo chose leniency and did not destroy the city or punish its inhabitants. In gratitude, the townsfolk opened up the city's halls offering the soldiers somewhere dry and warm to sleep and for a time calm reigned.

Chapter Six

Jerusalem ~ AD60

In the days that followed the attack on Daniel, the young man hovered between life and death and it was several weeks before they were certain that his life no longer hung in the balance. Despite the best efforts of the two physicians, infection set in prolonging Daniel's recovery, even with Hannah and her uncle sharing his care, never leaving the young man's side. Hannah spent hours watching over her brother's friend, while Gideon saw to others who needed his skills. Even when they considered the danger had passed and that it was safe to carry him to his own home, Hannah continued to help Elisheva often staying overnight, allowing Daniel's mother to rest.

They never discovered the identity of the assailants but Daniel's friends, already resentful at a system that seemed to be fracturing around them, used the incident to fuel their ire. What had been, until now, simply a group of disenchanted youths became far more serious; especially when they discovered that those of like mind, intent on undermining the Roman influence in their city, were innumerable.

Hannah was more concerned with them getting hurt. Not long after Daniel had gone home, she and Gideon spent nearly a whole day treating a variety of wounds after a discussion between opposing factions got out of hand, although Hannah was never really sure about how accurate a description the 'discussion' part was. To those involved, their reasoning was sound, but to Hannah it seemed as though they were just bent on creating mayhem regardless of the consequences. Days like this were becoming the rule rather than the exception.

Daniel eventually recovered, but the attack changed him. He had been a gentle soul who preferred reading and study to the more physical pursuits of his friends. Now he was harder and his eyes glinted with barely suppressed rage. The daily tasks of all these young men were arduous, their bodies robust and vigorous, add this to a mind burning with righteous indignation and you have a city seething with impotence, ready to support anyone whose aim is to oust those whom they consider to have outstayed their welcome.

Hundreds of men who had worked on the rebuilding of the Temple — now reaching completion — no longer had employment, their regular income gone. Although some did manage to get work repaving the city's streets, many did not. The gap between rich and poor suddenly loomed very large. Privations, previously confined to the overcrowded slums, were now a part of everyday life for all but the very rich; and ailments, once easily cured were becoming harder to treat.

Such hardships were excellent fodder for nationalistic groups such as the Zealots, already part of an underground revolution that had been operating for years but who had of late; found that their resentment could no longer be confined to dark rooms and secret meetings. Then there was the increasing popularity of the Sicarii, considered an extreme splinter group and deemed little more than urban terrorists by the Romans, and a faction who had no problem murdering anyone they felt to be a Roman collaborator, even in broad daylight. The biggest problem continued to be who to trust.

Hannah and Gideon now faced another concern — disease. Living in an area regarded as relatively comfortable, virulent epidemics were not usually something they had to deal with. Yes, there were always common maladies to be aware of and the occasional outbreak of fever; but the houses here were somewhat larger than those in the poorer areas, fewer people lived in them, the streets were clean and, in general, the inhabitants were healthy. Suddenly unknown infections and viruses were felling whole communities. Some were quite mild, the sufferer recovering quickly, but others developed illnesses that seemed impossible to treat and more than should have, died.

Customarily, Hebrews believed that any affliction was the result of God's displeasure and that only God could heal the victim. By the time that Gideon had begun his practice, however, they also accepted that physicians were instruments of God; a vessel through which God sometimes worked to heal the sufferer. Most could not understand what they had done to incur God's wrath, for despite living their lives as instructed in the Torah, offering sacrifices to God and spending time at prayer, citizens kept dying.

Gideon, a devout Jew, was not entirely convinced that his God was angry enough to allow so many innocents to perish, recognising that this was a temporal epidemic, not a celestial one. With all the other hardships they were facing, such as poverty, an inability to provide for their loved ones and lack of proper nourishment — and even though it should have been as instinctual as breathing — people became lax in their daily habits. Forgetting to cleanse themselves or their homes frequently, or to allow the air to circulate, or to throw out rotting food, encouraged small pockets of germs to multiply. Adherence to basic hygiene would have prevented, or at least reduced the severity of most of the cases.

Spending hours visiting houses where the sick lay, both Gideon and Hannah extolled the need to keep isolated from their families, anyone who showed even the slightest symptoms. Soon, those ailing became too numerous and it was obvious that a different approach was necessary. Gideon persuaded some of his friends, who lived on the edge of the enclave to move out of their homes, allowing the physician to use them as temporary wards for those who were sick. It was better to have them in one place, yet set apart, than spread over a wide area risking further outbreaks.

Making sure the houses were cleansed thoroughly, Gideon and his loyal assistant set up as many beds as possible within each dwelling and put victims who showed similar disorders together. There were some with a coughing sickness, others with what seemed to be an acute digestive disorder and yet others who were running a fever that refused to be controlled. For the most part all Gideon and Hannah could do was treat the symptoms and let the diseases run their course. It was harrowing for they were unable to save everyone. Before the epidemic was over, and whatever had caused it eradicated for now, a shocking number had died — neighbours, friends and family.

Gideon was very concerned for Hannah, as despite the knowledge she was gaining from the experience, she was still only a child and he worried that the loss of all these people she knew and cared about would prove too painful for her. Often during the months they had been fighting the outbreak, he had tried, very hard, to persuade her to go home and let him handle it. She had just as vehemently refused; knowing that there was no way her uncle could possibly manage on his own.

Difficult as it was, she was learning so much. No amount of reading, studying manuscripts or talking with her uncle could have prepared her for what she was dealing with on a daily basis. Constantly cleaning up after patients who were vomiting, or unable to control their bowels. Sitting with disease-ravaged people trying to convince them that they weren't going to die, knowing that there was a good chance they might. Cleansing the bodies of those who, unfortunately, did die and then preparing them for the burial rituals.

One evening, as Hannah was sitting in her uncle's rooms sipping hot milk after another gruelling day, her brother appeared looking grim.

"What is it, Aharon?" asked Gideon.

"I need Hannah, actually I need both of you, to come with me."

"What's happened, Aharon?" Hannah queried, bewildered by her brother's expression.

"Just come." Hannah and Gideon hurried after the brawny youth, through the darkening streets, quiet now, as most families would be eating. Hannah's bewilderment turned to fear as Aharon pushed open the door to their own home and stood aside to let his sister and uncle enter. Motioning towards the sleeping area, Aharon explained, quietly, that both of their parents seemed to have succumbed to the sickness.

Hannah shot into the small space, falling onto her knees by her mother's side. Resting her hand on her mother's cheek, she noted the hot and dry skin and the rasping breaths. Glancing across to where her father lay, Hannah realised that, if anything, his symptoms were slightly worse. Both slept, but the three watching, knew this to be a temporary state.

"How did I miss this?" Hannah whispered, brokenly. "They are my parents. How did I not see that they were unwell?"

"I suspect, because they didn't think they were." Gideon replied. "I was talking with your father yesterday and although he looked tired, his skin and eyes were normal. I have been observing everyone in our neighbourhood and anyone who showed even a hint of sickness has been treated immediately. This has been a sudden onset."

Hannah muttered something about collecting the remedies that she thought might be useful and before Gideon could stop her, was out of the door. Running down to her uncle's house, the child dashed into the treatment room, gathering up anything she thought might help, along with a pile of cloths. Rushing back to her home, she tumbled through the door, jars of herbs and tinctures tipping out of the basket. Gideon caught her before she landed on her knees and righted the basket, gently taking it out of his niece's trembling hands and unobtrusively picking up the items that had fallen onto the floor.

Filling a bowl with clean water and after stirring in a small amount of frankincense and myrrh, Hannah soaked two pieces of cloth in the mixture, squeezing them out and applying one to her mother's face and hands and the other to her father's. While she was doing this, Gideon added a few drops of mentha to the oil lamp, the scent permeating throughout the room and almost immediately both patients began to breath more easily.

Over the next few days, Hannah refused to leave her parents for more than a few minutes, watching for changes that would indicate whether they were getting better. She tried everything she knew to alleviate their symptoms, but nothing seemed to work. Avigail, Hannah's mother, along with so many of their friends, had been caring for others in the neighbourhood who had been afflicted, never expecting that she might fall victim to infection. Her father Efraim, in his capacity as a merchant, had been travelling for many days, returning home exhausted.

Under normal circumstances Hannah's parents were healthy enough to throw off the minor maladies that ran through their community on a semi-regular basis, this time however, the circumstance was not normal and the malady was not minor. Even the most robust of people had succumbed to the epidemic and just when Gideon thought it beaten, it would pop up again with a whole new variety of symptoms. In the end, all they could do was keep their patients comfortable, make sure they drank plenty of water and where possible relieve the worst of the illness.

Aharon was persuaded to sleep at one of his friend's homes, reducing the risk to his person, while Hannah and Gideon continued to share the burden of care between them. One evening, Hannah was sitting next to her mother singing quietly, a lullaby Avigail had sung to her daughter as a babe in arms.

"Hannah, please will you bring me my casket from the shelf up there?" Her mother pointed to a small intricately woven basket in which Avigail kept her most treasured possessions. Hannah did as she was asked, lifting the basket down carefully and handing it her mother, who had pushed herself up against the wall. Making sure she tucked another blanket around her mother's shoulders for warmth, Hannah curled up on the floor and waited. This delicate casket brought back memories of a carefree childhood, for she had loved it when her mother let her touch the items inside; pins, ribbons and keepsakes.

Avigail opened the lid and lifted out a silver pin. She gave it to Hannah saying —

"I want you to have this, it will keep your mantle securely clasped, you know the one you have is next to useless." Her mother grinned albeit weakly, the first smile Hannah had seen for days.

"This is so beautiful, but surely you will need it, my mother. I am too young for something so dainty." Unable to help herself, Hannah turned the pin in her hand, mesmerised by the design. It was a gorgeous piece, fashioned from several lengths of very slender silver strands entwined around a central sliver.

"I would like you to have it. My mother gave it to me and now it is for you. You are becoming quite grown up and it is time you started to dress in a more adult manner." Avigail winked at Hannah's disgruntled expression. To her daughter, the idea of being an adult meant that she should take on the womanly duties that she would need when she eventually became a wife.

"I'm never getting married, mother. I am going to be a great healer. I can't do both. Aharon can get married and I shall pass the pin on to his daughter. I think I might make quite a good aunt."

"Oh, I think you might find you change your mind, my dear, when the right man comes along." Hannah looked rather perplexed. Arranged marriages were the norm; a girl did not have the option of choosing her husband.

"I'm sorry, my mother, but I do not want to be given to a man, even though I might know and like him. For I know that once married, I will no longer be able to practise as a healer. Please don't make me." Hannah beseeched her mother, the emerald green of her eyes — so unusual in a Hebrew girl — deepening in her earnestness to make her mother understand how important her work with Gideon was.

"I will let it be for now, Hannah, but we must talk about this again soon." Avigail chuckled at her daughter's relief. Biting her lip, Hannah had the strangest feeling she was letting her mother down.

"Maybe you should keep this until I am older. Maybe then I'll be a better daughter." Avigail stared at Hannah in astonishment —

"You think that I am disappointed in you, my daughter?" Hannah just gazed back, unable to speak and a recalcitrant tear ran down her cheek. Not one for crying she scrubbed it away fiercely. Avigail reached her thin hand up to her daughter's face, cupping it gently. "Hannah, my beautiful child, you could never disappoint me. You are brave and strong, loving, thoughtful and compassionate. You care about your friends and family and you go out of your way to help anyone who needs it, often to your own detriment. I love you more than you will ever know and I am very, very proud that you are my daughter."

The long speech tired Avigail and as she finished speaking, the words caught at the back of her throat sending her into a paroxysm of coughing. Hannah held her mother, stroking her back until the bout subsided and then persuaded her to drink some of the tincture Gideon had brewed up. The mixture had a calming effect and soon Hannah could see that her mother was drifting back to sleep.

Drawing the covers back up over Avigail's frail body, Hannah sat for a minute ruminating over her mother's words, a warmth settling over her heart. Glad that she wasn't making a complete hash of being a good daughter, Hannah's lips curved in a sweet smile as she went to check on her father.

He still slept and the child studied his face for several moments. Efraim looked gaunt, his body, like that of her mother's, was also too thin from the effort of fighting the sickness. A cold finger trailed its way down Hannah's spine as she noticed subtle changes to both of her parents indicating that they were far sicker than she had allowed herself to believe. Panic coursed through her; she couldn't lose her parents, they couldn't die, she hadn't had them for long enough.

Hannah ran out of the door and down to her uncle's house bursting in without knocking. Gideon was in the middle of treating a small boy suffering from toothache and without looking up from his task, waved his niece into the other room. It was maybe half an hour later before he came through to find Hannah, who was curled up in a shivering heap by the fire, her arms wrapped around herself. Gideon could tell that the girl was barely in control of her emotions. Sighing — knowing its likely cause — he lifted her up onto his lap, holding her head against his shoulder.

"Are they going to die?" She whispered, desolately. Gideon's heart constricted. He had been hoping that she had been so caught up in treating those under her care that she hadn't registered the pathway of the illness.

"I don't know, Hannah. They are both very sick, far sicker than perhaps you had realised and their bodies are struggling to survive. All we can do is pray and hope." Hannah shuddered.

"Why would God let them die? They are good people, everyone says so." Plaintively asked.

"I cannot say," replied Gideon, "but maybe God wants them home. Your mother and father have worked hard for many years and have raised two children of whom they are very proud. Perhaps it is time for them to be with God now."

"B-b-but, we will be alone. God has plenty of people, we only have one mother and one father." She stuttered miserably.

"You are not alone, Hannah, I am here. Should we lose your parents, I will not let any harm come to you." Her uncle's gentle words washed over her and Hannah started to feel a little less bereft.

"Maybe they will get better…" her voice trailed off hopefully. Gideon hugged her close, resting his chin on her head.

"There is always hope, my dear. We can only pray and wait and see." He took a deep breath; knowing he had to be honest with her, "let us take just one day at a time."

Chapter Seven

Corbulo wintered his troops in Tigranocerta and for a while there was a cautious easing of their, normally very strict, vigilance. The soldiers returned to their every-day tasks — drill, sword training and regular patrols around the city and its vicinity. Somewhat battle weary, Maxentius enjoyed being able to address the more mundane duties expected of him as a centurion; these included the ongoing training of those soldiers under his command, general administration and discipline — should it be required. On top of this, along with the other centurions, Maxentius was involved in the organisation of provisions; both for while they were in Tigranocerta and for the campaigns that would likely follow.

The Roman Army's inveterate distrust of the Parthians was well founded, for not long after Tigranocerta surrendered, the Parthian king, Vologases I, tried to re-enter Armenia. Thankfully, a timely response from Verulanus Severus, who had a large auxiliary force under his command, put paid to Vologases' attempt. The Parthian ruler retreated leaving Rome, for the time being, in control of Armenia. After granting several areas in the far west to loyal vassals, Rome installed a Cappodocian noble, Tigranes VI as their new client king.

In recognition of his success, Corbulo was accorded the governorship of Syria. This large and wealthy province was seen as a just reward for so distinguished a military career. Entrusting the protection of the new king to a garrison comprising several thousand of his soldiers, Corbulo departed to take up his new position. A period of relative peace followed. None of the commanders was naive enough to presume that Vologases had given up his claim on the Armenian throne, but they knew he was currently distracted attempting to quell an insurrection within his own borders by the Hyrcanians, another citizenry trying to rid themselves of Parthian rule.

Still based at Tigranocerta, the soldiers were able to treat themselves to a little rest and recreation. At the end of a long day, they could go into the city and discover what delights it had to offer. As always with men on campaign — wine, women and song was their preferred method of relaxation and Tigranocerta was no different from any other large city across the empire, offering a variety of entertainment.

A young man with all the usual urges that beset young men, Maxentius was easily persuaded to accompany his comrades to one of the many taverns on their rare free evenings. He did not, however, frequent the lupanarium — the local brothel — even though it was common practice for Romans to indulge in such pastimes, tolerating the half-hearted ribbing he took from his fellow soldiers for his restraint.

This did not mean that he didn't enjoy the company of women — he was a warm blooded male after all — but he preferred a more gentlemanly courtship. One day, while checking the provisions, Maxentius had met a young widow named Narineh, whose husband had died from sickness two years previously. She worked in the kitchens that supplied meals for the garrison; a tentative friendship had blossomed and the two began to spend more than the occasional hour together.

Concerned that Narineh would assume that he could offer her more than just his company, Maxentius had explained, with due care for her sensibilities, the nature of his life and that regulations did not permit him to marry — or that if he did, their union would not be recognised. An intelligent woman, Narineh was under no illusions; shrewd enough to realise that her time with this handsome soldier was fleeting. For her it was enough that he treated her kindly and that they enjoyed their free hours together. That they became closer than perhaps either of them anticipated was something they never discussed.

Having grown up in the city, Narineh was familiar with the locale. She would pack some food and delight in showing him places few would ever find. Maxentius loved exploring and Narineh proved an excellent guide, full of interesting information about the history of this land. More than this, it offered Maxentius a different perspective on the people the Romans had conquered and how they had adjusted to life under occupation. This was something he never forgot.

Life at Tigranocerta fell into a familiar pattern. The soldiers began to settle down, expecting to remain in the capital for a while. In place of the temporary workshops they had been using to maintain weapons, armour and any other military equipment, more solid structures started to appear. A dedicated forge, a stonemasons, a carpenter's shop and many more. It looked as though the garrison might become a permanent fixture. Many of the soldiers welcomed the prospect, as they had become comfortable in the city. The available amenities made life far more agreeable than constant marching, tents, privations and indigestible food.

All the typical duties and tasks that go on in a garrison continued to be performed, but because they were enjoying a cessation of hostilities, the rigorous schedule of training was slackened. In order to keep the soldiers occupied as well as to prevent them from becoming bored — which had a tendency to lead to friction within the ranks — Maxentius and his fellow officers decided, in addition to their daily training sessions, to introduce a regular tournament.

Using standard military divisions, each centuria of ten contubernia became one team and with the garrison standing at around three thousand soldiers, they ended up with a substantial number of teams, thus, in the interests of fairness, one tournament lasted two weeks. All the teams chose a name — usually that of a decisively won battle. The contests began within the centuriae, individual contubernia facing a multitude of challenges in a round robin competition. The winning teams then faced off against each other and as they advanced through each level of the competition, the challenges became more arduous and complicated. Nor were the tasks purely physical, some involved mental acuity such as planning battle strategies, or handling logistics, there was even a challenge related to basic medical care.

These competitions had the dual effect of encouraging the soldiers to work together to beat the opposing teams and also made them think about the administration of a garrison, something many soldiers had no reason to do — that was what their commanders were for. Learning from the commander at Rhandeia, however, the centurions at Tigranocerta now believed that an understanding of every aspect of a working garrison was essential for maintaining efficiency. For the teams themselves, military pride was at stake not to mention the prize, which was a full day without any duties for the winners, whose tasks would be divided amongst the losing centuriae.

Somewhat inclined to ridicule these championships at first, as time progressed the soldiers began to relish the challenge, which had the unexpected benefit of producing a much more cohesive garrison. Owing to military scheduling, the number of teams changed per tournament, as at any given time centuriae could be deployed elsewhere, but this merely served to intensify the competitive edge of those who remained within the city walls.

As a bit of fun, one of the workshops forged a trophy that the winners could display until bested and the carpenters fashioned a roll of honour — a wooden board nailed to a post outside the building that the army had co-opted as their principia — onto which the name of whichever team had won that particular tournament was carved. It became a matter of principle for the soldiers to see how many times their team's name appeared on the board.

Light hearted though it appeared, there was a serious reason behind these tournaments. On the one hand, it gave the centurions a chance to see which soldiers excelled at which challenges, allowing them to channel their expertise in the appropriate direction when organising rosters. On the other, it also meant that they could observe any soldier who struggled with a particular activity, determining whether more training would likely increase his competence or, depending on the activity in question, whether it was prudent to avoid assigning him such duties altogether.

A rather sober young man, it was years since Maxentius had indulged in frivolous fun and games but, to his surprise, he found these tournaments to be most enjoyable and along with the other centurions contrived to come up with original and inventive ways to test the soldiers under their command. Most importantly there was a new respect between soldier and officer and the camaraderie across the garrison increased tenfold. For a time the atmosphere was almost buoyant.

While all this was going on and aware that the current respite was likely only to be temporary, especially with reports trickling through from Parthia indicating that Vologases was preparing for another onslaught, the commanders kept a watchful eye on their environs. Patrols increased, their range widened and on a regular basis, a centuria would venture much further afield, scouting far into the distance, sometimes staying out for several days, returning with detailed reports of possible Parthian troop movements.

The soldiers had been in Tigranocerta scant months when the relaxed command suddenly tightened and the soldiers were placed back on battle footing. Maxentius and his fellow centurions, glad that they had implemented the team challenges, were satisfied that their men were ready, should an attack prove imminent.

Chapter Eight

Jerusalem ~ AD61

Standing in the middle of her home, Hannah twiddled with the piece of material hanging from her fingers. She was at a loss, the house was scrupulously clean, everything was at it should be, but she felt as though there was something more she ought to be doing. It was the day of her father's burial. Her mother had died seven days previously and her father, although initially appearing to rally, once he knew his beloved wife had lost her battle with the sickness, gave up his own fight.

The girl had spent long hours sitting by her parents; talking to them in her gentle voice, soothing their fevered skin, helping them to swallow food and medicines in a vain attempt to nourish and strengthen them. Crooning lullabies to help them sleep; all the while desperately hoping she could coax their exhausted souls to cling onto life. Had sheer force of will been all that was required, Hannah's parents would have survived, sadly it was not enough.

Hannah had not been present at either death, although this was not for want of trying. Attentive to the whims of the disease they had been struggling to contain, Gideon had noticed that the signs indicating that his brother's wife was sliding away from this world were beginning to manifest and had dispatched his niece on a seemingly urgent errand. Returning home to find her home full of mourners, Hannah had been devastated and realising what her uncle had done, refused to speak to him. She had undertaken the burial ritual anointing her mother's body with aromatic oils, the calming scent of myrrh and aloes wafting across the room, before wrapping her in a simple shroud. Then, following tradition, Avigail, wife of Efraim, was laid to rest in the family tomb, alongside her own parents and the two other children she had lost in their infancy.

She had performed the same rite for her father, who had died while Hannah slept, something she had rarely done during the last few weeks. It was almost as though he knew it would be less distressing on his only daughter, leaving her this way. That was it; suddenly her parents were no more. Two vital people, whose love and laughter had enveloped their home, were gone as though they'd never been here.

Alone in the room, Hannah let her memories roll around her head. The house had always been full of noise, full of family and friends; the youngsters spilling out into the street, chasing each other up and down, or playing games together; huge platters of food being passed around, the men talking about whatever it was men discussed, the women chuckling about the antics of their offspring, or gossiping about the shortcomings of their men — everyone always welcome.

Now there was only silence, no laughter or chatter and everything really was far too tidy. No smells of cooking, no hug as she came through the door. No one to chide her gently for spending hours with her uncle, no one to encourage her to try to become more feminine, no one to tweak her nose and tell her she was the most beautiful daughter in the world. There was no one at all. Hannah shook herself, that wasn't quite true, she still had Aharon and she supposed, grudgingly, that she did have her uncle, but she was still mad with him.

Looking for his sister, Aharon came through the door, pulling up sharply as he took in her too pale face and drooping shoulders. She was a shadow of herself and he was concerned that if she wasn't careful she too would fall victim to the sickness. Quietly he made his way over to where she stood.

"Hannah, they are waiting for us."

"I'm not going," her reply was barely a whisper.

"It is expected, they have prepared a meal for us to honour our parents. We must go."

"I cannot." She lifted her head and the pain in her eyes nearly felled him. She was too young to have to deal with such grief and for a split second he was angry with his parents for leaving them, for leaving her.

"Please, my sister, just for a short while. You must eat and these are people who love us." He paused for a moment and then continued. "It is your duty Hannah, you must not shirk it and our mother would expect nothing less." He forced a note of coolness into his voice, hoping it might get a reaction from her. She gazed at him and he could see tears forming in her wide green eyes, but she blinked them back, determined not to cry. In fact, she hadn't cried at all. Gideon and Aharon were both worried for her; she had not shown one iota of emotion at their parent's deaths, although it was obvious she was still enraged with her uncle.

Hannah was using this ire to keep her going, to help her put one foot in front of the other. To lose one parent was hard enough, but to lose both and in the space of a week, the girl didn't know how to function anymore. On top of this, she had barely slept and had lost several friends, both young and old to the same epidemic. It was easier not to feel anything, that way she somehow managed to get up every day and carry out her regular chores before going along to her uncle's home. She might still be mad at him, but there was no way she was going to stop helping him.

Aharon's tone cut through the fog in her brain and she nodded.

"I apologise, Aharon. I was not thinking. I will do as you say." Her voice was stilted, empty and her brother's heart clenched. He held out his hand and as she grasped it, he could feel that hers was trembling. He squeezed it gently and drew her out of the house, along to the place where their parents' friends had laid out a mourning repast. The food was plain and simple, the mourners quiet. As Hannah and Aharon approached, they turned as one and waited in silence. Aharon thanked them for their kindness and for helping them through this difficult time. He said a short prayer, thanking God and asking that the food be blessed.

Unable to recall whether this was normal at a burial meal, Hannah thought Aharon's words sounded very dignified and respectful. She continued to grip her brother's hand tightly, unable to let go. Formalities over, the atmosphere relaxed and everyone started talking. Stories of Avigail and Efraim filled the air as those who had gathered celebrated the life of their friends. During the day, others joined them; their grief tempered by the joy of having known two people who had touched so many lives.

After a while, Raizel came to sit with her best friend, taking Hannah's hand in hers, not talking, just being there. Her presence soothed Hannah, it always had. There was something serene about Raizel; everything was less complicated when she was around. Hannah could not explain it, but her friend's quiet composure was a balm to her weary soul. Aharon came over with a platter in his hand asking whether they would like anything to eat. Hannah shook her head, but Raizel was having none of it.

"You must eat, Hannah. You need to be strong or you will be no use to others who are sick or injured. Your mother would be upset if she knew you weren't eating properly." Raizel spoke gently but firmly and Hannah acquiesced reluctantly, nibbling on some bread and fruit. Between them, the two girls cleared the platter and Raizel asked Aharon whether he would mind bringing them some more. He grinned at Raizel, who smiled back; their feelings clear on their faces, had anyone been paying attention.

The day wore on, Gideon disappeared for a time, needing to attend to a few patients but he returned as the sun began to dip below the buildings. All the food had gone, the wine had been drunk and everyone had left. Hannah was still sitting on the wooden bench where she had been for most of the day. She watched the light change and leaned her head back against the wall, waiting for the darkness to descend. Hannah loved the night sky, she could stare at it for hours, trying to imagine how many stars there were and who else across the world was looking at them.

Gideon came to sit next to her. She shuffled away ostensibly giving him room, but in reality putting distance between them.

"Hannah, you have to stop being so angry with me. I did what your mother asked of me, you must respect her wishes." His niece glowered at him, but did not speak. Her uncle sighed. "Come now, you are nearly ten and four years old, some of your friends are already betrothed. This behaviour might be acceptable for a petulant child, but not for a young woman who wishes others to take her seriously as a healer." He paused then continued —

"I know you wanted to be with your mother, but she did not want you to watch her die. Just before she went to be with God, she asked me to tell you that you should always follow your heart and that if you truly wanted to be a healer then you should strive to be the very best healer you could be. She also told me how much she loved you."

"She did?" Hannah murmured so quietly that Gideon had to lean close to hear. He nodded waiting, sensing that there was more. "I don't know what to do now they're gone. I have never had to worry about anything; they were always there to do the worrying for me. I can't cook, you know I'm hopeless," she gave a wry grimace, making Gideon chuckle. "I can clean and sew, but I don't know which stalls at the markets are the best for food, I never went with her. I never offered to assist her with anything more than my household chores." The child's voice rose in her anguish. "How can she have been proud of me? I was never there to help; I never did anything to make her proud. I have been selfish and now she's gone." Aharon had come to find out where his sister was and heard her last few words.

"Hannah! What is going on? You need to calm yourself; the neighbours will wonder what on earth is the matter. It is time you snapped out of this mood." Aharon spoke harshly and Gideon tried to speak, to explain, but his tall nephew waved his hand and rather rudely hushed his uncle. Standing in the street, hands on his hips, Aharon glared at his sister.

"I don't care about the neighbours." Hannah hissed, suddenly livid with her brother. He had always been her protector, watching out for her. How dare he speak to her like this? They had only just buried their father, barely twelve hours ago. Aharon had been so kind during the day, now this! What was wrong with him? Her temper began to bubble.

"Who do you think you are? What right do you have to speak to me this way? You are not my father! You are not my father!" She fairly shrieked the last sentence and flew at her brother, fists clenched and small though she was, managed to beat on his chest, railing at him. Aharon merely wrapped his arms around her, holding her tightly to him effectively stopping her flailing punches from reaching their mark.

Without warning, Hannah slumped, and the tears that she had refused to cry finally spilled over, cascading down her cheeks like a spring downpour. Aharon stood, letting her cry it out, never relinquishing his hold as she sobbed brokenly against him. Now she had started to cry, she couldn't stop and Gideon guessed that hysteria lurked close to the surface. Aharon, recognising the same thing, scooped up his sister and moved to sit next to his uncle on the bench. Settling Hannah on his knee, he spoke softly to her —

"You must try to stop now, Hannah, you will make yourself ill if you don't." He ran his hand up and down her back slowly and rhythmically, calming her. Knowing he was right, Hannah made a determined effort to stem the flood, hiccuping as she tried to swallow her tears. Gideon patted her knee.

"I know it doesn't feel like it right now, but tomorrow things won't seem so bad and the next day even less so. You needed to cry, it is unhealthy not to allow yourself to grieve. You were so tightly wound up, I was afraid you might snap." She smiled rather tremulously at her uncle.

"I am sorry I have been petulant, my uncle. I do not deserve your kindness." Gideon smiled at his niece and cupping her chin in his hand said —

"Do not think on it my dear. I have broad shoulders on which an angry niece can sit quite comfortably, until she comes to her senses." She flung her arms around him and hugged him tightly.

"I love you." She muttered into his chest, her face flushing as she said the words she had never uttered before. "I'm glad you are still here." Gideon chuckled

"I love you too, Hannah. Now, I think it might be a good idea for you to get some sleep."

"My head aches." Hannah said tiredly, rubbing her forehead, as she yawned prodigiously.

"Time for bed, my sister. Come." Aharon pushed her off his knee and made to stand up, holding his hand out to her in much the same way as he had done earlier and in much the same way she grasped it, her slender fingers curling around his huge palm.

"Thank you, Aharon." Smiling up at her brother who grinned back at her in the gloom. "Oh dear," she gulped, "everything seems so far away." Her voice fading and Hannah swayed as suddenly everything overwhelmed her. She would have fallen had Aharon not been quick to catch her; swinging his diminutive sister back into his arms, the rangy youth carried her home and laid her in bed. She never stirred, exhaustion finally staking its claim.

Chapter Nine

Armenia ~ AD61

Rome meanwhile had not been resting on its laurels. Detailed reports from Corbulo before he left to take up his commission in Syria had led them to strengthen their forces in Cappadocia. Quite opportune as it happened because several events occurred that brought the situation to an acrimonious head.

Tigranes VI, without any prior referral to Rome or her commanders in Armenia, decided to invade Adiabene, a province close to the southwestern border and under Parthian protection. The Roman army at Tigranocerta took no part; in fact, they were rather aghast at the temerity of the client king, for acting without approval. The governor of Adiabene begged Vologases for support. His plea encouraged the Parthian ruler to finalise treaty negotiations with the Hyrcanians, thus ending that particular rebellion and freeing up a considerable force able to launch an assault against Tigranes. Not content with that, Vologases also pronounced his brother Tiridates was, once more, the king of Armenia.

In the meantime, hearing reports of attack and counter-attack and aware of the vulnerability of Tigranocerta, the Roman army mobilised. However, although the garrison numbered around four thousand legionaries including auxiliaries and cavalry, the commanders were concerned that they were still too few to withstand a large-scale assault and were concerned that Tiridates might besiege the city. As Syria was closer than Rome and as the governor there was familiar with the Armenian situation, it was decided that a contingent should be sent to Corbulo with the request that he assign them more troops.

Maxentius, now the *primus pilus*, or commanding centurion of the first cohort of his legion — in the main owing to his outstanding military instincts, not to mention his courage on the battlefield — was directed to undertake the assignment. He would take a company of cavalry, for not only were the horsemen experienced scouts, but also it meant they could travel much more quickly. Corbulo wasn't just across the next rise. Antioch, the Roman capital of Syria was two weeks hard riding; although there were rumours that Corbulo was at Zeugma supervising the construction of a bridgehead. Even so, this was still a seven-day ride and then they would be marching the troops back, the task was neither speedy nor simple.

Plans were made, weapons checked, routes marked out and two days later, they set out. It would be a hazardous journey; as before entering Syria, they had to cross in and out of territory that was constantly changing sides. Maxentius guessed that it was preferable for a centurion to go than a commander, the lower rank being somewhat expendable.

In the two days prior to departing, Maxentius spent as many free hours as possible, with Narineh. Under no illusions as to the danger of his assignment, he didn't want to leave without explaining those risks to the woman he had, unexpectedly, become so close to. She deserved nothing less and even though they both understood the limitations of their relationship, Maxentius felt a certain responsibility towards her. Wanting to ensure she wasn't pestered by any of the other soldiers, he asked his friend, Tullius to watch over Narineh — the old soldier agreeing without question.

Narineh had already prepared herself for this day, for though she expected Maxentius to return, she realised that it was unlikely he would remain at Tigranocerta. Young as he was, he had gained respect amongst the commanders for his measured approach and tactical thinking, which along with his ability to understand the local populace, marked him out in the eyes of those looking to promote. A soldier of equestrian status, his expertise would be required elsewhere in the Empire. She would miss him. He had brought the light back into her life, but in her heart of hearts she knew that their time together was ephemeral, better to part now before their emotions became too entangled.

In the dawn light, Maxentius and his horsemen set out. It was a cool morning, with the promise of a warm day ahead. The light was magical at this time of day, the landscape spread out before them was slightly undulating, the long forgotten winter rains had encouraged the hardy crops to grow and areas of green stood testament to the efforts of both local and soldier. Much of their route would be across the arid plain, through which ran the Tigris and Euphrates rivers. This was where they would be the most vulnerable to ambush. Although technically Roman territory, the upper basin was close to the Parthian border and skirmishes were a regular occurrence. The soldiers were hoping to be able to travel at night for some of their journey to reduce the possibility of such encounters.

The weather favoured them and except for one or two minor fracas — easily dealt with — they arrived at Corbulo's temporary headquarters without incident. Apprised of the situation, Corbulo wrote to the Emperor Nero suggesting that as Syria was such a vital province and could not be left unguarded, perhaps a separate legate should be dispatched to Cappadocia to be responsible for the conflict in Armenia. At the same time, he sent two legions back with Maxentius to augment the garrison at Tigranocerta and moved his remaining three legions up the Euphrates to fortify the line as a precaution against a Parthian invasion.

Maxentius and the legions travelled as fast as possible, bearing in mind there were now over ten thousand men on the move. Every Roman soldier, however, was used to such journeys and they covered many miles each day. Evenings were spent chatting around campfires, discussing strategies and manoeuvres and Maxentius came to know and respect all of the ranking officers; unaware that in the not too distant future, one of them, a young military tribune, would have the power to save or destroy everything that Maxentius held dear. Maxentius would be very thankful that they had become, if not friends — a term hardened warriors never bandied about — at least good comrades during those long days between Zeugma and Tigranocerta.

Thankfully, the weather held, it was early summer and the days were warm and dry, making the long distances less arduous than they might have been. A mood of anticipation, even zeal flourished amongst the men, it was all very nice building bridges and fortifying frontiers but a battle, that was what a soldier longed for. That was why they had joined, in

their opinion anyway, the greatest military force in the world
— to fight. Their eagerness translated into haste and before
many days had passed they could see Tigranocerta on the
horizon.

Luckily, they arrived before the enemy and were quickly
installed within the city. While Maxentius had been away,
Tigranes, possibly realising the error of his ways, had begun
stockpiling supplies and ensuring that the city was strengthened
against any possible onslaught. Fortuitously the river
Nicephorius flowed alongside a considerable section of the city
walls and, where it didn't, a huge ditch had been dug. So now,
there were around fifteen thousand soldiers, plus auxiliaries and
cavalry, as well as hundreds of loyal Armenians who refused to
surrender their city.

Narineh met Maxentius the evening of his return, as she
finished her working day. They savoured their reunion, but
Narineh sensed that her solider was indeed slipping away. It
was a subtle shift and probably definable only to her, but she
made no comment, determined to enjoy whatever time she
believed was left.

Their preparations, military efficiency and sheer wealth of
numbers stood the Roman army in good stead when the
Adiabeni did lay siege — left to do so by the Parthians who
being cavalry-men, were inexperienced and — in all honesty
— generally disinclined to participate. It was a brave attempt,
siege-engines and ladders were moved into position, volleys
were fired over the walls, but the soldiers inside the city
withstood the attack and quickly drove it back.

The Adiabeni were further hampered when the Parthians,
advancing to support the siege, were compelled to abort their
mission because of something as simple as a shortage of fodder
for their horses, rendering them completely ineffectual.
Corbulo seized this opportunity to send an envoy to Vologases,
the outcome being that the Parthian king withdrew his general
from Armenia. The siege was broken.

There was great rejoicing in Tigranocerta, although all
inside were of the consensus that they would have won anyway,
being quite the superior force. Celebrations, the like of which
had not been seen for many a year, went on for days. The

centurions and their commanders were required to furnish Rome with reports, so spent long hours discussing the siege, its outcome and its implications for the region.

During this time, Maxentius was assigned a new command. He was to take a detachment of soldiers comprising a cohort, auxiliaries and horsemen to Masada, a military outpost in the Judaean desert, near the Sea of Salt. The soldiers would replace a detachment that had served their requisite four years on the post and would be returning to their legions. Maxentius and his cohort would travel part of the way with the two legions who were to be withdrawn to Rhandeia, then continue down through Syria, past Jerusalem and on to Masada. The journey was well over five hundred miles and would take around thirty days — conditions permitting. However, Maxentius was not averse to discovering pastures new and he had long since ceased to question any decision the army chose to make.

The biggest hurdle to all this was that Maxentius, although *primus pilus*, was still only a centurion and garrison commanders were usually legates — men of senatorial status. However, the military hierarchy had it in hand. Maxentius being of equestrian rank could be promoted to, what was in effect, a vice-commander, who took charge in the absence of a general. Usually this was for a legion and although Maxentius would be in charge of far fewer soldiers, it allowed for the possibility of him being assigned the command of larger units or even a legion in the future — should the need arise.

Military regulations and procedure satisfied, Maxentius prepared for his new posting. It was strange to be packing up after being so long in one place. He hadn't spent this length of time anywhere since he had joined the army just over three years previous. Maxentius experienced a certain sadness knowing he would have to leave Narineh, but it was evident to him that while he would miss her presence, saying goodbye would not bring him to his knees. He had long accepted that such a depth of emotion was not something he would ever encounter while in the army and neither did he wish to. To fall in love with a woman so completely was an encumbrance he could well do without.

They managed to snatch a few hours together, but farewells are painful and Maxentius did not want to cause Narineh any more grief than was necessary. She had already lost a husband. The two parted on the best terms possible and as Maxentius left Tigranocerta the following day, his one glance behind caught the eyes of a solitary woman standing on the city walls, her long dark hair lifting in the breeze, swirling around a body that was held immobile. He inclined his head and his lips curved in a slow sweet smile, probably one she would not see, then turned to face the next chapter of his life.

Chapter Ten

Jerusalem ~ AD63

Hannah smiled delightedly as her brother and his new wife thanked everyone for their blessings. She really hadn't been at all surprised, when six months ago, Aharon and Raizel told her that they were to be betrothed. For long enough Hannah had noticed that things had changed between them, no longer simply an older brother and a childhood friend; suddenly they were seeking each other out. Then there was the odd whispered word, certain nuances, sideways glances and secret smiles when they thought no one was looking.

Had Hannah and Aharon's parents been alive, Hannah herself probably wouldn't have registered the change quite so quickly. But they weren't and because she had come to rely on Aharon, maybe more than a younger sister should, she was aware that sometimes he wasn't where she expected him to be. She had grumbled about it to Gideon one afternoon, as their last patient was leaving, but her uncle merely reminded her that Aharon had his own life to attend to and couldn't always be at the beck and call of his sister.

Not long after this conversation she had seen the two together and everything clicked into place. She was pleased for them both; Raizel was her dearest friend and Aharon had long been her champion, more so now that it was just the two of them.

Gideon had taken on the role of guardian to negotiate the betrothal and the *mohar,* or gift, from the bridegroom to his bride's family had already been set aside by Efraim before he died and entrusted to Gideon. Apparently Efraim and Avigail as well as Raizel's parents had hoped for this match. Initially, out of respect for those grieving the young couple had decided to keep their blossoming relationship quiet; it also gave Hannah the chance to come to terms with the change.

It was now almost two years since they had lost their parents and for a long time Aharon and Gideon had been worried for Hannah as they watched her shrink into herself, forgetting to eat and not sleeping properly; she became like a ghost, a pale version of the vivacious girl they knew. Eventually, however, her natural resilience and love of life kicked in and she pulled herself together; and although she still struggled with her loss, for the most part she had moved on. She barely had time to think about it anyway as she was busy all day, every day assisting Gideon. Lately she had even acquired her own patients; usually women who preferred to discuss their symptoms with another female rather than Gideon. Of course, she still deferred to her uncle, but it was gratifying to realise that the locals accepted her as a healer in her own right and trusted her skills.

Recently, she had even persuaded Gideon to let her carry out the occasional operation, nothing too complicated, but she had proven herself more than capable and it eased his burden too. Gideon was feeling his age, for although still considered relatively young, he had begun to notice that his joints ached more than they ought and that he was beset by headaches rather frequently. He assumed it was simply a legacy of many years of long hours. Working in half-light and conditions that were sometimes less than satisfactory, along with the privations they were all facing as a result of the ongoing unrest. In truth, he was glad that Hannah had chosen to stay with him, rather than become a replica of her mother and take over the running of their household. Mind you, as Hannah often pointed out, if left in charge they'd have starved long ago, her astonishing lack of culinary expertise was legendary.

Conscious that her uncle was not quite so active as he had been, Hannah watched over him; trying to shoulder as much of his workload as she could without him realising. Aharon had assured her that their uncle was just getting on in years, but Hannah, fearful that they would lose him like they had their parents, kept a close eye on him.

Today was for joy though, so Hannah pushed her concerns aside and allowed herself to be swept along with the revelry. The ceremony under the traditional canopy was long over and Raizel, richly dressed in her bridal attire and still veiled, had been carried along to Aharon and Hannah's home, which would now be hers also. The couple had been left to consummate their marriage in relative peace while the festivities continued, the whole neighbourhood sharing in the wedding feast.

It was not unusual for wedding celebrations to last for seven days. Hannah wasn't sure she would be able to last that long, already exhausted and this was only the first day. She would be staying at Gideon's house for the week, leaving Aharon and Raizel to begin their married life without a third person in the house. Both had assured Hannah that she would continue to live with them, but the young girl didn't want to be in the way, at least for the first few days. Gideon was more than happy for his niece to stay with him; she was there most of the time anyway.

As she sat on one of the benches, watching the fun, her brother's friends came over to chat. Several of them were more than a little interested in the girl who had absolutely no idea how bewitching she was. At nearly ten and six years old, she was still petite, her chestnut curls — utterly untameable for the most part — usually spilling over her shoulders and down her back were, today, caught in a leather clasp. Her green eyes sparkling with laughter at the antics of some of the children, dropping on the ground to play whatever game they were drawing her into.

Hannah was not in the slightest bit aware that these young men were interested in anything other than friendship. She had known them all her life and to her they were like family. She still had no desire to marry, her work with Gideon absorbing all her attention and she was not prepared to let someone else dictate her future. Thankfully, Aharon was sympathetic and trusted that when the right man came along, all her nonsense would fall away and she would embrace the change. Mercifully, he had no idea just how great this change would turn out to be.

One of the men was called Tobias. He lived quite close to Hannah and Aharon and as children they had played together. Hannah could remember him pulling at her plaits and chasing her up the street with a bucket of water, laughing uproariously when she screamed for Aharon to save her before Tobias tipped the cold water over her head. Aharon had always included her in their games. She could run as fast as any of them and could climb a tree in half the time, the boys' tall lankiness, no match for her diminutive stature and agility.

Aharon worried that she had become too much of a tomboy, that playing with his friends and spending time with Gideon had made her an unlikely choice as a bride. It seemed however that these were the attributes that made her all the more attractive and, knowing his sister's opinion on the matter, he had begun fending off hints from several of his friends who wished to be considered as a suitable husband for Hannah. Even though he was well within his rights to arrange a match for her, he did not want to force her into anything. More than this, in his heart of hearts he knew Hannah was not ready, quite worldly in certain aspects of her life, she was still very naive when it came to matters of marriage and being a wife.

Tobias however was determined that Hannah should be his. He had watched her grow up into a beautiful young woman and he contrived to spend as much time with her as was acceptable without actually making his interest official. Hannah, in the meantime, took no notice; in fact, it was conceivable that she barely registered his existence, other than as one of their friends. Aharon had noticed, as had Gideon and they knew something would have to be done sooner rather than later before things got out of hand.

Tobias, along with so many of the young men from the neighbourhood had become deeply involved in the underground movements that hoped to oust the Romans. Running battles with the authorities and organised violence had become the norm and the men who had grown up under the shadow of oppression longed to be free of it. Youths who were once fun loving boys only interested in how they could sneak out of lessons were now hardened activists, sneaking into Roman controlled areas of the city and creating mayhem. Always angry, their lives no longer carefree, they watched, learned, listened and then acted — usually under the dictates of a local Zealot or Sicarii faction.

Hannah was saddened by these changes and frustrated that her friends couldn't keep themselves out of harm's way, a constant queue of men coming to Gideon's clinic to be treated. From cuts and bruises to more serious injuries, even this didn't prevent them from being caught up in the fight. She was also angry with them for the grief they caused their families and although she understood the reasoning behind their actions, it didn't mean that she wanted any involvement in it or with them.

Tobias too had changed, gone was the fun loving boy who enjoyed silly games and treated Hannah like one of the gang; he was now somewhat brutish and thoughtless. Much as he wanted Hannah to be his wife, he also believed her too independent, that she had more freedom than was acceptable and that she needed a stronger hand than her brother's to curb her spirited ways. This was exactly what Aharon didn't want. The thought of Hannah's zest for life being crushed was, to him, unconscionable. If she lost this essential part of who she was, she would no longer be Hannah. He also felt that Tobias was crass and boorish — certainly not the right person for Hannah and had dismissed the notion out of hand.

Hannah, of course, continued to treat all the young men the same as always, respectfully, and at arms' length. She would chide them gently if she felt they were becoming too familiar, but somehow managed to do so without them realising that she was spurning them and they all settled back into the comfortable and friendly relationship they had long shared. All that is, except Tobias. However, even he thought it rather insensitive to broach the subject today, it being Aharon's wedding. It was not done to steal the limelight from the happy couple. He would bide his time and speak to Aharon eventually. Hannah wasn't going anywhere.

As the sun began to dip towards the horizon, Aharon and Raizel reappeared amongst their guests, looking supremely happy and maybe a little flustered. Aharon could not let go of Raizel's hand and she obviously revelled in his touch. Their joy was contagious and the celebrations carried on well into the night. Hannah slipped away earlier than many of the guests, tired from the long day and maybe a little sad. She had gained a sister but she had now lost her brother, or rather their relationship was changing. His first concern was no longer her but Raizel and while Hannah accepted that this was as it should be, it was going to take some getting used to.

She traipsed into her uncle's house to find Gideon cleaning up his treatment room. He had left hours ago; calls on his time by patients stopped for nothing, not even a wedding. Hannah moved to help, but her uncle waved her through into the adjacent room, telling her that there was hot milk in the pot over the fire. Hannah poured some into two drinking bowls, adding a dollop of honey and sprinkling cinnamon over it then curled up on one of the chairs, letting the fragrant spice waft over her.

Gideon strolled through shortly thereafter to join her. The pair sat in companionable silence as they drank, enjoying the peace.

"Everything's changing," muttered Hannah after a while. "I don't like it."

"Life always changes, Hannah," replied her uncle, "and it is not necessarily a bad thing. If things never changed, we would never appreciate what we have. I think that throughout your life, you will face many changes, some good, some not so good, but all will make you stronger and more capable."

"Do you really think so, uncle?" she questioned doubtfully. "I don't feel very strong. In fact I feel like going to bed and not getting up again." Gideon chuckled.

"We all have days when we feel like that, my dear, but then we do get out of bed and life doesn't seem so tough and the next day is better and the next and soon we have forgotten what it was that laid us low." Hannah didn't look convinced, but her uncle didn't push it, simply patted her on the knee and suggested that she should go to bed, for it was late and it was likely that they would have patients on the morrow, as well as the ongoing wedding festivities. Hannah released a sigh that would have blown over a lesser man and nodded tiredly. Dragging herself off to bed, she nestled under the covers and was asleep before Gideon had tidied up the bowls.

Later, Gideon checked on his niece, she was sleeping peacefully. He went out into the street and spent long moments studying the stars; their vast yet delicate beauty making his worries seem inconsequential and he felt them flow out of him. His headache had returned, so he mixed up a draft he found efficacious for such agues, going back outside to sip it in the cool of the night, finally able to relax under that endless sky.

Chapter Eleven

Armenia to Judaea ~ AD62~63

The march from Tigranocerta to the encampment where Maxentius and the other two legions separated was uneventful. The days were hot, summer was reaching its height and it seemed that for a while, peace reigned across Armenia. Although the soldiers were not naive enough to think that this was a permanent respite, it did mean that they could lower their guard, just a little. Three days of brisk marching brought them to Amida from where Maxentius' contingent would head south, while the two legions ranged north to Rhandeia. Here Maxentius formally took his leave of his soldiers, who would not be accompanying him to Masada.

He had hoped that Tullius Rufinus, who had become his right hand man, might be assigned to this post also, but Tullius was at the end of his army career and would likely retire before the year was out. Tullius himself was very pleased to be going back to Rome, already planning what to do with his discharge benefit. The two were part of a close and steadfastly loyal group of soldiers who had done everything together for over four years, from daily drill, to reconnaissance, to long days of marching, to eating, to relying on each other in battle; inevitably, their bond was tight. All except Maxentius were headed to Rhandeia. The cohort Maxentius would command, consisted of detachments from two of those legions he had gone to request from Corbulo before the siege.

On the night before they went their separate ways, Maxentius and his men decided to toast their friendship, their careers, their successes and failures and their new beginnings — and anything else they could think of — with one, or maybe ten, too many goblets of wine. The next morning, in spite of feeling as though they'd been run over by a siege engine, the soldiers made their farewells and set off. It took several hours before Maxentius felt even close to being human again, thankfully they did not meet any insurgents and their day progressed without incident. He knew that if the detachment managed a good pace and the weather held, their anticipated arrival at Masada would be within the month.

Several days later, Zeugma loomed up in front of them. The detachment would break here for two days to rest the horses properly and restock their supplies. Maxentius had spent the journey between Amida and Zeugma getting to know his new command. The soldiers were a mixed bunch, many fresh-faced youths and others who had been in the army for years. Maxentius had been concerned that they would consider him too young or too inexperienced to have this position conferred, but as far as he could tell, they were just glad it wasn't them. Being in charge involved too much administration. Most preferred to fight, eat and sleep, uncaring of the necessity for reports and meetings and the constant referral to Rome.

His new command included quite a large number of recruits and Maxentius wasn't sure why they'd been assigned this post, it seemed a rather dull appointment for new soldiers. An isolated citadel in remote Judaea was not somewhere they could hone their skills. Still, as ever, his was not to reason why and to be fair, most had now seen some action, not only as they marched to Tigranocerta from Corbulo's headquarters in Zeugma, but also during the subsequent siege.

One of them, Gnaeus Marcus Aelianus, who was a little younger than Maxentius, had only arrived in Syria a few months before being dispatched to Tigranocerta. Nearly as tall as his new commander, Marcus Aelianus was a steady soldier from a rural background, used to hard work and wise beyond his years. Their difference in rank notwithstanding, the two had hit it off on the journey back from Zeugma and Maxentius had been very thankful that this young soldier would be part of his cohort. He already felt able to rely on him and instinct told him, that Marcus Aelianus would be a valuable ally. Never could he have imagined just how much.

The soldiers enjoyed their brief rest at Zeugma, but were soon back on the road. Their route took them down through Syria to Damascus via Palmyra, before entering Judaea, then onto Masada stopping at Jerusalem and Hebron on the way. Temporary camps were erected and dismantled most nights, but they did enjoy the occasional luxury of sleeping in a barracks when they arrived in towns guarded by a Roman garrison.

Their journey took them past many interesting places and Maxentius, endlessly fascinated by foreign cities — their history and architecture — managed to find an excuse to stop at some of them. Most of the soldiers had never seen anything beyond Rome or Armenia and these ancient cities, with their sophisticated Greco-Roman influences were an eye opener. The first was Palmyra, an established caravan oasis linking Persia, China and India with the Roman Empire and a rapidly expanding centre for trade. The city, which could trace its origins back over two thousand years, was dominated by the awe-inspiring Temple of Ba'al, dedicated a couple of decades previously. Palmyra had also been the base for Legio X Fretensis, who had been part of Corbulo's army, so the Roman soldiers felt a familial connection to the town.

Damascus was also somewhere Maxentius wanted to see. He had heard of this ancient city through associates of his father and knew it had been completely redesigned under Pompey to replicate that of a Roman town. As they entered through the immense triple-arched gateway leading onto the Decumanus Maximus — the main road running east to west through the city — it was clear that any civic development remained true to Pompey's model. Maxentius spent several pleasant hours discovering the delights of the city, even managing to explore the partially constructed temple to Jupiter that, apparently, was being built on the site of an Aramaic temple to Hadad. His enthusiasm was a source of endless amusement to his subordinates, who thought him rather eccentric — not that they said so of course.

By the time they reached Jerusalem, they needed to replenish their dwindling supplies — although they had been assured that the storerooms on Masada were plentiful — and they also took the opportunity to enjoy a spot of recreation. It had been a long journey; a three-day break would matter little and, Maxentius believed, would revive the flagging spirits of his soldiers. Although the city was deemed a melting pot and very unstable, none of the cohort noticed anything out of the ordinary. Taking their time, they all enjoyed exploring this most intriguing of centres, dominated by the spectacular Temple Mount, the renovations to which, now virtually complete.

Not far from Jerusalem, and reputedly the place he was buried, was the palace of Herod I at Herodium. It was in fact two palaces, both equally remarkable. Herod had expanded and then built upon a small hill, creating a platform around four hundred feet above the surrounding landscape. This was the main fortress, Herod's administrative centre and private residence. Below was the second palace, where Herod's guests and visiting dignitaries were entertained. There was even a pool, the size of which was testament to Herod's wealth and power, as it would have required a substantial amount of water to fill it, here in what was a relatively dry area.

The soldiers were stunned at such opulence, for even by Roman standards this was lavish. Their incredulity, however, did not prevent them from indulging in a quick swim and maybe some water sports — it was too good an opportunity to miss! Too soon, however, they were back on the road and made it to Hebron just before nightfall.

The final leg of their journey took four days, the terrain was not too arduous, but it was tricky here and there and they had to be extremely observant as the risk of ambush in this, more mountainous, region was high. Many Hebrews detested the Roman presence in Judaea and in so isolated an area the dead would be a long time unfound.

Finally, they arrived at Masada, marching up the steep winding path to the fortified West Gate. Getting their wagons up was particularly awkward, but their horses were patient and eventually it was done. Soldiers will usually find a way of surmounting obstacles given time and manpower. The outgoing commander, a legate named Decimus Julius Calvus, who had been on the plateau for around four years, greeted Maxentius and his detachment as they lined up for inspection.

The man looked wearied, his shoulders were hunched and he appeared scarcely interested in the new arrivals. Dismissing the soldiers, with instructions to one of his own centurions to show them their barracks, the commander escorted Maxentius to his office. This turned out to be a large room in what had originally been one of the administrative wings, within a complex that Julius Calvus referred to as the Northern Palace.

Tired as he was after a long day's march, Maxentius was mind boggled by the sheer size of Masada and he was looking forward to exploring the fortress in its entirety. Knowing it would have to wait, he contented himself with a quick peek into the rooms he was passing as he followed the legate along the corridors. Even the little he saw, along with the position of the fortress, was enough for Maxentius to realise why the Romans considered it so vital that this outpost remain under their protection.

After so many days of marching, it took Maxentius and his soldiers some time to settle back into garrison life. A week later, the outgoing commander and his soldiers departed, heading towards Jerusalem and then, for many, home to Roman Italy, retirement in the offing. Once they had gone, Maxentius turned his attention to his own soldiers who, along with the auxiliaries, currently numbered around seven hundred men. Here, so many miles from what they could consider — even vaguely — to be civilisation, he needed to keep them occupied for as much of the day as possible, to prevent them from getting bored and coming up with less acceptable ways to pass the time.

As when they were in Tigranocerta, he reinstated the tournaments, which when added to regular duties and patrols, filled the soldiers' days. He also wanted his men to understand the layout and complexity of the plateau, for although it was presumed unassailable, Maxentius did not wish to be caught unawares. This took some considerable time, as the citadel was immense. Two palaces, a synagogue, workshops, an armoury, barracks, cisterns, storerooms, bathhouses and several smaller palaces, there was even a swimming pool here too; not to mention secret stairways, watch towers and a casemate wall — which was so huge that you could live inside it.

Maxentius was in awe of those who had designed and constructed this fortress, for their skill was unparalleled. This was especially evident in what had apparently been Herod's private retreat at the northern end of the plateau, a feat of elegant engineering that saw three tiers literally hanging over the edge of the precipice. A huge sweeping balcony at the upper level gave anyone standing there a breathtaking view out over the desert to the Sea of Salt, its blue coolness shimmering in the distance.

While many considered this landscape harsh and unyielding, Maxentius loved its untamed beauty and he could often be found staring out over the vast wilderness, stylus in one hand, tablet in the other, ruminating over a particularly knotty problem. He claimed the view helped him to think, that such an expanse of nothingness focused his mind, a notion that merely compounded his soldiers' belief that he was more than a little unconventional. They did however respect him. Maxentius was a fair-minded commander, never expecting the men to undertake something he wouldn't do himself, quick to praise and should a reprimand prove necessary it was done with minimal fuss and without any loss of dignity on either side.

Further and as he had done in Armenia, Maxentius had taken pains to get to know the men now under his command, including the auxiliary staff. It took some doing, for they numbered in the several hundreds, but he had started memorising them as they departed Tigranocerta and by the time they had been on Masada for two months, he knew them all. To be fair, most he only knew by name, but that was more than most commanders bothered to remember. In this way, Maxentius hoped that the garrison would run as smoothly as could be expected and if any of the men had a grievance they would make the effort to come and discuss it with him rather than let it fester.

Therefore, it was not without a modicum of relief that the soldiers' days returned to those regular duties and tasks typical of a military base, a familiarity they had missed during the long journey. Dividing the men up into centuries, Maxentius appointed each group specific chores on a rotational basis, such as general maintenance of weapons and armour, cooking, laundry, even cleaning and upkeep of the buildings. Everyone was expected to do their bit, regardless of whether they were soldier or auxiliary. They lacked the usual domestic staff, so this ensured their quarters were kept in as decent a shape as a group of men could manage. In truth, army discipline came to the fore and, as with the tournaments, rewards were available to those who excelled. In an unexpected twist, the mundane nature of many tasks was improved by the light-hearted competition.

For a time, life could almost be described as agreeable.

Chapter Twelve

Jerusalem ~ AD64

Hannah and Gideon were wrist deep in blood, the youth on the table between them had so many wounds they didn't know where to start. Their meticulous examination revealed cuts, bruises and, what appeared to be crush injuries, the damage was horrendous. Hannah had never seen anything like it, even Daniel, whose wounds were terrible, hadn't been half as badly hurt as this man. In silence, the two healers struggled to stem the bleeding, sporadically going to wash their hands and arms and change their aprons, in the hope that this would reduce the chance of infection.

The young man was deeply unconscious, thankfully and, although he groaned occasionally, Hannah wasn't sure whether he had any awareness at all, or whether it was simply his subconscious responding to their ministrations.

Hours of painstaking effort seemed to be paying off for they had managed to arrest the flow of blood. Most of his larger wounds had been treated, but there was still the not inconsiderable matter of all the smaller lacerations and the crush injuries. Neither healer could imagine what had caused such damage and were stunned that he still lived. His breathing, although laboured did not sound restricted, so they believed his lungs were intact — one good thing — but his abdomen was oddly swollen and one of his arms lay crookedly on the table, possibly as a result of a dislocated or broken shoulder.

By rights, they should have taken a break, but neither was prepared to leave the other to bear this burden alone. Hannah stretched, arching her back and rolling her shoulders, her muscles aching from leaning over the table. Gideon rubbed his forehead with the back of his hand, his headache increasing in ferocity the longer he concentrated. In recent months, Hannah had become very concerned for her uncle who, to her experienced eye, was definitely not altogether healthy. Gideon, however, waved aside her unease, saying it was just his age and maybe it was because his eyesight was less than it had once been. Surreptitiously, his niece had begun to assume much of his workload; initially one or two patients here and there, increasing the number gradually until she felt her uncle would be able to rest during the day without actually realising why he had the time to do so.

There was a knock at the door, Hannah called a quiet "come in" and Aharon entered the room. Her brother looked haggard; it had been he and three of his friends who had brought the young man in, not even knowing who he was. They had come across him as they were returning home. Seemingly, there had been yet another riot, the outcome of which had left many dead and hundreds wounded. Aharon believed the man had tried to run and had been caught under a horse; Gideon agreeing that such an incident might have caused the terrible trauma. Aharon and Malachi had spent the remainder of the day trying to discover who he was and whether he had any family.

"His name is Nachum. We have no idea from where he came. He certainly does not live anywhere near us; no one recognised him as we were carrying him here. It is possible that he lives on the other side of the city, which begs the question as to what he was doing so far from home. I think it can only be as I suggested, he was part of the riot and simply fled in whichever direction looked the safest. That or he was an innocent bystander, in the wrong place at the wrong time."

Hannah listened to their discussion and glanced back at Nachum; he was so pale and still in a stupor, one he may never wake up from. She shuddered; it never ceased to disturb her how much damage men could inflict upon each other. Unwilling to hear any more about the riot, she turned her attention back to their patient. They needed to re-position the man's shoulder and work out what was going on with his stomach.

While her brother and uncle talked, Hannah made sure that Nachum's arm and shoulder were completely clean and then probed along the limb to pinpoint the problem. Whatever had happened hadn't torn through his flesh, but her gentle touch was able sense where the circulation seemed sluggish and she noticed that his fingers were very pale. Working her way up to the shoulder, she discerned that the joint had come out of alignment, which although painful was much better and easier to treat than a broken bone.

"I'm sorry to interrupt, but we must deal with Nachum now, everything else can wait until later. Aharon, would you be able to stay and help?" Spoken in undertones, Hannah flicked her eyes at Gideon as she spoke, tacitly hoping Aharon understood her meaning. Aharon, aware of his sister's anxiety for her uncle, inclined his head slightly, replying —

"As long as I don't have to stitch anyone up, I am at your service." Hannah heaved a sigh of relief and explained why she needed him.

"Nachum's shoulder bone is dislocated and although it just needs to be popped back into its socket, it requires quite a lot of strength and a smooth, continual pull. I do not think I can manage this."

Aharon looked rather confused, so Gideon demonstrated the technique and then readied the patient. Hannah raised the unconscious man into a reclined position and held him steady, while the physician wrapped a long sheet around the upper arm and underneath the shoulder. Asking Aharon to hold it taut at the opposite side of the man's body to prevent him from moving, Gideon lifted the elbow and slowly rotated the limb until there was an audible clunk.

Immediately, Nachum's fingers began to regain their normal colour and the shape of the shoulder was as it should be. Nachum himself hadn't even flinched during the procedure, which was of grave concern to both physicians. Gideon checked the joint and then satisfied that it rested correctly within its socket, immobilised it with a sling. Aharon asked whether they needed him for anything else and once persuaded that his sister and uncle had it in hand, left them to it, saying he'd be back later. The two healers were weary but their day was far from over.

"While he rests, we shall consider the problem of his distended abdomen." Gideon said and he talked Hannah through his diagnosis. "I believe that Nachum is bleeding internally. If he was caught under a horse, it is probable that one or more of his organs has been damaged, but because the skin here is not broken, we cannot be certain."

As Gideon carefully palpated the area, he leaned close to Nachum's abdomen listening for what would be considered irregular abdominal sounds.

"He is so swollen that I am unable to determine whether the tract responsible for expelling food and waste from the body has been ruptured. The only way to know for sure is to open Nachum up and check inside." As Gideon explained this, Hannah blanched and her stomach roiled. In all the time she had been assisting her uncle she had never been faced with such an operation, even though she was aware that he had performed several during his years as a physician. Gideon was still speaking, so she forced herself to concentrate on what he was saying.

"There is a slight chance that if the waste tract isn't torn, Nachum's own body might heal itself. The bleeding could stop on its own, but I do not think it likely. Sadly, Nachum's chances are slim to doubtful. What I do know is that with his other injuries, he is too ill for me to operate today; he would not survive. I think all we can do at the moment is let him sleep and observe him." Gideon sighed, wiping his hands on a damp cloth, studying the man on the table.

Taking a moment to gather themselves and both hoping that, given a little time, the internal damage might begin to reverse itself, Hannah and Gideon cleaned up the clinic. All their instruments were placed into a bowl of boiling water, the bloodied cloths, strewn around the floor were picked up and either dropped into cold water to soak or thrown into a basket by the doorway, ready to be burnt.

As gently as possible, they removed the dirty sheet from under Nachum, replacing it with a clean one and covering him with another. Then, while Gideon put some bread and vegetables drizzled in oil on a large platter and made a hot sweet drink, Hannah scrubbed the floor and washed everything they had used very thoroughly. Finally, they sat down, utterly fatigued yet knowing that this was only the first step. Nachum would need monitoring constantly, the risk of infection and shock as troubling as the possibility of internal bleeding.

Aharon returned shortly thereafter, accompanied by Raizel — who had cooked a proper meal for them all, making sure Hannah and Gideon each ate a good portion, while Aharon sat with Nachum. They had not been able to locate any family although Malachi was still confident, intending to go back to any of the neighbourhoods where they thought he might belong. Hannah's biggest concern was that even if they found his relations, they might well be too late. Pushing her disquiet aside, she rested her head against the back of the chair, enjoying the sensation of a full stomach. Raizel was an incredible cook, a skill of which Hannah, still unable to master even the basics, was in total admiration.

Aharon escorted his wife home about an hour later, instructing Hannah to come and get him if they wanted him to take a watch over night. Hannah and Gideon returned to their patient, who was still unconscious, although his breathing seemed rather less strained. His heart rate was erratic but quite strong and for a time they dared to hope.

Several days passed, during which Nachum barely regained consciousness. Gideon was becoming convinced that the young man would not survive, while Hannah refused to accept it. In the time she had been helping Gideon, she had never seen anyone die. She had helped before and after death, but she had never witnessed the moment when the soul finally gave up the fight.

Much of this was because Gideon did not want her exposed to such things. She might be ten and seven years old and had been assisting him for years, all her friends might be betrothed or married, but despite all these things Hannah remained quite an innocent in the ways of the world. It had taken her a long time to recover from the death of her parents and he could only imagine what a patient dying under her care might do.

In truth, he realised that it was important for her to understand the nature of death, but in Gideon's heart she was still his niece. That guileless little girl, who used to shove her long curls under a cap and scurry around his clinic doing anything she could to help him, and he did not want to be the one to destroy that naiveté.

They never discovered where Nachum lived or whether he had any family, but they did manage to find the man who had given Aharon the injured man's name. It turned out that he was a friend of sorts, the two having met at Temple, coming across each other on occasion, more by accident than design, eventually becoming more than passing acquaintances. The friend, Amos, visited Nachum as often as he was able, but it was increasingly difficult to traverse the city at night — usually the only time Amos was free. A curfew and patrols by the Roman army intent on maintaining some form of control, making even the most innocent venture quite risky.

In the event Gideon, whilst accepting that Nachum might be suffering from grievous internal damage, decided not to operate on the young man, acknowledging that the shock would kill him. Any further decision was taken out of the physician's hands when one night, as dawn approached, Nachum slipped away from this world, his body too badly broken to continue the duel with death.

Hannah had been asleep, curled up on her bedroll in front of the fire having watched over the young man for long hours. Gideon cleaned and anointed the body and said a prayer for Nachum's soul, maintaining a vigil until the sound of children in the street saw him ask one of them to fetch Aharon. Hannah still slept, she didn't even stir when Aharon came in half an hour or so later, her brother waking her so she could say goodbye. Hannah stood for several moments smoothing the long dark hair off Nachum's forehead, murmuring something under her breath, before helping Gideon to wrap the shroud around the body in readiness.

Hannah, Gideon, Raizel and Aharon followed the litter carrying Nachum to the place of burial. They were accompanied by a number of people from the neighbourhood in a gesture of respect, not only for the young man but also for Hannah and Gideon who had fought tirelessly to save him, their presence a balm to the exhausted physicians. As they laid him to rest, the small crowd began to sing a eulogy. It was a lament for the death of a soldier and although Nachum, as far as anyone knew had never been one, it seemed appropriate. The voices harmonised over the quiet scene and to Hannah, it was akin to a lullaby, the haunting melody soothing her, washing away the sadness. It was a lament she never forgot.

Chapter Thirteen

Masada ~ AD64

Two years! It had been two very long years since his arrival on Masada and no matter what Maxentius did to keep up the spirits of his soldiers, it seemed that this was a battle he was destined to lose. They were becoming slovenly, disillusioned and recalcitrant. He could understand it; the outpost was just that — an outpost — so remote that it was a good four days hard march to reach the closest decent sized town. Maxentius himself liked the isolation; he loved the silence that descended at dusk, the stark beauty of the landscape, the astonishingly blue waters of the Sea of Salt, the colours that flickered across the desert throughout the day, and the billions of stars that provided a breathtaking show of luminescence every night.

Not that he enunciated any of these thoughts, mind you. It was hard enough maintaining any level of respect from these men, to declare that he found the place utterly captivating would see them mount a mutiny, believing him to be mentally unbalanced.

Thankfully, he had Marcus. The young soldier had, unofficially, taken on the role of second-in-command, as the soldier appointed to this task was rarely sober. The stores on Masada were plentiful enough to feed several legions for decades, the stock of wine — considerable, and bored men require little encouragement to indulge. Maxentius had given up trying to place a guard on the doors for they were as bad as the regular soldiers. At least once drunk they slept, which gave those who were less inclined to imbibe, some relief.

To be fair, there were many soldiers who continued to carry out their duties and they had a reliable body of men who could be trusted to patrol the area competently. They still held the tournaments, although they had become somewhat sporadic, as Maxentius had discovered that groups of soldiers often took themselves off to the far end of the plateau to avoid being involved — preferring to laze about. The whole point was ruined if there were only half the competitors; however, for those prepared to make the effort the rewards were worth it.

Marcus continually proved himself a dependable and capable soldier and Maxentius was glad to call him a friend. It was he who suggested that it might be an idea to try to grow some crops on the plateau, there was plenty of water in the cisterns and it seemed that previous garrisons had made a half-hearted attempt. A stone trough with a hole near the bottom that could be plugged, allowed water to run into long gullies that stretched the length of what Marcus assumed to have been the planted area. An area of ground had been turned and a few pathetic looking plants tried to survive the harsh climate. Pomegranate trees were dotted around; their fruit most welcome and Marcus knew that if these trees could produce leaves and fruit, it was logical that other plants could be cultivated.

Employing soldiers whom he felt less likely to shirk their tasks, Marcus had begun a systematic planting cycle — much was trial and error but soon they began to reap the benefits. There were already chickens and goats, and one of the patrols had somehow managed to barter for the purchase of two oxen, who could be used to plough — and if that failed, would make good eating. Masada was also on a trade route and extra supplies could be haggled over when the need arose, or they could ride out to Engaddi one of the semi-local villages.

Although life in the fortress had settled into a routine, it wasn't comfortable, for Maxentius knew that the country was ripe for rebellion. Masada, however, was far from Jerusalem and, protected as it was by the massive casemate wall and multitude of watchtowers, not to mention the height of its sheer sides, it presented a formidable barrier to anyone thinking of launching an attack. The constant theme in the report of every patrol was the lack of anyone in the vicinity. Occasionally they came across the odd goat herder or a merchant following the trade routes, but rarely anyone else; certainly, there didn't seem much likelihood of anyone venturing so far from Jerusalem, despite the unrest there.

During these long months, word filtered through from Rome that, finally, Armenia had been pacified, although it was not the result Maxentius expected. The long requested legate for Cappadocia had arrived, a man by the name of Lucius Caesennius Paetus, who after the Parthians once again declared war, invaded Armenia with a considerable force, confident of victory. Despite supremacy of numbers, Paetus' tactics seemed irrational and this, combined with an apparent lack of any strategic ability, sent his legions into panic, culminating in them being besieged near Rhandeia. Paetus sent word to Corbulo but before the General arrived — with half of the Syrian army, rounding up dispersed soldier's from Paetus' army on his way — Paetus himself had surrendered. It was a humiliating outcome that shattered Rome.

Corbulo was, once again, placed in charge of the Armenian campaign, his position in Syria taken by one Gaius Cestius Gallus. Corbulo re-organised his legions, adding two more along with auxiliaries and contingents from loyal client kings. The Parthians when faced with such an overwhelming force readily capitulated and agreed to negotiations. Peace, albeit a compromised peace, was eventually declared, for although Rome maintained military supremacy in Armenia, a Parthian sat on the throne. This political concession, which led to around half a century of concord, also meant that Armenia came under increasing Parthian influence — but that, as they say, is another story!

As an army commander, Maxentius received detailed reports of all major military campaigns and was aghast at the waste of lives for no real gain at all. The only positive result that he perceived had come out of the whole debacle was that Rome re-organised and strengthened their defensive positions in the East and took control of the entire length of the Euphrates. Interestingly and unknown to all who had been involved in the Armenian campaign, this frontier would last for centuries.

Maxentius recalled those men with whom he had served and ruminated on how many may have been lost in the battle for Rhandeia. It was a sobering thought; a few misguided decisions and life could so easily be snuffed out. He determined that he could not allow such a thing to happen to the men who trusted their lives to him. Calling Marcus, he explained the result of the Armenian campaign and the two devised long-term strategies, which they hoped should combat any threat to Masada. All he required his men to do was to follow his directives and maintain their vigilance.

In the late summer of Maxentius' second year on Masada, a replacement detachment arrived. Mainly recruits, they breathed fresh vitality into the jaded ranks of soldiers. Very young and still enamoured of the military, not wearied from long marches or endless campaigns, their exuberance was infectious and life on Masada took a turn for the better. The recruits threw themselves into their duties; never needing to be reprimanded for slovenliness during daily drill; their weapons and armour gleaming from constant honing and polishing. This eagerness on the part of the recruits to prove their prowess to the veterans amongst them extended to the tournaments, which also took on a new lease of life — for those who had not been rotated out were not about to allow these novices to best them.

A young soldier called Quintus Sergius Crispus, the unofficial spokesman for this draft of soldiers, quickly became valuable to Maxentius and Marcus. A long-limbed brawny youth from Brindisi, he had no patience for sloppy ways or inefficiency and whether owing to their respect or fear of him, the recruits rarely disregarded his instructions.

Thus, it became a habit at the end of long dusty days, for Maxentius, Marcus and Sergius to meet to discuss their charges, often over a goblet of wine — or two — and for a time, the garrison enjoyed a relatively uneventful existence.

Jerusalem ~ AD65

Meanwhile in Jerusalem, the antagonism between the different factions and the Romans was no less fraught. By now, many of the groups who would normally have fought against each other had banded together against their common enemy, which included the current procurator — Gessius Florus — Rome and anyone who supported either. Florus was faced with what could be considered insurmountable challenges, all of which he chose to handle in an utterly reprehensible manner.

It must be admitted that previous procurators had also been rather short sighted in their handling of the increasing problems within Jerusalem. However, for the most part all had managed to conceal their iniquities and according to Josephus — whose narratives provide the closest thing we have to an eyewitness account of what happened — their actions paled into insignificance when compared with those of Florus, whom the ancient writer credits as being the primary cause of the Great Jewish Revolt. In the concluding book of his *Antiquities of the Jews* Josephus declared that it was as result of, but not restricted to, Florus' public greed, blatant injustice towards the Jews, excessive wickedness and violent abuse of authority. A gentleman he was not!

Thus, the seeds of dissent that had been growing steadily, blossomed into all out rebellion and the city was now on the brink of catastrophe. Although the small enclave where Hannah lived was relatively untouched by the turmoil, being somewhat removed from the centre of Jerusalem, it did not stop the young men from becoming entangled in it. Hannah was very much afraid that her brother and his friends would end up being caught and executed for their involvement. The latest person to hold them in thrall was a man named Menahem ben Judah, whose rhetoric could incite even the mildest of men, and whose actions would set in motion a series of events that would culminate in not one but two massacres.

Every day, Hannah and Gideon were kept busy treating a variety of injuries, ranging from small lacerations and bruising, to far more serious wounds, often working into the early hours of the morning. The two rooms Gideon used as his surgery were in no way adequate for the amount of people who came through his doors. Gideon himself struggled with interminable headaches; often so bad that he had to stop whatever he was doing, as the disturbance to his vision made it impossible to continue.

As she had been trying to do for the last year or so, Hannah unobtrusively shouldered his workload, recruiting the young son of a family friend as her assistant. The lad, Asaf, was willing enough, especially as Hannah gave him coin when she could. He was quiet and efficient and didn't yell or panic at the sight of the injured men or the copious amounts of blood that had become the norm, which was as much as Hannah could hope for.

This particular day the three of them had been so engrossed in trying to deal with the queue of people clamouring for attention, that they had forgotten to eat or take even the shortest of breaks. Eventually, realising that they would likely collapse themselves if they didn't rest, Hannah called a halt. She shooed Asaf off home, with strict instructions not to return until he had eaten some food and had at least an hour's sleep.

Then she went outside and asked for quiet.

"Please, I must beg your forbearance for a short while. We have been working since dawn and have not eaten. If we are to treat you all, we must take a break to refresh ourselves and have a meal." She smiled tiredly at those standing patiently in line. "I know how long you have been waiting and I promise that we will see you all." One or two muttered grumpily, but most appreciated how hard the two physicians worked and readily acquiesced to Hannah's request.

"Take your time…"

"Don't rush, we aren't going anywhere…"

"Make sure you eat properly…" and so on, their understanding making Hannah smile all the more.

Going back inside, she told Gideon that Raizel had left them some food in a basket by the fire. Two men were recovering in the small living area, not quite able to walk yet after their treatment; so Hannah divided the food between the four of them, before pouring out goblets of a hot sweet drink made with honey and spices.

Hannah studied Gideon, whose face was grey and drawn. He had never told her how bad his headaches had become, but his niece was not blind. She had been working alongside him for over a decade and could read him better than the manuscripts she still loved to pore over. Today, she knew he was in excruciating pain and also that he would never admit to it. Slipping some of her herbs, blended specifically to help alleviate such afflictions, into a little wine, Hannah quietly handed her uncle the drink, saying that this would help. Gideon glanced up at her and swallowed it gratefully, squeezing the slender fingers that rested on his shoulder, before laying his head against the back of the chair and shutting his eyes for a few minutes allowing the brew to take effect.

Hannah, meanwhile, went back into the surgery to tidy up. She removed the used and bloodied cloths and bandages, dropping some onto the fire and the rest into a bucket to be washed later. Then she cleaned everything in sight, the benches, the jars and the bottles before placing fresh sheets on the pristine table checking and re-checking until she was satisfied all was as it should be. She stretched her back and rolled her shoulders, lifting her arms high above her head trying to loosen the knots that were an inevitable part of her day.

Taking a deep breath, she stepped back outside and observed the, now even longer, line of people waiting patiently. She walked along, asking questions, looking at injuries or discussing symptoms, so that by the time she had spoken to everyone she had a fair idea about who needed what treatment.

Re-entering the clinic, Hannah took one more glance around and called the first person in.

Chapter Fourteen

Jerusalem ~ AD65

By the middle of the evening they had seen every last man woman and child, thankfully there were very few of the latter. Aharon had popped in at some point during the afternoon to tell them that Raizel would hold dinner until they were finished, for which Hannah and Gideon were most grateful. Asaf had re-appeared just as Hannah had resumed treating those in the queue and had proved his worth. His assistance also meant that they had been able to leave Gideon to rest. He had re-joined them sometime later, assuring them that the pain had subsided; Hannah wasn't convinced but was smart enough not to pursue the matter.

Wearily, they put the clinic to rights, re-stocking all the sheets, blankets, bandages, cloths, ointments, balms and unctions ready for the next day. Asaf was falling asleep as they closed the door, all of them ready for a hot meal and Hannah draped an arm around his thin shoulders, scurrying him home and handing him over to his mother, thanking them both as she took her leave. Asaf's mother, Tali, waved the girl's thanks aside, saying that Asaf loved helping and it was all she could do to make him have breakfast before he rushed along to the clinic every day!

"Still, I am glad he is not getting under your feet and making a nuisance of himself, and at least I know where to find him." Tali added.

"Well, I am very pleased to have his assistance, he makes my day very much easier." Hannah smiled ruffling Asaf's hair, to his utter mortification. She did not imagine the delighted grin that lit up his tired face though, as he slipped under her hand and disappeared into the house following the mouth-watering smell of hot food. Hannah nodded to Tali and retraced her steps to her old home. She rarely slept here now, more because she wanted to keep an eye on Gideon, but also in the belief that it was better to let Aharon and Raizel enjoy their life as, relatively recent newlyweds, without the presence of a sibling.

She did enjoy eating here though, for as has already been mentioned, should Hannah be left to feed Gideon and herself, it is likely they would starve, or at the very least come down with all manner of stomach ailments. She let herself in calling a 'hello' as she did so, finding her family already gathered and the food laid out; hot stew, plenty of bread and a flagon of slightly diluted wine. Raizel had also managed to find some pomegranates at the market. Hannah loved this sweet red fruit, declaring it to be the elixir of heaven and if at all possible, would eat the fleshy seeds individually, to the annoyance of everyone around her.

They chattered as they ate, filling each other in on their day. Until recently, Aharon had been employed in the rebuilding program, but discovering a previously untapped artistic talent, had turned to leather-crafting. To his own amazement, Aharon found that he loved this work and his enthusiasm was clear when he described his day. He, along with his colleagues in their small workshop, were never without orders. Not only for sandals and boots, leather was used for harnesses, saddles and bridles for horses and donkeys; muzzles for oxen; water bottles and wineskins; bellows; musical instruments — the list went on. Aharon much preferred this to the hard labour involved when he had been a stonemason working on the temple projects, it being far less dangerous and he no longer came home covered in dust and tiny cuts from flying stone chips.

Hannah and Gideon talked about the clinic and they all mourned the issue of the ongoing clashes and upheaval. By now such topics of conversation rarely caused even a modicum of surprise, as all were so accustomed to it that it had become almost mundane.

For once, however, surprised they were about to be and even more so because it came from Raizel. Quiet and unassuming Raizel who, although perfectly able to offer a counterpoint to most arguments, usually preferred to act as peace-keeper; and was still the voice of reason for Hannah, should that young lady get a wild idea into her head. For much of the evening, she had been fidgeting, for no reason that Hannah could see and it was so unlike her serene sister-in-law that she began to feel quite concerned. Eventually, Hannah could take no more —

"Raizel! Whatever is the matter? You are like a goat that has jumped into a fire pit! Are you unwell?" Raizel smiled rather sheepishly and, blushing prettily, looked at Aharon who chuckled and took her hand.

"She is not ill, Hannah, but she might be indisposed in a little while." Hannah stared at her brother and his wife, now completely bewildered.

"Indisposed in a little while? How on earth could you possibly predict that?" She expostulated as Gideon gave a bark of laughter, which earned him a glare from his niece. "You too, my uncle! What is going on?"

"Hannah, for a physician and someone who considers herself to be quite observant, sometimes you can be remarkably blind to what should be obvious." Aharon grinned at his sister. She frowned at him, looked at Raizel, then back to Aharon, suddenly registering that her brother's wife looked different; her cheeks were fuller and she seemed to be blooming. Hannah ran her eye over Raizel's body, noticing that her usually slender shape was no longer quite so slender. She had been so busy at the clinic that she had missed the signs.

"Oh my goodness! I cannot believe I didn't notice. Raizel, Aharon, I am so happy for you! I'm going to be an aunt?" The two nodded, unable to prevent the beaming smiles that lit up both their faces. Hannah caught Raizel in a hug and did the same to her brother, then went to the door and leaning out, shouted her news to the neighbourhood.

"I'm going to be an aunt." Gideon hushed her, good humouredly, but a few voices floated back along the quiet street

—

"Congratulations!"

"That's excellent news!"

"Thanks for telling us!"

"You sound very excited Hannah!" and so on until a grumbling voice yelled at them all to shut up, it being late and some people needed to sleep.

"Sorry Uncle Haim," Hannah called, "I'll call on you tomorrow to check on your foot." Raizel giggled. There was a gruff response then peace returned. 'Uncle Haim,' who as far as they knew was nobody's uncle, in fact they didn't think he had any family at all, had been adopted as such by the whole neighbourhood, and had been called 'uncle' as long as anyone could remember. Even though he grouched a lot, he secretly enjoyed the attention. Hannah had been checking up on him nearly every day as not only did he have a tendency to forget to eat, but also he had fallen recently and she needed to make sure the resulting cuts on his foot were kept clean and properly bandaged.

Raizel pulled Hannah inside, while Aharon poured a celebratory goblet of wine and the four fell to gossiping about the baby. Hannah asked her sister-in-law to come around to the clinic for a proper check-up, for even though expectant mothers usually just carried on with little change to their lives until the babe was due; Hannah wanted to be sure Raizel received the best care she could offer. More than this, monitoring women through pregnancy was something that Hannah felt was often overlooked. She knew that if the subtle signs and indicators that occurred at different stages were missed, complications might occur and she certainly did not want anything to happen to Raizel or her unborn child. Raizel blushed but agreed and a short while later, Gideon and Hannah took their leave.

Aharon came to the door and as Gideon set off along the street, Hannah stood a moment with her brother. Tilting her head so that she could look at him properly, Hannah's face was illuminated by the soft moonlight, her green eyes still shining with joy at their news and, unexpectedly, Aharon hoped she would find someone who would love her as much as he loved Raizel. Gestures of affection between the siblings were rare, but Hannah reached for Aharon's hand and squeezing it gently, whispered —

"I'm so glad Aharon, it is the most wonderful news. I am just sorry our parents did not live to see this. They would have been so proud and excited for you, not to mention how delighted they would have been to be grandparents." She swallowed a gulp, grief for their loss still lurked close to the surface, despite it being nearly five years since their deaths.

Aharon pulled his small sister to him, hugging her close in much the same way he had done on the day of their father's burial, realising with a jolt; it was indeed that long since. He had always looked out for her and until a few years ago included her in everything he did, but as he held her, he accepted that things had changed. They were no longer as close as they used to be and even though he knew that this was inevitable, he was momentarily saddened.

"Thank you, Hannah, but I want you to remember that I will always be here for you, just because I have a wife and soon there will be a child, does not mean you are less important to me — you are still my sister." Hannah stared at him, as inexplicably, tears brimmed in her eyes. Determined not to cry, she blinked them away and gave him one last tight squeeze.

"Thank you Aharon." She muttered and shot off after her uncle. Aharon smiled after her and went back inside. Raizel raised an eyebrow at him

"Will she be all right, my husband?" she questioned in her quiet way. Aharon nodded.

"I believe she will, my love. I just don't think she wants to accept that she's all grown up." Raizel smiled in agreement and held out her hand. Aharon went to her, and drawing her into his embrace, kissed his wife most satisfactorily.

"Is it still safe to…?" he asked rather diffidently. Raizel shrugged, it was their first child and she really had no idea, but surely something as natural as making love could not harm it.

"I believe it will be fine." She replied a soft pink colouring her cheeks.

"That's what I hoped you would say." Came Aharon's rather hoarse response as he carried his wife to their bedroll and proceeded to demonstrate just how much she meant to him.

Meanwhile, a little further along the street, Hannah found Gideon at home boiling some milk to make a hot drink. She collected their goblets from the bench, putting a dollop of honey and a spoonful of mixed spice in each one then holding them while her uncle poured in the steaming milk, the delicate aroma and gentle flavour soothing the weary minds of the two physicians.

"How do you feel, Hannah?" Gideon queried, knowing how his niece hated change.

"Thrilled, my uncle. I find I am quite thrilled. I believe I could be quite a good aunt and they are so elated. I will keep a close eye on Raizel though and I will ask Aharon to make sure she rests properly." Despite the best care that was available, mortality rates for women during childbirth were astronomically high and neither Hannah nor Gideon wanted Raizel to take any risks. Her uncle nodded in agreement and after a little more discussion, they called it a night.

Hannah slept in the living area, arguing that if they were needed in the night, she was younger and could get by on less sleep. Initially Gideon had tried to argue with her but she was implacable and in the end, he'd given up. In truth, the headaches that plagued him were often worse at night and he knew he would be next to useless should their services be called upon.

The weeks passed by with what felt like lightning speed. Raizel did present herself for examination and Hannah was pleased to see that everything appeared to be progressing as normally as could be expected. She gave her sister-in-law strict instructions to rest for at least one hour during the day and to try to retire to bed a little earlier. Raizel didn't seem pleasantly disposed to following such orders, but Hannah spoke to her brother, impressing upon him the importance of his wife taking things a little easier and Aharon, by dint of coming home at lunchtime and sitting with her, managed to get his wife to slow down a bit.

It was maybe two months after Aharon and Raizel had shared their news that life for Hannah changed again. It had been a very long and arduous day. Three men, whom both physicians knew, had been brought in with quite nasty injuries and it had taken nearly all day to patch them up. Aharon had stuck his head through the door at some point telling them that Raizel had organised the evening meal and to just come when they were done. Thankful that she didn't have to try to cook, Hannah had winked an acknowledgement to her brother over the cloth tied around her nose and mouth, her eyes being the only way she could communicate while operating. Aharon had become quite adept at reading his sister's expressions though and, message received, he'd sauntered away whistling, never giving it another thought.

It was mid-evening before he realised that his sister and his uncle hadn't appeared and although this was not unusual he couldn't shake the sense that something wasn't right.

"I'm just going to check on them," he called to Raizel and walked down the street, his long strides bringing him to the clinic in seconds. Just as he opened the door a small figure barrelled into him, nearly knocking him off his feet.

"Asaf? What's wrong?" Aharon picked up the lad who looked petrified. Now Aharon was really worried and without waiting for an answer hurried through into the first room. No sign of either Hannah or Gideon so he continued through to the living space. Hannah was on her knees next to her uncle who seemed to have slumped in his chair, his head leaning at an odd angel.

"Oh, Aharon! I'm so glad you're here," she gabbled, "I don't know what has happened. One minute he was fine, we were talking about the day we've had, then next he just sort of collapsed." Aharon could see that his sister had tight control of herself but that she was on the verge of a panic attack. He came to where she knelt and lifted her off the floor.

"Do not fret, Hannah" he said his voice calm and reasonable. "Go and get some fresh air, I will see what can be done with Uncle." She shook her head

"You can't…you don't know…what if…" coherence, never his sister's strong point had completely abandoned her and she could not seem to form the words that she needed, to tell him that she was the one with medical knowledge and she had no clue what had happened.

"Trust me, Hannah. I will call you if I need you." He pushed her, gently, towards the front door and turned his attention to Gideon. His uncle's eyes were open and he was breathing, a little erratically, it must be admitted but he was breathing. Thinking quickly, Aharon took hold of the man's hand and pressed it very gently, feeling faint pressure in response.

"Gideon, if you can hear me, squeeze my hand." He said in a calm voice. He felt the pressure again. So far, so good. "If you are in pain, press my hand. If not do nothing." He waited — nothing, he waited a little longer just to be sure — still nothing. "You have no pain." He made it a statement not a question and was rewarded with a very slight nod. Taking a deep breath Aharon tried to decide what to do, remembering Gideon's headaches he said, "Do you think this is because of your headaches?" Searching his uncle's face he noticed that he had raised his right eyebrow and took this to mean it was possible.

With no idea what had happened or how to treat it, Aharon simply made sure his uncle was sitting more comfortably and then went to find Hannah, who was sitting on the bench outside, staring at nothing. Asaf was nowhere to be seen; hopefully he'd run home. Hannah heard her brother's footfall and spun around, questions spilling from her mouth. Aharon put his hand up to hush her and she bit her lip, falling back against the seat and waiting for him to speak.

"I do not know what is wrong, but he indicated that he is not in pain. Mind you, while I am no physician, I can see that this is serious. Gideon thinks it may have something to do with his headaches." Hannah nodded —

"Years ago, when he was teaching me from his manuscripts, Gideon told me of a strange illness which is a kind of brain fever." Aharon looked confused and his sister tried to clarify. "I believe it happens when the blood no longer circulates properly, maybe it gets sluggish and it makes everything else sluggish too. I think speech can also be affected, but I can't remember, neither can I recall whether there is a remedy. I'll have to see if I can find anything in his medical texts."

Hannah was white faced and Aharon could see that she was trembling. He sat down next to her, slinging his arm over her shoulder and drawing her against him. She felt too thin and, absently, he worried whether she was eating enough.

"Do not fret, Hannah, Gideon is strong. We will find a way to help him overcome this." Hannah didn't reply, she was leaning on him trying not to cry, wishing her mother were there to hug her and tell her everything would be all right. She was a grown-up now and crying was for babies, but Gideon's attack had frightened her. She knew he had become increasingly unwell, but because Gideon had downplayed his symptoms, had not thought it quite as severe. After a few moments she muttered —

"What do we do? I cannot lift him and he seems to have lost the ability to move. Until I can work out how to treat this, I will need help. I want to look after him. Would you be able to help him into bed?" Aharon nodded and the pair went back inside to check on their uncle. Hannah knelt back down in front of Gideon and taking his big hand in her small one, said —

"Uncle, I think that you may be suffering from a brain fever. I will read through your manuscripts to see what treatment is suggested, but for now, Aharon is going to help you into bed."

Gideon was obviously trying to communicate but his words were incomprehensible and half of his mouth had drooped. He tried to get up, but did not have the strength. Hannah spoke soothingly —

"Please do not fret, we will watch over you. The best thing right now is that you rest." Her demeanour seemed to convince him and Gideon leaned back in his chair.

Aharon was once again astonished by how his sister could calm even the most distressed of patients, with just a gentle touch and her quiet voice. Made even more amazing when he remembered how she used that voice to shriek at him if he yanked her plait or pushed her into the stream when they played as children near the edge of the city; sounding more like a donkey braying than a young woman from a good family.

While Aharon lifted his uncle onto his bed and ensured he was as comfortable as possible, Hannah ran down to her old home and told Raizel what had happened. Raizel then said that she would bring the dinner to them; Hannah chose to wait, helping her carry some of the food.

Leaving Aharon and Raizel to have their meal, Hannah slipped into her uncle's room with a bowl of warm soup and some bread which she had pulled into small pieces and dropped into the soup, softening it and making it easier to eat. Aharon had settled their uncle into a reclining position, propping him up with plenty of pillows. Without any fuss, Hannah drew up a chair and began to spoon the food into Gideon's mouth in extremely small portions. He managed to swallow some, but soon it was obvious that the effort was exhausting him.

Hannah patted his arm and told him not to worry, that he'd be able to try again later. Tucking him in she left him to rest, taking everything back into the main living area. Aharon and Raizel were chatting in undertones and both turned as she walked into the room.

"He hasn't been able to eat very much at all, but he is very weary, so I think he just wants to sleep now." She informed them. Raizel said she would go and sit with him while Hannah ate. The girl's appetite had left her, but Aharon convinced her that she would be no use to anyone if she had no energy, keenly aware that his sister would want to keep watch over Gideon that night. He just hoped that her vigil would not be in vain.

Chapter Fifteen

Masada ~ AD65

Maxentius stood on the huge sweeping balcony where King Herod had once stood, and looked out over the vast desert. It was still dark — although he perceived a slight lightening in the black emptiness — and he, along with a small contingent of soldiers, intended to travel down to Engaddi, a settlement not far from Masada, to barter for food and other supplies, before it grew too warm. The stores on Masada were plentiful, but none wanted to use them unless necessary, further it was much more pleasant to eat fresh food and the markets there offered a wide variety of fruit and vegetables.

As with the tournaments, it had become a challenge for those soldiers on kitchen duty to see which group would provide the tastiest meals and since this distracted the men from less law-abiding pursuits, Maxentius wasn't going to stop them. Sergius — who had become unofficial deputy to Marcus — would accompany him, but knowing that they would be gone for most of the day, Maxentius would leave Marcus in charge. The soldiers were reverting to their slovenly ways, despite the threat of harsh punishment should standards be allowed to slip, and Maxentius did not trust most of them when left to their own devices, relieved that he had a very reliable second-in-command.

Maxentius was at his wits end, and as a last resort for he certainly did not wish to appear an ineffective commander, had been considering whether there was any point in sending a missive to Rome. He was loath to do so and it was not as though the soldiers disobeyed him as such, more that they just stretched the letter of the law to its very limits. Troubled by the prospect that this lackadaisical attitude left them vulnerable, Maxentius was thankful that because of its isolation, an attack on the fortress was improbable. He had also increased the watch, ensuring that there were always at least one soldier posted on every tower day and night, their view across the desert virtually limitless.

As he gazed out across the desert, Maxentius witnessed the dawn break over the outcrop, fingers of light pushing back the shade of darkness. Soft hues bled across the rock mutating from pink and purple to gold. Maxentius never tired of it, for this was a spectacle unspoiled by time, its permanence in a world of uncertainty — comforting, its ceaseless path enduring for eternity.

He remained motionless until the last shadow had been banished and then drawing a sigh that seemed to come from his very core, turned his back on the beauty of nature and began his day. Those journeying to Engaddi left shortly thereafter, their stomachs nicely filled from their first meal. The village was about twelve miles away so, as they were few in number and for convenience sake, they rode; it made the journey much quicker and they needed horses to pull the supply wagon anyway.

It was a pleasant morning and they reached Engaddi by the fourth hour, spending a little time chatting with the townsfolk, another of Maxentius' initiatives. After so long in Armenia he understood and empathised with those who lived under foreign jurisdiction. Their distance from Jerusalem meant that these people were scarcely aware of the upheaval that was tearing that city apart, content to carry on with their lives untouched by turmoil.

Maxentius wanted this to continue and made it a priority to visit the neighbouring communities on a fairly regular basis — most were just hamlets, but a few larger settlements like Engaddi were beginning to spring up. On the one hand it reinforced the presence of the Roman soldiers, but on the other, it gave him the chance to spend time among the locals, getting to know them, solving minor issues and matters of discontent before they became major problems. He also wanted them to know that as long as they carried on as normal and posed no threat to the garrison, they would be left in peace.

He had achieved some success. Of course there were those who much preferred that the Romans leave their country — none were particularly impressed by the way the procurators were running Judaea — but if they had to have soldiers on their doorstep, at least this latest contingent had made the effort to be cordial.

Eventually though they had concluded their discussions, all matters that had been raised by the townsfolk had been dealt with more or less to the complainant's satisfaction and the supply wagon was full to bursting. Thanking those he had been talking with for their time, Maxentius politely took his leave and the group set off back to Masada. As they rode along, Maxentius sent a few of the men out to scout the area on the off chance that bandits were roaming the countryside. They reported nothing untoward and they arrived back at the lonely citadel just as the sun was beginning its downward trek.

The horses were now corralled within a fenced area at the base of the rock, under the watchful eye of several trusted soldiers and horsemen. It was cooler at the bottom, more sheltered during the hottest part of the day and it was far less dangerous than trying to persuade the animals to navigate up and down the narrow path to the plateau. The wagons were also stored here and the soldiers unpacked the supplies distributing them evenly throughout the group. Then the tired men trudged up to the citadel. It was steep and winding and they had to go single file, but at least the day was no longer quite so hot and the path was in the shade.

Willing hands helped divest them of their burden when they reached the top, the watch having warned the rest of the soldiers of their imminent arrival. Maxentius thanked those who had made the journey and then strode over to his office to check in with Marcus. His second was still working, reports always needed to be completed and although he knew they had to be done, Marcus, who considered them a wholly unnecessary evil, hated them with a passion and was endlessly amazed that Maxentius always seemed able to breeze through them.

Nothing of any note had occurred in Maxentius' absence and the two friends completed their business, before joining the rest of the soldiers for a hot meal. Here on Masada there were huge kitchens, originally meant to provide food for Herod's vast entourage and any visiting dignitaries. With such facilities available to them, Maxentius felt it better that all the meals were cooked here, although given their numbers, each meal was served over several sittings — a tenth of the garrison cooking for the remainder on a rotating schedule.

After making sure those who were on evening duties or were due on watch had gone off to their appointed tasks, Maxentius, Marcus and Sergius retired to the balcony room with a flagon of wine and were able, finally, to relax. As had become their habit, they discussed their day. Maxentius confirmed that all seemed as expected in Engaddi and that the surrounds were untroubled, while Marcus complained long and bitterly about reports — which the other two, having heard it all before, just ignored — simply topping up his goblet with wine and continuing as though he hadn't spoken. They chattered long into the evening and as the moon rose sending a silvery glow over the fortress, quiet laughter could be heard as their tales became more far-fetched in direct correlation with how much wine they had consumed.

The next day, slightly sore heads aside, it was business as usual. Maxentius had divided the main duties of the garrison between the three of them, designating Sergius the role of workshop supervisor. From a family of artisans, Sergius was already a skilled craftsman before joining the army, able to turn his hand to anything of a practical nature and he relished the job. Workshops were vital to the smooth running of any garrison and the carpenters, stonemasons and metalworkers had claimed several smaller outbuildings. Armour, weapons and tools were maintained and repaired and the engineers had somewhere to store all their paraphernalia, away from the main living quarters.

Soldiers are not noted for their gentle handling of anything and there was always equipment that needed overhauling. Moreover, most of the fixtures and fittings remaining in the rooms and storehouses had been made for a king — whose intent was to impress rather than worrying about durability — and tended to be broken easily. Sergius had requisitioned many of the sturdier or larger pieces and set his men the task of creating more sturdy furniture.

Marcus was in charge of inspection, training and drill, as well as animal husbandry and the garden beds — both of which flourished under his watchful eye. Maxentius in the meantime managed all the paperwork — schedules, rosters, supplies and, to Marcus' eternal gratitude, reports and any other missives.

Recalling, again, the legate's objectives at Rhandeia, Maxentius was also intent on making sure every solider was capable of every task or duty. Further, with the assistance of Marcus, he had made the effort to determine which soldiers had an aptitude or preference for certain tasks, appointing them as supervisor for that particular activity, in the hope that this would prompt some pride in their work.

In addition to their regular duties, the three men had taken it upon themselves to explore this outpost. There were so many buildings within the fortress that they wanted to be sure they knew every single corner, if for no other reason than to be able to root out those who tried to shirk their duties. A frequent claim by soldiers was they became disoriented in the maze of rooms and corridors that made up the several palaces; at the same time, coincidentally, that they were supposed to be engaged in a chore considered more than a little tedious. Therefore, whenever they had a spare hour during the day they would investigate the next building, wing, or set of rooms. It took a long time but eventually they felt that they were familiar with the intricate layout of the citadel, unaware of just how beneficial their knowledge would become.

While Maxentius accepted that trying to make life interesting for his men was becoming more problematic, he was, at least, thankful that they were not in fear of their lives or having, on a daily basis, to face an enemy baying for their blood. Something he took pains to remind them of at frequent intervals. This is not to say that he didn't ensure a strict adherence to training. He was, after all, a soldier and regardless of circumstance, he knew that a soldier should always be at peak fitness and battle ready. It was just becoming harder to enforce.

The months ticked by slowly and news began to filter through from Jerusalem advising that the situation there was deteriorating rapidly and that the current procurator was losing control. Maxentius had not met him or his predecessor, but nearly four years previously, when he had passed through the city, one of the more circumspect Roman centurions with whom he had chatted several times, had hinted that each new procurator was worse than the last. Corrupt practices aside — something no one was ever surprised at — none had made any attempt to understand or address the grievances of the Jewish populace and dissent was rife. Maxentius had been impressed by the centurion's insight and the two men had kept in sporadic touch, exchanging missives when possible.

The winter was harsh that year and although the constant storms did mean that the cisterns were filled nearly to their brims, they made life on Masada almost unbearable. By its very position the citadel bore the brunt of the howling winds and lashing rain and there were weeks when it was impossible to step outside without fear of being blown over and instantly drenched. When spring finally broke winter's grasp, it was very welcome indeed; and on the plus side, as the days grew warmer a profusion of flowers in a variety of colours carpeted the plateau, alleviating the dusty landscape. The change of season brought with it a feeling of promise and a much more positive atmosphere began to pervade the community of wearied soldiers.

Therefore, you can imagine that he was more than a little delighted to receive a directive from Rome, informing him that at the end of the year he would be returning to the capital of the Empire to be assigned a new posting at that time. Most of those whom he had commanded since they left Armenia would also be leaving, the fact of which he had no intention of informing them quite yet, as would Sergius — Maxentius' cleverly worded assessments indicating that the young soldier would be far more useful in active campaigns rather than protecting isolated outposts.

Determined not to let their standards slip any further and desirous that the incoming commander would not find this garrison lacking in any way whatsoever, Maxentius — using the possibility of a transfer to a far more preferable location as an enticement — persuaded his soldiers back into the disciplined lifestyle they had tried so hard to eschew.

In fairness, not all of them had become lackadaisical, most enjoyed the strict routine; for if nothing else it made the long days fly by and some actually relished the slower pace and less dangerous lifestyle, having been in more battles than they cared to count. Maxentius, for the most part, was proud of his soldiers and had been quick to reward those who were prepared to put in extra effort, accepting that this posting was mundane and boring in the extreme for young men who had joined the army for the thrill of warfare but had ended up in a remote backwater.

The chance of a change, of a posting to a place where there were trees and grass, even rivers and lakes, encouraged the soldiers to adhere to their rigorous schedules hoping for a favourable evaluation when Maxentius completed his appraisals and for a little while, order reigned.

Chapter Sixteen

Jerusalem ~ AD66

It was late afternoon; the sky was a cloudless blue and the day mild. Spring had finally arrived, bringing with it an abundance of new growth. The leaves on the trees scattered throughout the neighbourhood were budding in vivid green and the air was scented with balmy fragrances from their bright blossoms.

Hannah was sitting with Gideon on the bench outside his rooms. Her uncle had recovered somewhat from the brain fever, but it had been a slow and for Gideon, frustrating, process. Despite it being almost a year since his collapse, Gideon still struggled with even the most basic of physical tasks and was no longer able to perform operations or treat anyone suffering from serious injuries. He was, however, still able to diagnose illnesses and suggest remedies.

Initially the entire left side of his body had been incapacitated and he had lost the ability to speak clearly. Eventually he had regained most of his speech albeit sometimes rather slurred — especially when he was tired — but his left arm and left leg remained weak. Occasionally Hannah and Aharon noticed that he could not recall certain events, but they did not draw attention to it, hoping that this too would rectify itself sooner or later.

Hannah had spent many hours caring for her uncle and once he appeared to be recovering, began a regimen of exercises, which she hoped might help strengthen his muscles. She had also persuaded him to let her massage his limbs for she knew that they could become wasted if unused.

For a man who, until recently, had been fit and healthy, Gideon endured her ministrations with fortitude and had to admit that she had worked wonders, but he was so weary. The effort simply to wake up and get dressed exhausted him and he could see little respite. Always a practical man and of course as a physician he understood his limits, Gideon's concern now was for Hannah, whom he knew would be badly upset when his time came.

He had taken Aharon into his confidence talking privately with his nephew, telling him what he thought was close, making him promise that whatever happened, he would not let Hannah fend for herself. That if for any reason he and Raizel decided to leave Jerusalem, they would take Hannah with them. Aharon, of course had no intention of leaving the city, or abandoning his sister, but he could see how important it was for Gideon that he agree and so gave his uncle his word.

Meanwhile and on a happier note, around three months previously, Raizel had come to term and after what seemed to Hannah to be a long labour, although the other women who attended said it was quite normal, gave birth to a son. Thankfully both survived to Aharon's relief and unending joy. Fearful of the risks, Aharon had wanted to stay with his beloved wife during the delivery, but custom and the presence of enough mothers who understood the process, dictated otherwise and he had been shooed out, spending the whole time pacing up and down the street in a cold sweat.

Named 'Efraim' after Aharon and Hannah's father, the child had become the most important part of Gideon's day. Raizel carried her son along to his great uncle in the late afternoons, settling him securely into Gideon's large frame. The sight of the child never failed to lift Gideon's spirits, even on his darkest days and his family hoped the baby might help to hold their uncle a little longer in this world.

Hannah was no less enamoured of her nephew, fascinated by his perfect features all in miniature and tried to see him as much as possible; often popping along to her old home, just to watch him sleep. These precious moments every afternoon, had become a time when everything else faded into insignificance, when she could relax and enjoy the simple pleasure of being with this child.

Today was no different and Raizel appeared on cue, carrying a wriggling bundle, the only visible part of which was a smattering of dark brown hair and two tiny fists. The child's mother looked weary and she was thankful to hand her son over for a little while. Hannah made sure Efraim was tucked against Gideon, remaining with them, aware that her uncle tired easily and that although tiny, the baby was like a fish when he chose, squirming to escape from his wraps.

Hannah ran her eye over her sister-in-law, noting the fatigued cast to her face and mentally made a point to tell Aharon that his wife needed more sleep. Her brother was very good at ensuring Raizel did not over-do things, but they lived in a world where women looked after all the domestic chores whether they had to care for a baby or not. He probably didn't even consider that the things Raizel had always done would be far harder to do when trying to fit them around Efraim's needs.

"Raizel, go and lie down. Please do not use this time to do more chores; they can wait. You need to rest whenever you can and we are quite capable of watching Efraim." Raizel smiled wearily and, promising to do as Hannah requested, went back to her home. Hoping her friend would try to get some sleep, Hannah turned her attention to the two men next to her.

They were the complete opposite of each other, one big and burly and the other so small that his feet and hands were barely the length of his great uncle's thumb. She cooed at the child and blew on his palms, making him gurgle while he tried to reach for her long curly hair, which as usual, was falling out of its plait. Efraim took great delight in twisting it in his little fingers and without warning pulling it hard. Hannah had grown wise to his antics and remembered — just in time to prevent him from achieving his goal — gathering her hair back out of his reach.

The three spent a happy hour or so watching the world go by, chatting to neighbours as they passed, many of whom took the time to talk with Gideon, a friend to all and the man who had likely treated them at some time or another. Dusk had fallen by the time Aharon arrived to collect his son, his face lighting up at the sight of the child. By now, Hannah was cuddling him and Aharon was struck by how comfortable his sister looked holding a child, suddenly hoping she would experience the same wonder that both he and Raizel felt.

Hannah was dancing with Efraim, making both the baby and her uncle chuckle and as she spun around she caught sight of her brother coming towards them and beamed at him with unaffected happiness. Aharon smiled back, registering, with a sense of shock, that his sister really was quite beautiful and that this might well be why all his friends and even those whom he considered to be barely acquaintances kept asking him for her hand. Tobias, especially, insisted on pressing his suit, but so far Aharon had denied it, his opinion of the young man in no way changed from when he had first indicated that he wanted to marry Hannah.

Pushing these thoughts aside for now, he lifted Efraim from Hannah's arms, dropping a quick kiss on his sister's head and thanking her for looking after him.

"You must have a care for Raizel, Aharon." Hannah spoke softly but her eyes held him, trying to make him understand the import of her words. Aharon frowned a little and started to speak but his sister interrupted. "She is very tired. I know it is three months since the birth but it is hard for her to do all her regular chores as well as looking after Efraim, who demands more and more of her time. I know this is how it has always been, but not only is she my best friend, now she is also my sister, as well as your wife and I am worried about her. I help where I can, but I am needed here and of late, I have scarcely any free time. I realise that you have to go to work, but maybe in the evenings, you could help a little."

She hesitated, letting that sink in and then continued.

"Please don't let her know you are doing it or that we have spoken, for I do not think she is even aware of it herself and she would hate it if she thought I was interfering or that you were worried. Little things here and there, like tidying away after a meal, or getting this cheeky little baby ready for sleep…" tickling said baby who chortled with glee. "…not going out every single night, and letting her sleep longer in the morning. Do you think you could?"

Aharon nodded, biting his lip, sensing that Hannah was chastising him without appearing to. As he ran his mind back over the last week or so he remembered thinking that his wife seemed listless, but he had been so busy with work and his meetings that he hadn't dwelt on it. How selfish of him, leaving her alone for long hours, while he discussed rebellion. She could be forgiven for thinking that he didn't care.

The thought that his actions, however unintentional, might be hurting Raizel, cut Aharon to the quick and muttering a begrudging thanks he rushed home to find his wife cooking their meal. Hannah watched him until he disappeared through their doorway and hoped he would do the right thing. She loved her brother, but he had been so caught up with his Zealot friends that those things most important to him were in danger of becoming neglected.

She grinned at Gideon winking impishly as she shared her thoughts. He nodded sagely and the two fell into easy chatter — well Hannah chattered, Gideon mostly just listened, letting the young woman's musical voice flow over him as he leaned back, resting his head against the wall. A little later Raizel brought a bowl of stew along for them, with a platter of breads, saying that she would collect their dishes later. Hannah told her not to bother, that she would carry them along when they had finished. About to retrace her steps, Raizel paused and glanced at her husband's sister, saying quietly —

"Thank you, Hannah." Hannah raised her eyebrows curiously and Raizel merely shook her head. "You know what I'm talking about. You are a good sister." Hannah blushed assuming that Aharon had either said something to his wife or that Raizel, who could read her husband like a prayer scroll, had worked it out for herself.

"I'm sure I have no idea what you mean," Hannah murmured, dipping her head to hide her expression. Raizel pulled her into a warm hug.

"You mean more to me than I can ever say." Leaving Hannah standing stock still, her mouth agape. Raizel gave Gideon a hug also, and hurried home, where she was surprised and relieved to find that her husband had put Efraim to bed and was preparing a hot drink. Relaxing in the peace of their house, Aharon drew his wife close and whispered his love for her, as she rested her head on his shoulder, revelling in his attentiveness.

Hannah and Gideon finished their meal, Hannah washing the dishes before stacking them ready to take back to Raizel. It was the end of another long day, although it had mostly involved dealing with children's ailments rather than injured men, for which Hannah was grateful. Leaving Gideon to enjoy the mild evening air, she went inside to make sure everything was cleaned, washed and set up ready for the morning.

Once satisfied that she had done all she could, she prepared a drink of the hot sweet infusion she had begun making for Gideon after his illness. She added the blend of herbs that helped his discomfort; for the headache had never left him and this way he got a restful night. Taking this and a goblet of hot milk for herself, she went back outside, picking up a blanket as she passed the pile on the shelf, to wrap around her uncle, as he seemed to feel the cold more than he used to. They had no need of talk, welcoming the quiet of the street, their immediate neighbours presumably either eating or preparing to sleep. The cost of oil for lamps aside, most were up with the dawn and by nightfall were ready for their beds.

Hannah leaned back against the cool stone wall and watched the stars wink into existence. Their ethereal light a perfect backdrop to the moonrise. Often lost behind the city's buildings, tonight the moon looked as though it was beginning its journey right at the end of their street, close enough to reach out and touch its celestial brilliance. It was utterly magical and Hannah almost forgot to breathe, so captivated was she by the sight.

Gideon smiled at his niece, her face illuminated by the glow of the moon, her green eyes enthralled. As he watched her, an odd sensation that could only be described as euphoria began to spread through him. Recognising it for what it was, he suggested to Hannah that she take the dishes along to Raizel before it got too late. Nodding, she collected the little pile and just before she dashed along the street she squeezed his hand.

"I won't be a moment. Will you be all right out here?" He nodded and, unusually for her, as she fought shy of overt displays of affection, she dropped a kiss on his cheek and whispered, "I love you, Uncle Gideon," then disappeared in the gloom. Gideon felt his heart crack. How could she know? No — there was no way she could know — accepting that it was probably subliminal; Hannah's soul perceiving a subtle change, which had yet to register in her consciousness.

It was time to relinquish his grasp of this life. Gideon was ready to go, he was just sad to leave his niece, but she needed to move out from his shadow and become the physician he knew she could be. He was weary, his body was failing and his mind fought to hold onto the information that used to come so readily. He gazed up at the incredible sky, with its billions of stars shimmering in a sea of obsidian, whispered a heartfelt prayer and let go.

Chapter Seventeen

Jerusalem ~ AD66

It was several minutes before Hannah returned, having been caught up in conversation with Aharon and Raizel. As she wandered into the house intent on brewing up another hot drink, she called something to Gideon and when he didn't respond, assumed he had nodded off. Something made her pause and she walked slowly back to the bench where her uncle was sitting. Kneeling in front of him, she took his large hand in her slender one and brushed her fingers across his face.

He was still warm but she knew. She found she couldn't move, she needed to tell Aharon, but it was as though time had stopped and everything around her had stilled. She curled up on the pathway, her head resting against his legs and shut her eyes.

"Don't leave me, my uncle. I am not ready to be without you," she sighed, her words lost in the hushed air. As she knelt, the silence wrapped itself around the two of them, one in this world, one in the next and through it, she imagined she heard him reply, her name murmured and his prayer that she would be happy, drifting back to her on a gentle breeze. Unable to help herself, Hannah began to cry, tears pouring down her cheeks; a neighbour who happened to be coming towards the pair, recognised the girl and unwilling to disturb her grief, hurried to find Aharon.

Aharon shot along the street, taking everything in at a glance and disentangling his sister from her uncle, carried her back to his home. Leaving her in the capable hands of his wife, Aharon returned to the bench and gently lifted his uncle, who for so tall a man now weighed surprisingly little and, laying him to rest on his own bed, covered the body with a blanket. The house was cool; Gideon could have one last night in his own home. Securing the house, he went home to find Raizel rocking Hannah as she would Efraim, his sister still sobbing brokenly. Crouching next to them, he stroked Hannah's hair —

"Try not to be too sad, Hannah. Gideon is at peace. He was very tired you know. He told me that he thought this day was not far away. I think he was ready to be with God."

"I know that Gideon was devout, so I hope there is a God and that our uncle is with him," his sister stuttered, "but I don't think I am so sure anymore. What kind of God takes everybody away?" Then, tremulously, "What am I supposed to do without him...?" her voice trailed away as the enormity of her loss sunk in. Infusing practicality into his tone Aharon replied —

"Hannah, you are ten and nine years old. By rights you should be married and running a household." Hannah curled her lip at his words and it was all Aharon could do not to laugh at her expression; she never let him forget her opinion on marriage. Biting his lip to control his mirth, he continued, "Gideon believed you to be more than capable of taking over his practice, to continue his work and to go further than he ever hoped to." She stared at him, reading in his eyes the truth of his words.

"I believe this too, Hannah." Raizel interjected in her quiet way. "You are already a good physician, Gideon expected you to be great. It is too easy to stand behind him, letting him be your shield, your guide. You are a strong woman and I have faith that this strength will help you go on and honour Gideon's name." Hannah twisted in the chair to look at Raizel. Her sister-in-law was a reticent soul and rarely said much but when she did, everyone listened. While Hannah was mulling this over, Aharon glanced at his wife over his sister's head and smiled his approval of her words, the pair sharing a look of complete rapport.

There was a huge sigh and Hannah drew herself up.

"You are right and I will do my best not to let our uncle down," she said, pleased to note that her voice was steady. "But I think I'd better wait until tomorrow, I feel rather peculiar" She made to stand, but everything around her seemed to be slewed at the oddest angle and she could tell that her brother was speaking to her, but his words were distorted. She tried to reply, but her mouth felt as though someone had stuffed it full of bandages and the last thing she saw was Aharon's face as he caught her.

The next day Hannah woke in less than familiar surroundings and lay for a moment trying to work out where she was. Then everything flooded back, Gideon was dead and she needed to prepare yet another body for burial. More than this, suddenly, she was the physician, she was the one to whom people would turn when ill or hurt. Yes, all right, she already had several people — women mostly — who sought her out, but they all knew that Gideon was there behind her with a breadth of knowledge that she could rely on should an unusual case present itself. Now it was just her.

Panic and grief threatened to overwhelm her, but she was determined to fight it. She would not fail her uncle, she would do everything she could to be who he believed she could be and she was not going to cry anymore. He deserved better than that! Hannah dragged herself out of bed, hearing a murmured conversation and the sound of a small baby demanding to be fed. Feeling rather awkward, she shuffled through to where Aharon and Raizel were eating a meal, knowing that she must look like a wreck. Aharon frowned a little when he noticed her and his expression hurt, unknowing that it was worry not annoyance.

"I'm sorry to be a bother, Aharon," she whispered. "I didn't mean to…" hesitating, uncertain what it was she'd actually done this time, "…cause you a problem." Her brother gaped, at a loss until Raizel, intuitive as always, intervened.

"He is not upset with you, Hannah. We are both worried about you. You collapsed last night and then we couldn't wake you. You have slept for nearly twelve hours." Hannah stared at Raizel in astonishment.

"So this is not the first meal?" she queried, waving her hand at the food. Raizel shook her head.

"No, this is the midday meal. Come, join us and then we will go and take care of Gideon. Aharon will watch Efraim." Hannah sat with them, suddenly ravenous and inhaled the delicious selection of food. Efraim, who was in Raizel's arms, spotted the woman whose hair was so much fun to play with and, crowing with mischief, desperately tried to grab Hannah's riotous curls. His antics made them all laugh and the rather strained atmosphere was broken; the three adults started to chatter about everyday matters that kept them going until the platters were empty.

Hannah cleared everything away, then took her leave saying
—

"If you will excuse me, I will go home. I need to wash and change before we begin to prepare Gideon's body."

"I will be along shortly," was all Raizel replied, understanding that Hannah wanted a little time on her own with her uncle. Aharon moved to go with his sister, but Raizel stopped him,

"She needs to do this on her own, Aharon. We have to let her." Aharon stared after Hannah, then looked down at his wife for long moments. Unexpectedly, he dipped his head and kissed Raizel soundly.

"What was that for?" Raizel queried, a little breathlessly as she ran light fingers through his hair. "Not that I'm complaining."

"How do you always know?" his wife shrugged and assuming Aharon did not expect an answer, simply leaned in and hugged him. "I am so glad you are mine, my love," he said, holding her close. Raizel chuckled artfully.

"Oh, I think you will find that it is the other way around, my beloved husband. You are, in fact, mine," returning his kiss with interest. "Now, I must sort Efraim out before I join Hannah. I trust you will watch over him while I am out." Aharon nodded, and while Raizel did whatever she needed to do, he finished some of her chores, much to his wife's delight.

Meanwhile, Hannah had slipped quietly into her uncle's home, which she presumed was now hers. She had been living there for long enough anyway. Taking the time to wash thoroughly and rinse her hair, Hannah dressed in a clean undershift and tunic and then, after rubbing some sweet oil through her unruly locks, twisted them into a tidy plait.

She stood at the door to Gideon's sleeping quarters, bracing herself, then straightened her shoulders and moved towards his bed, lifting the blanket from her uncle's body, she was thankful to note that it hadn't begun to swell and that there were no flies. She went through to the clinic and filled a bowl with water, adding a few drops of frankincense, myrrh and aloes. Collecting cloths and two linen sheets, she returned to the bedroom and began to prepare Gideon for his onward journey.

Moments later, Raizel arrived and the two women worked together quietly. Neither spoke, words did not seem necessary, but there was a tranquility in their silence. It did not take very long, after which they sprinkled the ritual oils over the linen before binding the sheets around Gideon's body. Unable to help herself, Hannah dipped a kiss on her uncle's forehead and even though she was more than a little ambivalent about the existence of God, murmured —

"Be at peace, my uncle," so quietly that Raizel wasn't sure she had actually spoken. Both women stood back, heads bowed, then as one left the room. Raizel said that Aharon and a few of his friends would carry the body to the place of burial and that they would go just before dusk. Hannah nodded, not trusting herself to speak.

"Will you come home with me?" her sister-in-law questioned.

"No, I will stay here. I do not wish to leave him alone and there may be a need for my services. I cannot ignore anyone who requires my help. Go, you have a son who needs you. I will be fine." Raizel hesitated, "Truly Raizel, Gideon's presence still lingers and I find comfort in that." Raizel gave in and kissing Hannah on the cheek, disappeared out of the door.

Hannah went into the living area and set about doing all the things she did every day. Laying and lighting the fire; hanging the huge pot full of water over the flames; placing cloths, bandages, bowls and instruments on the bench, just in case. Making sure that the jars and bottles containing oils, balms, ointments and tinctures were in order and all had been filled. Satisfied that she could do no more, the young woman poured a goblet of cool lemon drink that she found refreshing and went to sit outside on the bench.

It was hard to believe that a little over twelve hours previously she had been chatting with Gideon, gazing at the moon and admiring the stars. In a split second, everything had changed and Hannah ruminated over how often this had happened to her in recent years. While in her heart of hearts she knew such change was inevitable, she still hated it.

Everyone she loved had either died — she believed before their time — or moved on with their lives and as she pondered these things, a flicker of something flittered through the periphery of her mind whispering that it was because she was not worthy; that for her, happiness would always be ephemeral. It was so fleeting that Hannah blamed her grief and her flighty imagination, refusing to acknowledge it and buried it so deeply that she almost forgot about it. Occasionally, however, it would return to haunt her, until one day someone whom she loved beyond measure, would suggest that she learn to trust her heart.

Bringing herself back to the here and now, Hannah was thankful to be distracted by a few families who required her help. Most were minor ailments, but enough to keep her busy for the remainder of the afternoon. Just as the sun began to drop below the buildings, Aharon and five of his friends appeared. Respectfully and with dignity, they moved Gideon onto a wooden pallet and carried him to the place of burial. People streamed out of houses and from other neighbourhoods. Gideon had been loved by many and all wanted to say farewell.

They walked in a slow procession and came to the tomb where Gideon's parents and grandparents had been laid to rest. In truth, this was a very small cave, really more a hollow in the rock, just beyond the city wall, but it was cool and a body would not be desecrated. The men placed the body inside leaving Hannah, Aharon and Raizel alone. Hannah had brought one of Gideon's manuscripts, one describing how different civilisations imagined the journey their dead took to whatever afterlife they believed in. It was a subject that had fascinated her uncle and a text that she had copied out for herself years before. Hannah had rolled it tight, binding it with a narrow piece of coloured cloth. As she laid it on her uncle's body, she said

"Now you will know who was right, my uncle." Then tucking a sprig of rosemary into the shroud, left, without looking back. Aharon and Raizel glanced at each other somewhat perplexed, but used to Hannah's unconventional ways, simply said a prayer and followed her out into the waning light.

Those who had come to pay their respects began to sing, but this was no mournful lament, rather it was a celebration of a life well-lived and of a man well-loved. Voices blending in a song of praise that lifted the spirits of those around them and when the last note died away, grief had given way to joy.

Chapter Eighteen

Jerusalem ~ AD66

The weeks after Gideon's death flew by and for Hannah it seemed as though she barely had a chance to turn around, never mind have the time to worry whether she would be able to cope without her uncle. The clinic was always full, a constant stream of young men who insisted on clashing with the Roman soldiers and anyone else who supported the governing body of the city. Violent fracas were a common occurrence and Hannah often worked long into the night trying to treat all who knocked on her door, somehow managing on very little sleep.

The young physician was most grateful to have Asaf, who was a diligent boy and had learned enough to deal with minor wounds. Hannah had come to believe that Jerusalem could not withstand such turmoil and was saddened that the city she loved so much was being eroded from within and she guessed that it wouldn't take much to bring it to ruin.

The cause of the latest rampage could be laid squarely at the feet of the city's procurator. During his tenure, the corrupt practices of Gessius Florus and his seemingly blinkered determination to ignore any and all internal discord between his politics and the populace had alienated pretty much everyone. It was as though the procurator *desired* rebellion and Hannah's fears were well founded, for Florus' imprudence was about to set off a chain of events that would have catastrophic repercussions.

Florus — after being bribed of course — had ordered the release of brigands and robbers, subsequently allowing them to roam freely and continue their thievery, on the understanding that they would share with him any booty. This, along with the exorbitant taxes imposed on the Jews and the obvious class divide, continued to be a source of antagonism. Florus exacerbated the situation by showing favour to citizens of Greek and Syrian heritage, who had long disdained the Jewish people. This was never clearer than the recent atrocities in

Caesarea, where simmering rancour had spilled over into outright barbarity on both sides. Although complaints were sent to Cestius Gallus — Florus' immediate superior, now comfortably ensconced in Syria and away from the upheaval affecting Jerusalem — unfortunately, he proved to be wholly ineffectual and unable or unwilling to curb the procurator's ways.

Hannah was fighting a growing sense of foreboding and mind-numbing fear. She knew that her brother was deeply involved with those who wanted to oust the Romans, in the hope that they could reclaim their city, their land, and she feared for his life, not to mention those his friends whom she had known since they were all children. The so called meetings — now merely a euphemism for the brutal clashes incited by the more radical members of the groups — had increased in frequency and Hannah often wondered how anyone still dared walk the streets, so numerous were the brawls.

One evening, Aharon came home covered in blood, almost causing Raizel to faint from shock. It turned out it wasn't his, he had tried to help in the aftermath of a riot and the blood was from those who had been injured. For Hannah it proved too much and, with cool politeness, asked her brother to come along to Gideon's house, once he had soothed his wife's distress.

Aharon knew he was in for a scolding, but he could not have imagined the fury with which his sister censured him as he walked through the door.

"Aharon! What is wrong with you? Have you lost your mind? I never imagined that you, my brother, could be so utterly thoughtless and insensitive. You are a husband and a father. Yes, yes…" pacing back and forth and waving her hand in the general direction of the Temple, "…I understand that you believe in this rebellion, but have you ever, for one single moment, thought about the backlash that might well befall Raizel and me, never mind little Efraim, if you are caught?" About to protest that they were safe, Aharon suddenly paused. Crucifixion was the preferred retribution for traitors and those

134

in power had no care as to whether those punished were men or women and any children would likely end up as slaves.

Hannah was so angry that her words were almost a physical assault and when she finally wound down, she was shaking like a leaf, leaving her brother feeling as though he had indeed been battered. It had the desired effect, for Aharon realised just how terrified she was. The last thing he wanted was for any harm to come to his family, but it had been easy to pretend that they were safe, living some distance from where most of the strife was centred. The idea that any of them might suffer for his actions nearly brought him to his knees. He knew that there was talk of going out to the desert and although a hostile environment, maybe this was the answer, a way to protect his loved ones.

It took Aharon a long time to calm his sister and to convince her that he would never let anything happen to them. Hannah, however, was an intuitive woman and she had listened to the men when they discussed the volatile situation; her ability to fade into the background lulled them into forgetting her presence. She knew that the stability of their city was hanging by a very slender thread and that it would take little to incite anarchy. Bad enough that most of the young men she had known all her life were among the insurgents, but that her brother might be killed was more than she could cope with.

As she finally regained control of her temper, Hannah explained this to Aharon, her flat and empty tones worse than her anger. He broached a subject he never thought they would discuss.

"Would you consider leaving Jerusalem?" Hannah stared at him, waiting. Her brother continued, "There is a place many miles from here, which is hoped might become a safe harbour, should life in the city become untenable or unsafe. Rumours have been circulating for quite some time and although I do not know why this place has been suggested, it seems worthy of further examination." Hannah listened and, although until recently she would have refused to contemplate such a notion, and that the whole idea sounded too good to be true, the more her brother talked the more inviting it sounded.

Hannah had never been someone who needed all the facilities and amenities available in the city. She could manage with very little and was happy as long as she had enough to get by and was able to replenish her remedies when necessary. All she really wanted was for her family to be safe. As she mulled over Aharon's proposal, it came to her that there probably would be people living near this haven who, eventually, might allow her to treat their sick. It would be a refreshing change from trying to keep men alive after being trampled, beaten or worse.

Brother and sister talked for a long time and a plan began to formulate in Aharon's mind. The outcome of which neither in their wildest imagination could have predicted.

Realising the utter futility of all-out revolt, King Herod Agrippa II exhorted his subjects to consider the consequences, that to provoke Rome could only end in disaster. He tried to persuade them that the preservation of Jerusalem and the Temple was more important than engaging with an invincible foe. The king's words held sway for a brief period and life in Jerusalem reverted to minor chaos as opposed to outright pandemonium. The protests did continue, but as they tended to target the government officials and soldiers, Hannah's neighbourhood, at the far side of the city, enjoyed a respite. Sadly, it did not last and events were about to take a fatal turn, precipitated, once again, by their hated procurator.

Apparently, the antagonism of the Jews to his financial profiteering, his release of robbers, and general nefarious behaviour had little impact on Gessius Florus; for had he one iota of wisdom, he would have discerned the utter insanity of his next exploit, which went beyond the pale. Ostensibly, in response to a demand from Nero to settle an outstanding tax debt, the procurator decided to 'appropriate' huge quantities of silver from the Temple.

His behaviour caused uproar and those who had been vacillating as to whether the Zealots and the Sicarii really had a solid argument, no longer had any decision to make. To make matters worse, rather than try to deal with the issue in a reasonable fashion, Florus quashed any protests by the simple method of turning his troops loose in a killing spree. For the Jews this was the final straw and, incensed beyond reason, they rose up, annihilating every Roman soldier stationed in Jerusalem.

In response to Florus' pleas for assistance, Cestius Gallus sent a supplementary contingent from Syria, but the agitators had mobilised into a cohesive force and met them head on at the Battle of Ben-Horon taking great delight in separating them from their lives also. With each victory, support for the rebel cause grew exponentially, as did the numbers of those prepared to fight, and soon the Jews believed that they might actually defeat the Romans.

Meanwhile, the Zealots, led by a radical named Menahem ben Judah had developed a plan, the same plan that Aharon had mentioned to Hannah. It was not quite however, the simple remove to a place of safety that Aharon had first believed it to be. This so-called refuge wasn't just some desert sanctuary; it was Herod's fortress at Masada, a fortified citadel currently guarded by a Roman garrison — at least five hundred soldiers, probably more. Menahem, along with one of his relatives, Eleazar ben Yair, knew that there would be a sizeable cache of weapons there and following their recent successes, were not about to let a few more soldiers stand in their way.

Accepting that he was as involved as his friends and comrades, Aharon realised that he would be expected to join the raid on the fortress. It was a journey that would take several days, crossing harsh and hostile terrain, and it was conceivable that some might die along the way. Menahem, however, was nothing if not influential and after less than a day, hundreds of men who had listened to his exhortations were persuaded that gaining these weapons was crucial if they wanted to bring Rome to its knees.

Despite major misgivings, Aharon was not going to leave his wife, son and sister in Jerusalem to face the consequences and spent the rest of the day explaining everything to Raizel and Hannah. Now they had the whole story, his sister was sceptical as to the sense of the scheme, but like Aharon could see no way around it. Moreover, she knew he would never leave her alone in the city; it was far too dangerous and should the Romans regain the upper hand, retaliation would be swift and severe.

Raizel would never question Aharon's decision, for she had faith in his judgement and in all honesty would prefer to face uncertainty with him, than be left alone. The three talked long into the night and by the morning, they were agreed. Aharon spent the next day with the other Zealots, discovering that the Sicarii, under Eleazar would remain in the city to counter any response from the procurator — a logical move. Menahem informed them that they would set out two days hence and that they should set everything to rights, for there were no guarantees that they would return.

Raizel's mother, Aliza — who, coincidentally, happened to be very distantly related to Eleazar — lived in a village along the road to Jericho about five miles outside Jerusalem and Raizel managed to send word of their plans, begging her mother to join them. Aliza chose not to accompany her daughter, concerned about the long trek and believing that she was in no danger living so far beyond the city walls.

Hannah had already begun to organise her stock. With a clearer idea of what they might face, she knew that it was likely her skills would be useful, nay necessary. Attacking a company of Roman soldiers was, in her opinion, foolhardy in the extreme but she was determined to be prepared should the worst happen. After what she had witnessed, Hannah really didn't care about the soldiers themselves, her people had been subjugated for long enough and although violence in any form was abhorrent to her, she was also a realist. If this was the only way, so be it.

Throughout the next day, Hannah tidied up her dwelling, packing up her few clothes and any of Gideon's manuscripts that she thought might be useful. She remembered to tell Tali what was happening, that Asaf's services would no longer be required and explained it all to Asaf too. The boy's father had been killed in a protest years before and, despite his youth, he was wise to the reasoning of the rebels. Back at her home, Hannah checked her supplies; measuring out oils, balms, ointments and unctions into smaller jars and collecting what she hoped would be sufficient cloths and bandages.

As she packed away the last of her supplies, Hannah took a walk through the dwelling, recognising that it would be difficult to leave the house that had become her home. It would be the end of a chapter in her life, one that — for the most part — was filled with happy memories.

Two days later, in the dark watches of the night, scores of men, two women and a baby, slipped out of Jerusalem. Their departure was staggered so as not to draw notice, the Zealots having arranged to meet at a point along the route. Aharon had procured a donkey from somewhere so that Raizel could ride for much of the journey, as carrying Efraim over such distances would have been gruelling. It also meant that Hannah was relieved of the weight of her jars and bottles, Aharon having stacked them into one of the baskets.

Their journey took several days, more because they had to be attentive to their surroundings than because of the actual distance. Such a large group of men, traversing the desert together would have looked very questionable; so they tended to travel from before dawn until around the third hour. Resting during the heat of the day and then continuing once the sun began to set, walking until quite late in the evening. Wild animals and bandits were their biggest concern, but there were enough men to ensure anyone or anything with a mind to attack would think better of it. They carried weapons, which although crude, were enough to cause serious injury should their use become unavoidable.

Late one afternoon, they reached the small town of Engaddi, on the shores of the Sea of Salt. They would rest there for the night and then those tasked with plundering the weapons would make their way to the fortress the following afternoon. Their intent was to strike at dusk and be back before the moonrise.

Hannah was beginning to think that the whole enterprise was a huge mistake and muttered as much to her brother, out of Raizel's hearing.

"These Romans are guarding an outpost Aharon, there will be a Watch. How on earth do Menahem and his band expect to get up there without being seen? This is madness." Aharon was no less concerned, but the need for weapons far outweighed their sense of impending disaster and desperate men will stop at nothing to achieve their goal. He tried to allay Hannah's fears but his sister could tell he shared her trepidation.

A few would remain in Engaddi and Hannah was relieved to hear that Aharon was one of them. He along with around seventy other men, had been designated the task of preventing any escapees, who fled in their direction, from reaching the comparative safety of the desert. Hannah shuddered to think what that meant and tried to close her mind to the images that insisted on forming. It was one thing to kill in the heat of battle, a whole other thing to cut men down as they tried to flee. Still, she supposed she could understand their rationale.

A large number of those who would be part of the assault were men she knew. Men with whom she had grown up; men, who as boys she and Raizel had played amongst. It hurt her heart that they might be injured or killed and she just had to hope that, if called upon, her skills were expert enough save them.

Now, all they could do was wait.

Chapter Nineteen

Herod's Fortress, Masada ~ AD66

It had been a very long week, Maxentius was more than a little frustrated having had to dole out harsh punishments to several of his soldiers who had flouted the, not particularly strict, rules by being drunk on duty four days out of the last five. He was at the end of his tether and at a complete loss. It didn't seem to matter whether he tried friendly persuasion; coercion or something in between, nothing seemed to get through. He had removed most of the wine, thinking he had hidden it where no one would think to look, only to discover — the very next day — that they had found and raided the stock.

He knew that it was tedious here, so far from civilisation, but he had done everything in his power to make life interesting and challenging for his men. Many appreciated his endeavours and undertook their duties with a measure of diligence, but their efforts were completely undermined by the recalcitrants among them. Along with Marcus and Sergius, Maxentius had spent hours trying to solve the problem; even the threat of capital punishment — rarely invoked — for insubordination had little effect. Some soldiers obviously considered decimation, be-heading or hanging, preferable to life on Masada.

The sad thing was, Maxentius knew that even those who failed to behave in a manner expected of the Roman military were not actually bad soldiers, just discontented, jaded and discouraged — what they needed was a good battle. Finally, accepting that he was getting no-where, he had drafted a missive to be sent to Rome with the next dispatches; indicating that if the situation did not improve he would have no alternative but to levy more stringent penalties. Further, the transfer of a large corps should be arranged immediately.

He had also received troubling news from his comrade in Jerusalem, regarding the increased level of violence, including a polite and carefully worded warning to his superior that Masada might be an irresistible target for the insurgents and that he, Maxentius, might like to consider placing the garrison on a heightened state of alert. Maxentius had shown the message to his two friends, the three men aware that the Watch had a habit of slacking off as soon as the rest of the garrison retired for the evening; preferring to gamble rather than to stare out across the vast emptiness that was the Judaean Desert.

Concerned enough about the contents of the letter not to ignore it, Maxentius had called an immediate inspection updating his soldiers on the latest news from Jerusalem and suggesting in tones that brooked no argument, how vital it was that they maintain the highest levels of surveillance.

During the past few nights, Maxentius had taken it upon himself to patrol the fortress at random intervals and had been satisfied that, for once, his men had heeded his orders. This night, his intent was to check after midnight, the time when exhaustion crept up without warning. Thus, as the day passed into evening, Marcus, Sergius and he were enjoying a relaxing goblet of wine and a platter of fine food when all hell broke loose.

Five hours earlier ~ Engaddi

The men were prepared, their weapons — such as they were — gripped in ready hands. From the shade of a building, Hannah watched them leave, her stomach in knots. It would be a very long night.

The afternoon sun was warm as the horde of men departed Engaddi on their four-hour trek to Masada. After long discussions, Menahem had decreed that although attacking in the dead of night was the less dangerous option, he didn't want to have to locate the armoury in the dark; therefore they would attack at dusk, counting on the evening shadows to conceal their arrival. While many hoped that they would be able to slip in and out without the Watch raising the alarm, most knew it was a vain hope. They knew how efficiently these garrisons were run and even though remote, it did not mean that the soldiers would be any less cautious.

The great throng of men hurried along the winding tracks, hugging the steep sided rocks where possible, disturbing the occasional goat as they passed. As the afternoon began to wane, the huge plateau loomed up in the distance. Its height was daunting, but by the time they approached, the sun was descending towards the horizon, the sky turning a soft pink and the sides of the vast outcrop were darkening rapidly. Slowing their steps, the men circumnavigated the rock, noting the two favourable access points.

Menahem gathered them together and in undertones gave his instructions, which took some time, as there were more than three hundred men. The group entering with him would ascend via the winding track and head straight for the weapons that Menahem understood to be stored at one end of the barracks, situated about halfway between the two gates. A second group would gain access through the western gate, at the opposite side. Their job was to distract and divide the soldiers, hopefully giving Menahem enough time to breach the armoury. The last, and very much smaller, group would remain at the base of the rock to calm the horses — who were already becoming restless — and to prevent anyone from escaping.

The climb to the top would take at least an hour and they needed to remain undetected for as long as possible. Cautiously, they scrambled up the precipitous tracks and as the sun sank lower, the men reached their destination, managing to break through the gates without disturbing anyone — which did give them pause, but they just assumed God was on their side   spilling out over the plateau, killing anyone who stood in their way.

Finally, it was the screams of the wounded and dying that drew the attention of the rest of the garrison and a shout went up, soldiers appearing from every direction. Of course, they had no weapons and no armour, all of which was stored away, never anticipating that they would be taken unawares. Angry mutterings about the ineptitude of those on Watch were lost in the cacophony of the melee. The soldiers desperately tried to form a cohesive body, their rigorous training taking over, but without weapons, they were defenceless.

Maxentius, Marcus and Sergius barrelled out of the commander's quarters, brandishing their swords, which, thankfully they kept with them at all times. Entering the fray, the three men attempted to draw the attack giving the other soldiers the chance to get into formation. Bodies lay all over the plateau but in the fading light, it was difficult to distinguish whether they were friend or foe. Maxentius could smell the blood and he could hear agonised groans as his men fell, injured or worse, across the dusty ground in front of him. It was a rout — the men who had ambushed them had somehow avoided being seen and not a single warning had been issued. If he had had the time, Maxentius would have been incandescent with rage at such lax behaviour, but now everything in him focused on staying alive.

The skirmish seemed to go on for hours, but it couldn't have been very long, the bandits had the advantage from the minute they had burst through the gates. Tiring, Maxentius had become separated from his comrades and was being backed along a corridor. Despite getting in several good parries of his own, doing serious damage to at least four of them, his opponents were relentless and somehow they had knocked the sword out of his hand. Detachedly, he realised that the weapons these men were using, although crudely made, were no less effective than the sharpest Roman gladius. Fists and feet were also very useful in tight spaces and Maxentius felt as though they would burst his body so savagely did they beat him.

A sound behind distracted them as a deep bellow echoed along the narrow passageway. Sergius! Thanking all the gods for his loyal subordinate, Maxentius managed to get his fingers around his sword, lifting it and swinging the blade at his attackers, forcing them to retreat, as the young solider, who continued to bawl appalling invective, came at them from the other side. Slowly the two men began to gain the upper hand, ably assisted by Marcus who suddenly appeared, covered in blood, but still able to fight. The resonance of metal against metal was magnified in the narrow space, which combined with the peculiar swish of metal against flesh and the grunts of those fighting created a ghoulish rhythm, the macabre melody of death.

144

Abruptly everything ceased. Those with whom the three Romans had been duelling dropped, critically wounded, and Marcus ensured that they would never get the chance to ambush anyone again. The muffled pounding of footsteps reverberated around them, but whose they were and where they were going was beyond the care of the three in the corridor.

Sergius dropped his sword, the noise deafening in the unnatural silence, dark red blood pooling on the exquisite black and white tiled floor as it dripped from a vicious gash across the young soldier's abdomen. Maxentius caught his friend as he slithered down the wall, virtually carrying him into the first room they came too. Rarely used, it was large and airy with few furnishings. This wing of the palace was quiet and Maxentius hoped that if they could stem the blood flow from Sergius' wound and that they could rest undisturbed for a time, they might chance an escape.

Sensing movement in the shadowed doorway, Maxentius glanced up his heart beating too rapidly; fear that their attackers had returned coursing through his veins. He noticed a figure, he thought it was a woman, but knew that was impossible. She was wearing the most bizarre clothing, wholly unrecognisable to him and he considered himself quite worldly. As she turned, they locked eyes — hers were a luminous green and he was unable to tear his gaze away. Unsure whether she was real or an illusion conjured up by his exhausted mind, Maxentius tried to beg for her silence with his own eyes. It seemed that she nodded and then was gone, the whole thing over in a split second.

He had no time to question her presence, as Sergius required his full attention. Unrolling one of the rugs, uncaring that its plush richness would be ruined by the blood seeping from the young soldier's injury, he lay Sergius down. Wrenching open the door to a cupboard that stood against one wall, he discovered all manner of cloths, sheets and blankets. Grabbing a handful of the cloths, he pressed them against the wound hoping this would slow the bleeding, asking Marcus to fashion another few cloths, or roll one of the blankets, into a pillow to place under Sergius' head.

Sergius was obviously in extreme pain, his face was as white as the cloths Maxentius was using, and his breath was coming in shallow gasps. Maxentius was helpless, there had been a medicus — or doctor — with the garrison, but he had no idea where he was or whether he'd even survived. Once again, he registered the quiet and he contemplated the likelihood as no one had come to find them, that they might well be the last men alive on the citadel.

Although, this was comforting in one way — for it meant that there was no one to prevent them leaving — in another, being one of possibly the only three surviving Roman soldiers in so isolated a place presented a whole other series of problems. Even if they escaped, how far would they get? Especially as they were all injured. Maxentius could see that Marcus was covered in lacerations, some of which appeared to be quite deep. He himself had received a severe beating, as well as several gashes. Unless by some miracle they regained enough strength to be able to slip through the gate under cover of darkness and walk the distance to Engaddi, they were all doomed.

In the quiet, Maxentius thought about his family. They would mourn his death and his heart ached that he might cause them such grief. Determined not to wallow in self-pity, Maxentius asked Marcus whether he had any family; his second-in-command affirming that his mother and father lived in the countryside outside Rome, that they were from farming stock and he had been their only child. They chatted fitfully, for at least this meant each knew that the other was still alive. Sergius had fallen into a stupor; his breathing erratic and his agony clear in his low groans.

To Maxentius' unending surprise, Sergius survived the night. Ignoring his own pain, the commander had risked a cursory check of their immediate vicinity and had discovered a flagon of water in the adjoining room. Pouring some into a small bowl, Maxentius persuaded Sergius to drink some of it. He used a little more to rinse the cloths, cleaning the young man's wounds, removing the blood and pus as best as he could. He knew that they needed food, but the kitchens were at the other side of the courtyard. Not only did he not have enough strength to stagger that far, but also he had no clue whether anyone else was in the fortress and did not think he could make it there and back unseen.

The days melded into one and he had no idea how long they lay undetected. That Sergius continued to draw breath was a constant source of amazement to his commander, but they were all losing strength and eventually, despite Maxentius' best efforts, all three slipped into oblivion.

Chapter Twenty

After what they considered to be an extremely successful ambush, the rebels took stock. Several of their number had been killed and a fair few were badly injured, although their wounds were nothing compared with the horrific trauma they had inflicted upon their enemy. As most of the Romans had been unable to get to their weapons, they had been simply cut down indiscriminately. Those soldiers, who had eluded their assailants and managed to escape, had fled into the desert, their chances of survival — unfavourable. The plateau reeked of blood and death and Menahem had decided that since the citadel was now vacant, they might as well just stay there to re-group and plan their next move.

The rebel leader sent several scouts to go and inform Aharon, and the seventy or so men who had remained at Engaddi, of the outcome of the ambush, encouraging them to travel to Masada with due haste. When Hannah walked through the east gate early the next morning, she had to fight wave after wave of nausea; the devastation that met her eyes was beyond description. Pale and shaken, she had looked at her brother, words had not been necessary and although Aharon had expected there to be a few deaths, this was on an unimaginable scale.

Hannah knew the dangers of leaving bodies unburied and, since their illustrious leader seemed less than interested in the state of the fortress, immediately started ordering the men about. One group to clear the dead, another to find some water to begin to swill the blood away, and yet another to seek out a convenient area to where they could remove the wounded. She dispatched Aharon to find rooms for himself and Raizel, in order that her sister-in-law could rest and take care of Efraim, who had behaved remarkably well for so young a baby.

The land around Masada was very dry making the burial of so many, impossible. Even though it was against tradition for those among the dead who were Jews, Hannah instructed that all the bodies must be burned. There had been some consternation about this until, eventually, she had rounded on the complainants, placing her hands on her hips and drawing herself up to her full, rather diminutive, height, hair whirling around her head and her eyes spitting green fire.

"Fine! If you, who have just broken the sixth commandment, are so worried about the burial ritual, get yourselves down off this rock and dig the graves, one for each body and that includes the Romans. Then, when you've completed that, I want you to get your sorry selves back up here and start clearing the rest of the plateau. Once the blood has been washed away there will still be plenty to do." She glared at the men in front of her, daring any of them to question her dictates. A few of them, rather sheepishly, murmured something about building a pyre and shuffled off, the rest following in their wake, looking for all the world like naughty boys who had been caught stealing sweetbreads from their long suffering mothers.

Despite the carnage surrounding her, Hannah grinned to herself and carried on with what she had been doing. Shortly thereafter, another of the men, Simeon, came to advise her that he had found a set of rooms in one of the palaces that might prove suitable as temporary chambers for the wounded. She went along with him and inspected the space. It was almost perfect. Adjoining each other were two very large rooms, with high ceilings and enough windows to make them light but not over bright. A small antechamber was tucked in an alcove off the first room, offering a place to store all she would require. It even had a large stone bowl that she could use as a sink. Nodding at Simeon, she asked that he find as many pallets as he could and distribute them throughout both rooms.

Meanwhile, Hannah went to check on those who had been injured. They were still lying outside, in the shade of the massive casemate wall and she guessed that, in all, there were about a hundred. Mercifully, most were walking wounded, afflicted by minor lacerations and the odd gash. Knowing that these men did not require urgent treatment and that she could deal with them quickly and easily, Hannah issued her instructions —

"The first thing you need to do is to go and find some water. I understand there are several cisterns on this citadel, any one of them will do. Wash yourselves thoroughly, please make sure you have removed every last speck of dust and dirt from your skin. Then come back to me and I will dress your wounds."

As they plodded off to do her bidding, Hannah turned her attention to those whose injuries were far more severe. Counting forty men, she hoped that the pallets would arrive soon, preferring to wait until they were in the cool of those rooms before she started to clean them up. Out here in the open, the dust would just blow straight back into any cut or slash. Checking them over carefully, she saw that approximately half had suffered less brutal damage and immediately decided to split them up. Those whose injuries she felt necessitated closer observation would go into the furthest room, the rest in the first room. Unable to do any more for them until they had something to lie on, she chatted with the men who were awake, trying to assess their pain levels.

Soon, Simeon returned with a goodly number of helpers, all carrying wooden pallets. Hannah had absolutely no clue where they had found them, probably the barracks; it would make sense. She directed them into the rooms, asking them to put twenty pallets in each one. While they were doing this, she hurried over to an area she had come across by accident after becoming disorientated trying to fathom the maze of corridors and courtyards in the smaller of the two main complexes. It looked like a laundry and consisted of several generously proportioned sinks and a fireplace — so huge that Gideon's treatment room would have fitted into it. At one side of the sinks stood a large cupboard, in which she discovered an ample supply of sheets, cloths and blankets.

Yelling for some assistance, Hannah hauled a pile over to the other palace and began to make up the beds. The faithful Simeon and two of his comrades went to fetch more and soon they had made up all the beds — each now sporting two sheets, a sort of pillow and a blanket. Then she asked whether her aides might help get the injured men into bed indicating those to be carried to the far room.

While they were getting settled, she retraced her steps to the laundry, next door to which was a kitchen. Searching through cupboards and shelves, she found what she was looking for — salt! Then filling a huge jar with water and collecting a smaller flagon from a bench, she staggered back to the temporary clinic, unsure whether she would actually make it with such an awkward and heavy burden. Aharon, coming out of the rooms he had commandeered, noticed his sister struggling and intercepted her. Taking the great jar out of her arms, he walked with her across the plateau, placing the unwieldy vessel on the bench in the antechamber at her request. Slightly winded, Hannah said gratefully —

"Thank you, Aharon, I wasn't really sure whether I could manage but it seemed easier than traipsing back and forth all the time." Aharon chuckled knowing how impatient his sister got when she thought there was an easier way.

"Before I go, are there any more heavy jars you need me to fetch?" he inquired, laughter warming his tones.

"I am fine for now, thank you," she grinned. "How are Raizel and Efraim?"

"She's sleeping, as is Efraim" Aharon replied. "Hopefully she will feel up to joining us for a meal later."

"Don't you mean you hope she feels up to cooking a meal?" Hannah asked, archly.

"No, that's not what I mean at all," she raised an eyebrow at him. "Truly, two or three of the men have offered to organise it. Apparently, there are huge storage rooms, filled to bursting with food and all manner of other goods, so they think they can produce something edible." Hannah wasn't convinced but there was no way she was going to get involved — if she tried to cook she would likely poison them all. Thanking her brother again and saying she would pop over to see Raizel later, she turned back to the task at hand and Aharon left her to it.

Dissolving some salt into a bowl of water and carrying it, along with several cloths, through to the far room, she began to clean and assess the wounded men more thoroughly. It took a long time. First she cleaned every nick, cut and abrasion and then added a coating of her salve, covering that with a piece of clean cloth, finishing up by bandaging everything securely in place. Some of the men had more bandages showing than skin, but she wanted to be sure she did not miss even the slightest scratch. Of those men more seriously hurt, a few might need their wounds debriding and then stitching up, but she wanted to give them a day and a night to settle before she decided. It was a painful procedure, for it involved cutting away the dead skin and then suturing the sliced edges together. Even with a draft of poppy juice, it would be excruciating. She would only do it if absolutely necessary.

Despite the circumstances, the room was peaceful. All Hannah could hear was the rather erratic breathing of the men and the odd groan as one of them tried to shift position. She was in a rhythm now and continued to work steadily until every last man had been treated. It was dark outside when she eventually finished and her last patient was Tobias; he was unconscious, but she didn't think he was too badly hurt. His skin was clammy and his heart was beating a little too fast, but his injuries did not appear to be life threatening.

Tired beyond reason, Hannah took a final walk through the two wards, checking each man to make sure there was nothing that she needed to panic about then she trudged out into the cool evening air and came to a standstill. Spread out above her the velvety night sky was breathtaking; the stars looked close enough to be plucked down, a gossamer blanket of glistening lights. It was hard to equate such beauty with the horror she had witnessed this day and for some absurd reason it made her want to cry.

Blaming exhaustion, Hannah found her way over to Aharon's rooms and checked Raizel over, satisfied that her sister-in-law was simply tired from the long journey. Efraim was chortling to himself, lying on a thick rug on the floor, looking more wide awake than the three adults surrounding him, put together.

Aharon had filled a platter with some food for Hannah and she wolfed it down, surprised to note that it was actually quite palatable.

"Thank you my brother, I was ready for that. If this is the quality of the meals that those men are able to provide, we should get them to cook every day." Raizel spluttered with laughter at the idea that men would be happy to do domestic chores, while Aharon fought to maintain a neutral expression, unwilling to get dragged into a discussion about the roles of men and women. "I will sleep near the sick rooms tonight Aharon, in case I am needed, but tomorrow, I must find my own quarters. I cannot imagine that we will leave this rock in the immediate future and I have no wish to sleep so close to those men long term." Aharon acknowledged the sense of her argument and asked that she let him check whichever rooms she decided upon, more for her own security than anything else.

"I would quite like to find something near the laundry and the kitchens if possible. They open onto a courtyard; perhaps there are some rooms around it that migt prove adequate." They chattered about this a little longer, until Hannah bade her family goodnight and wearily made her way back to the other palace.

The night, like a cloak of ebony silk, settled around her and for a moment she stood and let the magnificence of her surroundings register. She was in the middle of one of Herod's most isolated yet opulent fortresses; but all she could think about were the men under her care and how tired she was. She hoped that before they decided to leave here that she might get the chance to have a quick explore.

One more check of the injured; all were asleep and none appeared to be in any more discomfort than expected. Asking the man on watch to call her should she be required, she found her way into a room three along from the sick room, where earlier she had spotted a rug as well as a very long and comfortable looking, cushioned bench-like seat. Dragging the rug up onto the seat for extra warmth, Hannah wrapped a blanket that she had lifted from the pile in the ante-chamber, around herself and curled up — falling asleep before she realised her eyes were closing.

Chapter Twenty One

It was a long night; Hannah was called several times and in the end did not go back to the comfortable bench. Rather she found a low stool, managing to steal a few moments of rest between looking after her patients, by dint of leaning back against the wall in one of the wards. A few of the men were causing her real concern and she lost count of how many times she had to wash wounds, before re-applying salve and fresh bandages.

Around dawn she fell into an exhausted doze only to be roused less than an hour later by the sounds of everyone else on the plateau waking and starting their day. Giving up, Hannah dug out some clean clothes and dragged herself over to the laundry; closing the big wooden door, she stripped off and indulged in a proper wash. Feeling slightly more refreshed, she went to the kitchens and picked at some of the bread lying on a platter, mulling over what she had to do that day.

Finding her own bedchamber was important, but that could wait until she had examined the wounded and dealt with anything else that required her attention. During the night while attempting to snatch some sleep, Hannah had begun toying with the idea of trying to find two or three rooms together and making one of them into a treatment room, or at least somewhere she could stock all her remedies and so forth. While the rooms in the main palace were useful as a temporary sick bay they were quite a distance from this kitchen and the laundry next door. Accepting that there were probably similar domestic facilities in the other palace, Hannah had already surmised that it was a much larger building and access to where she currently stood was far easier.

Pleased with her scheme, she gathered another pile of sheets from the laundry and made her way back to the sick rooms. The next few hours were spent repeating what she had been doing all night. Among those who were more seriously hurt lay Daniel, the young man whom Hannah and Gideon had fought to heal around six years previously — only six years, yet it seemed like an age.

He floated in and out of consciousness, but had spoken a few words; most of which revolved around how much he had enjoyed killing a not inconsequential number of Roman soldiers. That he had taken such gruesome delight in slaughter, shocked Hannah and in the face of his vehemence, she was moved to comment, quite reasonably she thought —

"Daniel, while I appreciate your need for revenge, relishing your actions makes you more barbaric than those thugs who injured you all those years ago and they weren't even Romans. These soldiers have done you no harm, they were simply protecting an outpost."

Daniel stared at her, colour flushing up his pale cheeks and, shamefaced, he had the decency to hang his head. Hannah pressed his hand.

"I know you were — are — angry, Daniel, but I do not want you to lose your humanity. You are a good man, who was subjected to a heinous attack, but it was years ago and none of these men were to blame. Remember in all of this, that they likely have people who love them who may never even know where or how their sons or brothers died." Then, infusing practicality into her voice "now, we will say no more, I just want you to get well. How is your pain?"

"Quite bad," he acknowledged. Hannah could see that their conversation had tired him and he was slipping back into unconsciousness. She held a small bowl enabling Daniel to sip some of the poppy juice, then laid him back down, covering him with a sheet and pulling the blanket halfway up, within reach if he felt chilled.

"Sleep now Daniel, it is the best thing for healing. I will be near should you need more pain relief." He half smiled as his eyelids drooped and was asleep before Hannah sat down at the next bed. She spoke to as many as she could while treating them. Some were either in too much pain or did not wake and she made a mental note to check them regularly, determined that no more would be seized by death.

As Hannah had suspected, there were a few whose wounds would need stitching, but she intended to leave that until the next day. She was too tired to consider such a delicate operation, especially as she would probably need to slice any shredded or necrotic skin away first. Eventually, she had examined them all. The sun was high overhead and she realised that she was very hungry.

Making her way over to the kitchen, she rooted about and found some of the food left over from the previous night. Pulling up a stool, she sat at the long table that stood in the middle of the room and devoured the whole lot. It was here her brother found her a little later, as she was washing it down with a goblet of heavily diluted wine.

"Hannah! How are they?" Aharon asked, tipping his head in the general direction of the wards. Hannah gave him an update and then asked after Raizel. Aharon assured her that his wife was back to normal, in fact, she had declared herself determined to cook the main meal that evening.

"Oh thank goodness for that." Hannah grinned. "Once Raizel sees what's available in this room alone, never mind the stores, there'll be no stopping her." Knowing how much his wife loved to cook, Aharon could not help but agree; then asked his sister whether she had yet looked for rooms of her own. Hannah shook her head.

"I will do so this afternoon. I have spent all morning with the injured and feel that I should run my eye over them again before I look for a chamber, as that in itself may take some time. These palaces are so big and I keep getting lost." Aharon laughed at this, Hannah was quite capable of getting lost in a two-room house, so the layout of the building on the plateau would likely prove a challenge.

"Don't forget to let me know when you find somewhere. Please Hannah," as she frowned at him, "I would like to be sure that you will not be…" he hesitated, "…disturbed." Hannah was about to scoff at his strictures, but she caught his concerned expression and suddenly remembered that she was an unmarried woman in a remote fortress full of single men.

"Fair enough, my brother," she acquiesced, "I promise to do as you ask." Formally spoken, Hannah softened her words by giving Aharon a quick hug. Surprised, for Hannah usually avoided such familiarity, Aharon returned it and then saying he would see her later, returned to whatever he had been doing.

Gulping down the last drops of her drink, Hannah tidied up her dishes before strolling back across the plateau. It was a beautiful day and she paused, taking a few minutes to look around her. She did not know whether any of the buildings had names, although she recognised the barracks and the armoury standing between where she currently stood and the palace where her patients lay.

Aharon had told her that they believed the complex where she had just been eating had been Herod's private family palace and the larger one was probably the ceremonial and residential palace. Hannah could see both the west and east gates at either side of her, nestled in the massive wall. There was also a planted area a little way up the plateau to her left. Obviously, someone had been tending the crops here for they looked to be flourishing.

A couple of oxen, as well as a goat with her kids, chewed at a patch of vegetables and Hannah debated whether anyone had thought to provide them with a drink. Then she noticed a large stone trough, brimming with cool clear water and realised that this place was well set up for both animals and plants.

Just beyond the barracks, scattered across the middle of the plateau were several pomegranate trees. Hannah was ecstatic; she loved pomegranates with their luscious red seeds like miniature edible gems coated in a hint of sweet sticky juice. She walked over to the closest one and stood in its shade while she admired the rest of the citadel. Scrubby bushes rather than trees, Hannah was only able to stand upright underneath its canopy because of her slight stature, the dappled shade offering cool protection from the afternoon sun.

Glancing around she spotted a large urn and without pausing to consider that it might be required elsewhere, turned it upside down and sat on it. Leaning against the trunk of the tree, she relaxed for a few minutes allowing the gentle breeze to waft over her.

In the early afternoon, after another hour or so with the wounded, Hannah finally got around to hunting through the

157

private palace for some rooms to make her own. Across the courtyard from the kitchens, a long passageway hinted at the possibility of several, so she decided to check it out. The first two rooms were tiny, more like alcoves really; she had no idea what on earth they could ever be used for, so she ignored them.

As she was making her way along to the next room, she noticed something splattered over the beautiful black and white tiles. Approaching cautiously she realised that it was blood and a lot of it. She hesitated, for as far as she was aware all the rebels were accounted for, and it had been assumed that the Roman soldiers had either been killed or had fled. A glint caught her eye and she noticed a sword leaning against the wall, also covered in blood.

Ignoring the rational voice in her head that kept insisting she go and get Aharon, Hannah walked slowly forward, peering into the next room. It was empty, but as she glanced in through the doorway nearest the pool of blood, she was aghast to see three men lying unconscious on the floor. Biting down on a terrified shriek and, uncaring that she could be placing herself in mortal danger, Hannah dropped to her knees to check whether any of them still lived. She was astonished to find they were all breathing, barely to be sure, but they were breathing. After a cursory examination and knowing that regardless of who they were she had every intention of trying to save them, Hannah shot across to her brother's quarters bursting in without knocking, entreating him in staccato sentences before she was even through the door.

"Aharon! Please come. Three men. They are unconscious. Injured. I must help them." Aharon raised his hand to slow the rush of words, staring at his sister in confusion.

"What are you gabbling about, Hannah? Slow down, I cannot understand a word you are saying." Hannah took a steadying breath and repeated her request,

"Aharon, I have found three men who are badly wounded. I need you to help me get them into proper cots." Her brother gaped at her in shock.

"Who are they?"

"I have no idea, just three soldiers." She shrugged. To her it didn't matter who they were, she just knew they needed her skills or they would die. She wasn't sure whether any of them had a chance anyway, but she wasn't letting them go without a fight.

"If they are Romans, sister, I will call Simeon and Malachi and we will finish them."

"No!" Her reply was sharper than she intended, she softened her tone, pleading, "Aharon, it is three days since this rock was ambushed and I know what damage the Romans inflicted upon our people. I have spent hours trying to heal them, but I will not stand aside and let you kill three unarmed men in cold blood. That is murder and against our laws." She took a breath "You cannot."

Her brother stared at her for long moments, debating whether or not it was worth arguing the point. She would never forgive him if he followed through with his threat and he really wasn't up to dealing with her ire. His sister watched his face; desperately hoping her brother would accede to her demand. She knew the second he'd decided and flung her arms around him.

"Thank you, Aharon! Oh thank you so much."

"Do not make me regret this. Even wounded these men are dangerous."

"Trust me, my brother, this is one of the best decisions you have ever made." She kissed him on the cheek and shot off in the direction from which she had come, yelling out for help to move three pallets into the room.

Perturbed, Aharon followed Hannah along to the room where the three men lay, taking in everything in one glance. Even without any medical experience, Aharon knew that all three were gravely ill and the youngest looked to be lying across death's threshold. He paused, wondering whether Hannah realised how sick they were, but before he had chance to voice his concern, she murmured that even though she doubted that the one with the stomach wound could survive such an injury, she wanted to do everything she could for him, for all of them.

"If nothing else, Aharon, I can ease his pain, so if I do lose him, his death will be less agonising." Trying to force her riotous chestnut curls back into the semblance of a plait, Hannah concentrated on what she needed to do. Simeon and

Malachi had brought in three cots and she was covering them with thick blankets and double folding a sheet over something that she had fashioned into a pillow.

"Just have a care, my sister. Please have a care." Aharon pressed her arm and she nodded abstractedly, her mind focused on the task in front of her. Aharon left her to it, making a mental note to tell his wife what her friend was doing.

Hannah bustled about placing clean fresh sheets over the blankets and then stood back to let her two assistants, very carefully, lift each man onto a cot. Covering them with yet another sheet and a soft blanket, she began to prepare her remedies. Salt dissolved in water with a few drops of myrrh and frankincense added to help fight the infection. A batch of the salve she had been using on the other injured men would be suitable too. Then she added some drops of poppy juice to a flagon of water and honey, hoping it would help dull their pain.

Drawing a deep breath, Hannah lifted the tunic of the youngest man, who had been placed on the pallet closest to the door and nearly vomited. She knew it would be bad but it was worse than she could possibly have imagined, and again, she was confounded that he had survived for three days without treatment. Blood mingled with a stinking, greenish, yellow pus, oozed from the wound. Gritting her teeth, she swallowed and taking short shallow breaths began to clean it. It took some time, for the gash was long and deep and some of the skin had to be cut away as it was too shredded ever to heal. The man never stirred, his breathing almost imperceptible and his heartbeat seemed little more than the fluttering of a butterfly's wing.

Eventually, satisfied that she had cleaned it as thoroughly as possible, she pushed the salve deep inside, enough to fill the affected area and then covered it with a cloth soaked in the same mixture. Spying several other injuries, she cleaned them all, adding more salve, bandaging everything in place, making sure they were just tight enough to stop the salve soaked cloths from slipping off.

Washing her hands thoroughly, she moved onto the next man, repeating her actions, checking every single cut. The

160

young man was covered in them, some deep, some superficial. Hannah slathered all of them with the salve and bandaging everything neatly. Finally, there was only one man left. He appeared to be older than the other two, although not by much.

His tunic was covered in blood but, following a quick examination, Hannah realised that much of it was probably that of his comrade. The soldier had a considerable number of nasty slashes, but it was his chest that bothered her. His breathing was not only erratic, but also very laboured and the colour of his skin wasn't normal. Needing to observe him for at least a day, she decided just to deal with his lacerations. She cleaned, and then coated each one with salve, bandaging any that required it, before carefully massaging some arnica into his chest. This was an oil known to reduce bruising; it couldn't do any harm and hopefully it might alleviate some of his discomfort.

As Hannah was wiping her hands on a cloth, the soldier regained consciousness, his eyes finding hers and their fathomless emerald depths transfixed her. As she stared at him, an odd sensation ran through her, but unable to pinpoint what it was, she pushed it aside, concentrating on the soldier. Confusion and fear flickered across his face as he made a valiant effort to sit up, but she pushed him back with a gentle hand.

Unsure about where he was or what was happening, all Maxentius was aware of was an almost intolerable pain. He was struggling to breathe and his head felt as though it might splinter. He tried to move but his limbs refused to respond. He stared at the woman, who took his large hand in her small, cool one and spoke in gentle tones —

"I do not know whether you can understand me," she said slowly, "but I am here to help you." He looked at her steadily and inclined his head very slightly. She smiled and pointed to herself.

"My name is Hannah."

Utterly captivated, Maxentius continued to stare at her. She was quite the most beautiful woman he had ever seen. Her

161

gloriously rich chestnut hair curling around her delicate face, her soft smile and her warm expression beguiled him; and as she spoke, her extraordinarily green eyes held his gaze, willing him to trust.

In that moment, in an isolated fortress, in the throes of agony and unknowing whether he would live or die, Maxentius lost his heart.

Chapter Twenty Two

Masada AD66 ~ Day Three

Still speaking slowly and never relinquishing his hand, Hannah explained how she had found them, going on to tell him what treatment she had administered. She had no idea whether he grasped her meaning, but she had to try.

"Both of your comrades still live, but he…" pointing to the youngest soldier near the door, "…is grievously injured. Be assured that you will not be killed." Regarding him steadily, entreating him to believe her. Maxentius listened, and thought he discerned the essence of her words, but his head was pounding and he was struggling to concentrate.

"Thank you for your kindness, Hannah." He muttered through clenched teeth, stumbling a little over the unusual name, hoping she might comprehend him. He was aware that she was still holding his hand and found that her touch soothed him. She smiled again and Maxentius felt his heart do the most peculiar sort of hiccup.

"Please rest. I am close by and I will be checking on you often." She squeezed his hand, then unable to stop herself and for reasons she had yet to discern, Hannah cupped her hand on his cheek. "You are safe now." Releasing his hand, she reached out for a small bowl. Its contents smelt a little strange to Maxentius and he tried to shake his head, but the pain was too much and as nausea roiled through him, he could not prevent a low groan. Hannah looked him straight in the eye saying —

"This will ease your agony and give you a peaceful sleep. Trust me, I will not poison you." Maxentius stared back, searching her face and reading the truth written there. He took a sip and shuddered as the liquid slid down his throat. "One more…" he frowned, "…please." Grunting, he took another sip and lay back on the makeshift pillow. Hannah drew up both the sheet and the blanket, tucking them snugly around him then used a damp cloth to wipe his face and hands. Maxentius watched her as she worked, enjoying the coolness of the cloth on his fevered skin.

As she finished, Hannah took his hand once more, this time in both of hers and even then his hand felt huge. To Maxentius, everything was rather hazy and he presumed it was whatever had been in the drink. He heard her quiet words as though from a great distance.

"I must go. I have others for whom I am caring, but I will be here when you wake." He tried to smile, but oblivion had other ideas. Hannah watched until she was sure his breathing had steadied. It sounded very strained and she decided it was probably better just to monitor it until she had his pain under control and his other injuries had begun to heal.

Before she went back to the other palace, Hannah re-examined the soldier's two comrades. The one with the terrible gash was deeply unconscious, but he wasn't tossing for which Hannah was grateful. His comrade was also still asleep, but Hannah deemed his injuries to be survivable. Resting her hand lightly on the chest of each man she registered that although both of their heart rates were rapid they weren't too irregular and she believed they would rest peacefully for a little while.

Tidying her things and bundling up the soiled cloths to be washed — or more likely burned — Hannah left the room pulling the door closed behind her. In the corridor Malachi lurked. Rather bewildered, the young physician asked what was wrong.

"Aharon asked me to watch over you." Hannah gaped at the man and grimaced in frustration.

"I am perfectly capable of looking after myself, thank you! Does Aharon really think that any of those three men are in a fit state to hurt me?" She expostulated. Malachi shuffled uncomfortably. Aware that he was only following orders, Hannah sighed and tried to calm her annoyance. "However as you are here, I shall be pleased if you will guard them now." Malachi started to back away. "No, Malachi, they are just as deserving of protection as our men. They did not ask to be attacked and since it appears that they were unable to get to their weapons, our men ambushed soldiers who were, essentially, defenceless. It was not a fair fight and I am not going to let anyone else die if I can help it. If I hear that you or

164

anyone else have harmed these men you will have to answer to Aharon."

Spoken evenly, it was clear that Hannah meant every word and Malachi nodded reluctantly.

"Do I have your word, Malachi?" she pressed.

"You have my word, Hannah daughter of Avigail. I will guard them with my life." She beamed at him and squeezed his hand.

"See, now that wasn't so hard was it?" Malachi blushed and chuckled. He, as with many of those on the plateau, had known Hannah for years and amongst their large circle of friends and family, her persuasive abilities were renowned. Grinning, Hannah left him to his duty and hurried along to Aharon's rooms to update him on the three soldiers before returning to the other wounded men. Aharon was still concerned, but once his sister had explained the situation and that Malachi was now watching them, he was less so.

Hannah, meanwhile, gave her brother no time to question her actions; she was out of the door and on her way back to the large palace before he had time to draw breath. She spent the next few hours examining all the injured. Perceiving that, as she had anticipated, at least two had cuts that required stitching, she took the time to explain the necessity of this to both unfortunate souls, while she was checking them over.

"It will hurt and, although I will give you something to dull the pain, it will not erase it altogether. It is because of the nature of your wounds, this is the only way they will heal properly." Both men had blanched when she described what she intended, but at least they had all the information, much better than just turning up with a pile of scary looking instruments and a cloth to bite down on. She assured them that she would only do it if absolutely essential, more to give them a little hope than anything else, already aware that she would have no choice.

By the time Hannah had finished, the day was nearly over. Needing a moment to gather her thoughts, she stood in the fresh air, stretching her aching muscles and dreaming of a lengthy and uninterrupted sleep; unable to remember the last time she had managed a proper rest. Before leaving Jerusalem, she had been called upon every night for weeks, in order to treat those who had suffered some form of abuse either from inter-factional fights or because of riots.

As she contemplated this luxury, she noticed that from where she was standing — it must have been a high point on the plateau — she could see the Sea of Salt, the sun's dying rays sparkling on the expanse of blue and the harsh colours of the land surrounding it, softening to a warm pink in the fading light. Although desolate, to Hannah, it was breathtakingly beautiful.

Turning away, she walked slowly back over to the other palace and found Malachi sitting on a bench that he must have had dragged out from one of the rooms. He was dozing, but her footfall roused him and he came awake instantly

"It's only me, Malachi," she said, "thank you. All will be well for a little while. Go and get yourself some food. I will find you if I need you." He looked uncertain, but she shooed him away. Malachi, who had received his initial instructions from Aharon, decided that it might be sensible to apprise that young man that Hannah had dismissed her guard. Aharon assured Malachi that he would check on his sister and thanked his friend, asking that he and Simeon share the watch over night. Malachi went on his way and, having heard that Raizel had taken over the cooking was looking forward to a very tasty meal.

Aharon strolled along to the rooms that Hannah had appropriated and found her cleaning and binding the wounds on the youngest soldier. Attracting his sister's attention, Aharon motioned for her to step outside. In the comparative seclusion of the courtyard, he asked what she thought she was doing sending Malachi away. Hannah folded her arms and studied his face expecting censure, yet only solicitude was reflected there. She heaved a sigh —

"Aharon, you need to trust my judgement. What on earth do you think any of these men could do to me? One strong puff of wind would flatten them. You have to believe me when I tell you that I am in no danger." Aharon started to interrupt but Hannah wasn't having it. "I know that you are only worried for my safety, but they will not hurt me and I am perfectly capable of screaming the place down if I feel in any way threatened."

"You never see the evil in people do you, Hannah." Aharon said. It was a statement not a question. "How can you find it in you to treat these men? They are enemies of our people. Why do you even care what happens to them?" His sister didn't hesitate.

"Because if I refuse to help anyone who needs me, I cannot call myself a physician. Who they are or what they have done must not affect my care of them. I treat the injury, not the person. Otherwise I am not true to myself, or to my calling, or to Gideon — who taught me to remain impartial; that no matter the circumstance, no person or group of people should ever prevent me from rendering aid to another."

Hannah spoke with calm deliberation and as happened so many times before, Aharon was taken aback by his sister's maturity. She probably had more wisdom in her little finger than most of the rebels who had stormed this fortress put together. Aware that she would carry on regardless, Aharon nodded, simply reiterating his wish that she be vigilant.

"Malachi or Simeon will be on watch throughout the night, Hannah. They will be close if you need them."

"Thank you Aharon, I do appreciate that you worry for me." Smiling at her brother, Hannah turned back into the room, concentrating on the job at hand and immediately forgetting that he had been there.

Aharon, meanwhile, decided it would be a good idea to ask Raizel to leave out a platter of food, as he knew Hannah would forget to eat if someone didn't remind her.

Once she had checked the three soldiers, washed their wounds, re-applied salve and bandages, Hannah sat for a while simply observing them. Current incapacitation aside, the one with the bruising, seemed to have an air of authority and she mused over the possibility that he might be the commander of the garrison, or at least some kind of official. The other two seemed too young to be in charge of anyone, especially the one with the abdominal wound who looked little more than a boy. Hannah had never been this close to a Roman — soldier or otherwise — and she was fascinated by how different their features were from those of her people.

All three were very tall and, she thought, very handsome. Obviously fit, for none had an ounce of excess fat on them, their muscles were well toned and from this she surmised that they took proper care of themselves. Their faces were quite angular and of the three, the older two had thin, straight noses, the younger soldier's being slightly bent, possibly it had been broken at some time in his youth. Their hair was very short, closely cropped, and despite the stubble now growing on their chins, it was clear that under normal circumstances they would be clean-shaven. This last attribute seemed strange to Hannah for, without exception, the men she knew all sported facial hair. She spent rather longer studying the older man, as there was something about him that intrigued her, although what it was and why, she was unable to divine.

While she was pondering these things, the object of her attention woke, his eyes immediately searching for hers. She felt that sensation again, it rippled along her spine but was gone almost before she realised it had happened. She moved closer.

"How is the pain?" she asked quietly. "Do you want a sip of that draft?" Speaking slowly hoping he understood. He shook his head.

"Not yet. Maybe later." He said haltingly, the effort draining him and Hannah patted his arm.

"Do not try to talk, just rest. Would you like some food?" she acted the motion of eating and he shook his head. Hannah tutted, "You should try something, it is days since your last meal. You need food for strength. Might you try a little…for me?" Maxentius stared at this elfin-like woman, knowing it was beyond his power to refuse her anything she asked. He nodded, gingerly; it was as much as he could manage. She beamed at him and it seemed to the weary soldier that the room lit up. Presuming it was the fever that was making him so addled, Maxentius ignored it and tried to concentrate on what she was saying.

Hannah just chattered away about the three soldiers, their injuries and how she was treating them. Maxentius had learned some Hebrew, but he was far from fluent and only grasped about a fifth of what she said, but he could have listened to her talk forever, entranced by her lilting tones. He tried forcing himself to detach. He was a captive and a Roman; she was freeborn, a Hebrew and seemingly a member of the rebel gang who had ambushed the fortress. It was futile to think about her. His heart, however, had other ideas, even though he was not prepared to pay heed to his heart quite yet.

Hoping that she could find something that would tempt the soldiers, Hannah went over to the kitchen, discovering a platter, which she presumed Raizel had left for her. As she inhaled it, without much care as to what it was, she noticed a large pot of stew by the fire. Spooning some into three smaller bowls, Hannah hoped that the smell alone would be enough to persuade the three men to eat even a small portion. Gathering these and some bread, she hurried back to the little room, knowing that she should not linger, there were other patients to whom she must attend.

Placing the bowls on top of the cupboard, she took one and a piece of bread and sat back down next to Maxentius.

"This is good. Please try." She dipped the bread into the hot meat juice, handing it to Maxentius. The soldier took a small bite and nearly moaned aloud. It was delicious, so delicious that he managed to empty the whole bowl, suddenly realising just how hungry he was. If Hannah hadn't stopped him he would have gobbled it down, but she explained, or hoped she had, that after so many days without sustenance, to eat too much too quickly would make him very sick.

Once she had seen to Maxentius, she woke the second soldier and did the same. Marcus was completely bewildered, having no recollection of how he came to be in one of the side rooms, on a pallet, with a strange woman feeding him stew. While Marcus ate, Maxentius explained, briefly, what had happened; and as Hannah listened to the foreign sounds, she worked out the inference of their conversation even though she had no knowledge of their language.

Sergius was still in a stupor and Hannah could not wake him. Preferring that he slept, she merely lifted his head and tried to get some water across his lips. She knew that if he did not drink, his body would stop functioning. She managed to get him to swallow quite a bit and then she re-checked his wounds. The gash was still oozing the yellowish discharge and she spent a long time cleaning it as best she could. Then re-applying the salve and binding the cloths in place she let him rest.

"I will be back soon." She said, remembering to speak with deliberation. Maxentius nodded and, after making sure the lamp was trimmed, Hannah left them in peace.

Marcus and Maxentius talked for a little while in undertones, although Marcus struggled to focus. Neither particularly clear on their situation, except that presumably they were now captives of a desperate band of men. They were both very worried about Sergius, for even though Maxentius could see that Hannah was a clever physician, some wounds could not be healed. All he could cling to was his belief that his friend's youth and general fitness would be in his favour.

Chapter Twenty Three

Masada AD66 ~ Day Three

Meanwhile, Hannah was back in the other palace. Most of her patients, while obviously a long way from recovery, were at least in no danger. It would just take time and she still had to be conscious about the risk of infection. Several were causing her some concern and she was quite fearful for two or three.

Checking them all, she was satisfied that they were as stable as she could expect and she dispensed a little of her poppy juice draft to all of them, knowing that it would give them an untroubled rest. The dose was very diluted, for although highly effective, Hannah knew it contained addictive properties and the last thing she needed was for these men to become dependent on it.

By the time she had examined them all, it was dark. Someone had lit a few oil lamps, placing them around the two rooms, providing just enough light to allow movement without tripping over a pallet. Hannah had been so absorbed by her work that she hadn't even noticed who it was, but was grateful, even though she carried her own lamp, so that she could see what she was doing. Taking one last walk along both rooms, she told those still awake that she would be back later and left them to rest.

The night air was mild and the moon was rising, the glow from the pale orb illuminating the citadel, creating all manner of interesting shadows. Too tired to appreciate it, Hannah made her way back to the room where the soldiers lay. Placing her lamp on the cupboard, she noticed that all three slept. Unwilling to disturb them, she simply listened to their breathing and brushed her hand over their skin, checking for fever. The youngest was tossing a little and she managed to get a few drops of the poppy juice down his throat, sitting with him until he settled.

Unwilling to leave them, she spotted a roll of material in one corner; it looked like a very heavy blanket or maybe a rug and it was lovely and warm. In the soft glow of the lamp Hannah fashioned a pillow from a sheet before wrapping herself in the blanket. Curling up in the corner, she slept.

Sometime in the night, Maxentius woke. Disorientated, it took him a moment to remember where he was. The pain in his head did not seem as bad, but the ache in his chest hadn't abated and breathing was no less uncomfortable. As he lay there, letting his eyes adjust to the dim light, he noticed a small bundle in the corner of the room. He was sure it hadn't been there when he went to sleep. Bewildered he stared at it, stifling a shocked gasp, when suddenly it morphed into a person.

It was the woman, Hannah. As Maxentius watched her stand up, he realised that she was exhausted. Her posture was that of someone bearing a heavy load and even in the gloom, he saw that her face was etched with weariness. She stretched, arching her back and he was sure he heard her joints crack. Closing his eyes, he felt the swish of air as she walked by his pallet and he was overwhelmed by the most fervent desire to ease her burden.

He had fallen back to sleep when she returned and Hannah, of course, knew nothing of his thoughts. She had been to check on the other men and one or two had fallen into delirium from infected wounds, so she had stayed with them until she felt the bout had passed. It was the early hours of the morning now and the young woman realised that she had to try to get some more sleep, if she was to be clear headed enough to stitch those wounds.

She checked the three soldiers, the youngest was muttering and his skin was hot to her touch, so she spent a few moments cooling him down with damp cloths and got him to drink a little more poppy juice. She didn't want to disturb him any more than necessary though, hoping that at least a disturbed rest was better than none at all, so refrained from inspecting his abdomen.

As she replaced the lamp on the cupboard she sensed movement and noticed that the elder of the three was awake. Crouching down next to him, she took his hand.

"Do you have pain?" she asked in low tones. He nodded carefully. Remembering that he hadn't taken any of the poppy juice earlier, she got him to drink a decent amount, checking his temperature as he did so. He was warmer that she would have liked but it was not really surprising after everything he had been through. Pouring some fresh water into a bowl, she did the same with him as she had with his comrade, soaking a cloth and using it to cool his heated skin, then rinsing it again, wiped it over his hair, cleaning out any residual blood and dust.

"You are tired." He stated, enunciating his words clearly, hoping he was using the right ones. She smiled at him, still holding the hand she had just been washing.

"A little; please do not worry about me, it is nothing. I will be fine. You just concentrate on getting better." She paused a moment, biting her lip, weighing up whether she dared ask what she wanted to know. He raised an eyebrow in query, so she gave in. Did it matter anyway? "Would it be impertinent for me to ask your name, Sir?" Maxentius struggled to understand what she said and his expression told Hannah of his confusion. She pointed to herself —

"I am Hannah." Then she pointed to him, raising her hand and shrugging her shoulders, the gesture clarifying that she did not know his name. He smiled then, a slow sweet smile, which completely transformed his rather grave countenance and Hannah stilled. She could not take her eyes from his face, his smile had stopped her heart and she forgot to breathe, as everything around her seemed to be poised on the brink of something momentous.

"I am Lucius Maxentius, commander of this garrison." He spoke with deliberation and no small amount of pride. Forcing her attention back to what the soldier was saying, Hannah made herself take a breath and repeated the curious words. It took her a few attempts to get them right, but Maxentius nodded when she finally mastered them. She pointed to the other two. "Marcus and Sergius. Our formal names are longer, but may be difficult to remember," again, carefully articulated.

Hannah practised these names also, giggling a little as she kept tripping over her pronunciation. Maxentius smiled again; bewitched by her animated features, her impish smile and her vivid eyes, discernible to him even in the low light. Hannah yawned; rolling her shoulders to stretch her aching muscles and although Maxentius had no desire to let go of her hand, knew that she needed slumber.

"Go, you should rest. My pain is not as bad and I think that now I will be able to sleep a little longer." She rested the back of her hand against his forehead, his skin was still warm but not overly so and the tired woman thought she might risk another couple of hours' sleep. She smiled down at the man on the pallet.

"Thank you, Lucius Maxentius, Sir. I am glad to know your name." He inclined his head and she released his hand, moving over to the huddle of rugs on the floor, snuggled into them and was asleep in an instant.

Masada AD66 ~ Day Four

For Hannah, the next day, was a duplicate of the one before. She did her rounds of the wounded, checking, examining and cleaning their wounds, applying salve, bandaging their damaged bodies, and changing sheets. She worked out that the fire in the laundry was never allowed to go out and that there were enormous buckets that could be swung over the flames in which she could heat water. She managed to wash soiled sheets, cloths and bandages, spreading them out along the walls, to dry in the sunshine.

Hannah knew that this was the day she would have to stitch those wounds that required it and, after gathering all her instruments, ointments, salves and balms together, she asked Aharon and a couple of the other men whether they would assist her. Obed and Levi were the two whose injuries required this treatment and she knew it would be agonising. Going over the procedure with them again, so that they understood, she filled a bowl with some hot water brought from the kitchens, adding salt, frankincense and myrrh. Then she gave both men a large dose of poppy juice, waiting until the opiate took effect, saying she would treat Obed first.

Giving Obed a twist of cloth to bite down on, she asked Aharon to hold his shoulders and one of the other men — she realised it was Binyamin, Malachi's friend — to hold his legs.

"It is vital that you do not allow Obed to move, for my instruments are sharp and I would rather not inflict any more damage or pain than is absolutely essential." All three men looked bleak as she said this, but did as she asked. The third man, Noach, who had agreed to help, stood to one side, ready to take over from either Aharon or Binyamin if required.

Once satisfied that they were ready, Hannah began. As the knife slid into his skin, Obed groaned and tried to writhe away, but Aharon and Binyamin did their job, and kept the patient restrained.

Hannah worked as quickly as possible, but it was not something that she could rush, the edges of Obed's wounds were ragged and it all had to be cut away. He had three gashes that needed stitching and it took a long time. Hannah paused every now and again, checking to make sure Obed was still alive and to give him more poppy juice. Several of her patients were awake and those who could see what was going on were riveted, a sort of strained hush falling over the room.

Eventually, she was done and pulled the final stitch, knotting off the thread, before coating the neatly sutured edges with salve, mixed with a liberal amount of honey to keep the skin softened and boost healing. Obed had slipped into a stupor while she had been working, which for him had lessened the trauma, but Hannah had to make sure that he would wake up. Leaving him to rest for now, she turned her attention to Levi, operating on him in the same manner. Levi only had one large cut that required attention and even though it was excruciating, his ordeal was over much more quickly.

Trembling a little from effort and concentration, Hannah took a deep breath as she secured the last bandage in place. Turning to Aharon and Binyamin she thanked them.

"You both have been invaluable to me. I cannot express my appreciation enough. It would not have been easy for me to operate without your help." Aharon squeezed her shoulder in acknowledgement and, noticing that Binyamin was looking a little queasy, Hannah suggested that he go and get some fresh air, advice he took readily.

Deciding to let Obed sleep until she had checked the rest of her patients for the second time that day, Hannah collected up everything she had used, placing her dowels and her knife into a bowl of fresh clean water, to which she had added some vinegar. Leaving them to soak, she checked the other men. Confident that she had done all she could for the moment, Hannah followed her own advice and went to stand in the fresh air for a few moments.

It was a glorious day; a slight breeze had begun to drift in from the Sea of Salt, making the leaves on the pomegranate trees dance, creating intricate shadow patterns across the plateau. It was quite warm, but not unduly so, and Hannah realised, that despite feeling utterly drained, she was actually quite content. She thought she had probably done enough to save all the Hebrew rebels and although Sergius worried her, she didn't hold any fears for the other two Romans. Firstly, their injuries were not quite as ghastly, but also both seemed endowed with robust spirits.

She heard footfalls and spun around to see Aharon coming towards her.

"Hannah, Raizel has prepared some food. She asked me to tell you that it is in the kitchen."

"I'll be over shortly," she replied, smiling at her brother, gratefully. "I just want to check on Obed." Aharon nodded and strode off towards the private palace. Turning her back on the stunning vista, Hannah re-entered the ward and, pulling her stool over to Obed's side, examined him quickly, noting that his heart rate was relatively steady and that his skin wasn't too clammy. Placing her cool hand against his cheek, she spoke in low tones, calling him. He stirred, blinking in confusion and then as memory resurfaced, gulped in panic. Hannah took his hand —

"It is done Obed. You were very brave and now you will heal. I will not touch your bandages until the last hour and if you will drink a little more of this draft, you will be able to sleep without discomfort." The man whispered his thanks, grimacing as he tried to move. Hannah helped him to get more comfortable, then held the bowl while he drank the pain numbing juice. Drawing up a clean sheet and laying the blanket over his lower half, she watched until his eyelids drooped and his breathing settled in to a steady rhythm. Going over to Levi, she did the same and both men were soon fast asleep.

In the antechamber, Hannah poured out the now bloodstained water, rinsing off her instruments and washing them thoroughly before wrapping them in a cloth. Gathering these and yet another pile of soiled cloths, bandages and sheets, she made her way back over the plateau.

Much later, after sorting out everything in the laundry and having eaten the food lovingly prepared by Raizel, Hannah went to see how the three soldiers were doing. When she had popped in earlier, they had still been fast asleep and unwilling to disturb them, had simply pulled the door almost closed and left them in the quiet.

Although both Maxentius and Marcus had their eyes open, Hannah recognised that neither man was wholly awake. Sergius was muttering and tossing, his frail body obviously desperately attempting to fight off the infection that was sapping his strength. Hannah frowned, uncertain how to tell the other two what she feared, hoping against hope that he would suddenly turn the corner and begin the long haul back to recovery.

Washing her hands, Hannah went to Sergius first; folding back the sheet, she took care to leave the lower half of his abdomen covered and then lifted his tunic. Gently unrolling the bandages, she dropped them in a conveniently placed basket, before removing the large swatch of cloth that protected the wound. Yellow pus and blood was congealed at the opening of his wound and the smell from the poison was rancid. Hannah swallowed and breathing through her mouth tried to remove as much as she could without waking the young man.

Her attempt was in vain and Sergius came round, the grey pallor of his face etched with agony. Hannah could have cried, this poor boy — blithely ignoring the fact that this 'boy' was actually older than she — to be so badly injured, so far from home. The enormity of what she was trying to do threatened to overwhelm her and she bent her head taking deep breaths. Determined not to falter, Hannah steeled herself and, placing her hand on his arm, looked him in the eyes.

"Sergius," stumbling over his name, "Sergius, I am sorry, I did not mean to wake you. Sip this draft, it will help." As she reached for the poppy juice, Sergius spoke, his words slurred. She stared at him in bafflement, but then Maxentius responded. Sergius looked at his commander, then at Hannah and then back to Maxentius who, Hannah noticed, nodded his head. Capitulating, Sergius allowed Hannah to help him drink the cool liquid. He shuddered, as he tasted the odd flavour and then exhaled a deep sigh that seemed to span a whole lifetime, as the physician laid him back against the pillow.

Hannah watched the soldier until his face relaxed, then continued with her task. The room was quiet; the only sounds the erratic breathing of the three Roman soldiers. After removing as much of the infection as she could, Hannah slathered salve into and around the gaping injury, bandaging it firmly, before cleaning and binding all his other, less vicious, injuries. Finishing up, she checked the other two and as with all the other men under her care, rinsed their wounds and applied yet more salve, making a mental note to blend some more. Marcus slipped back to sleep as she tucked the blanket around him, but Maxentius was still awake. As Hannah was about to leave, he spoke.

"I wonder, would it be possible to walk outside?" She gawked at him. Really! Hardly a day since he was so ill she thought he would die and he fancied a stroll? He smiled diffidently "I miss the sky." An odd phrase she thought and unsure whether she would be able to help him, didn't see why not.

"Are you sure? You are very weak." He nodded. Hannah asked that he give her a moment and quickly ran over to the kitchen to dump all the soiled cloths and bandages in the sink, calling to Raizel as she passed that she was going to help one of the soldiers onto the plateau. Raizel came to the door shouting after her sister-in-law, but Hannah had already disappeared across the courtyard.

Shaking her head and biting down on a grin, Raizel hurried over to her quarters to advise Aharon that his sister was about to go outside with an enemy soldier. Exasperated, yet not particularly surprised, Aharon made his way to the sick room intent on giving Hannah a piece of his mind at her blatant disregard for her own safety. He slowed his steps as he approached, listening to his sister's soft voice, coaxing the man to take it carefully. A low groan indicated that the man still suffered greatly, as two heads appeared through the doorway. The rangy soldier was leaning on Hannah, walking gingerly as though each footfall hurt, she was talking to him all the while, their pace slower than a snail's.

"Hannah, would you like some assistance?"

"Oh Aharon, no I think we will manage. Thank you though," waving aside his offer.

He watched their progress, amazed that the soldier had been able to get this far. They reached the corner and were about to turn along the passageway that led to the plateau, when the soldier stopped. He spoke and Hannah waited, her arm around his waist, her face looking up into his. Aharon studied her expression as something, an indefinable shift, skittered across his subconscious, but he couldn't hold it. Ignoring it for the moment, he strolled over to the patient and his healer.

"Do you need me now?" He asked, not ungently. Hannah beamed at her brother.

"Oh, Aharon, you're still there! The commander, Lucius Maxentius — yes that is his name. I know it sounds strange does it not?" in response to a raised eyebrow, "would like to reach the plateau just for a few minutes, to feel the sun, but I am afraid I am not as strong as I thought I was. Please, would you help?" She beseeched him not only to help but also not to reprimand. He noticed how pale she looked, recalling that of all those on this citadel, she, a young woman, was the one who probably had the hardest job. Around forty rebels and three Romans required her constant attention and no one had offered to assist her. He felt guilty and this guilt overrode any qualms about doing as she asked. He tucked an arm under the soldier's arm supporting his upper body.

"Please, do not go too fast, Aharon. I do not wish to cause him any further pain." Hebrew and Roman walked unhurriedly out into the open air. Maxentius lifted his face, the sun touching his skin, the breeze keeping it cool. The Roman turned to Aharon, as Hannah's brother settled him on a stone bench just at the end of the passageway

"Thank you, Sir. This is a great kindness." Aharon dipped his head in acknowledgement and telling Hannah to come and find him when the prisoner was ready to return to his room, stalked away. Hannah grinned, in no way repentant and settled herself next to the burly soldier.

"Are you warm enough?" she asked solicitously. He watched her speak and she illustrated what she meant with a rather amusing mime. Maxentius nodded and they sat together for quite a while, watching the world go by. Her proximity to this solider was doing weird things to Hannah. Her stomach fluttered and her heart refused to beat with anything like its normal rhythm. She had no idea why and didn't think it was anything like fear. She didn't believe that this man would ever harm her, although quite why she should think this was a whole other issue.

She chattered aimlessly, not expecting any response, just a way to make him feel at ease. Maybe an hour later, she observed that Maxentius was looking weary and ran to get Aharon. Her brother helped the soldier back to his cot, and Hannah gave him a little poppy juice to ensure he slept more comfortably.

Her day not over, Hannah trailed back over to the large palace to check on Obed and Levi as well as her other patients. Most were beginning to exhibit signs of healing, although there were still some who were too listless for her liking — showing little interest in food or the comings and goings throughout the day. She sat for a while with each of these men, frustrated that she couldn't locate the cause, but determined that it could not escape her scrutiny for long.

Chapter Twenty Four

Masada AD66 ~ The days that followed

A number of the rebels seemed inclined to remain on Masada. The fortress was well stocked with all manner of supplies and they presumed that so far from Jerusalem, it would be considered a waste of time for the authorities to hunt them down. Moreover, Menahem had returned to the city, with most of his supporters, intent on wreaking as much havoc as they could. News filtered through but it was sporadic and Hannah didn't really care. She had enough to do, without worrying about what was happening miles away.

Hannah's days fell into a pattern; she would check all her patients, Hebrew and Roman, repeating the same treatment, ensuring that any chance of further infection was kept to a minimum. Obed and Levi began to recover, the stitches doing their job. Two of the three Romans also began to heal although, as with the few Hebrews who worried her, both still required close scrutiny. Maxentius' bruising seemed to be getting worse rather than better and Hannah realised that there had to be another, underlying issue that she had not picked up. Maxentius while obviously uncomfortable and in considerable pain, was more worried about Marcus and Sergius than himself.

Every afternoon, when she had finished her chores, Hannah would help Maxentius out onto the plateau. Now, he was able to get all the way to the pomegranate tree and Hannah would encourage him to sit on her upturned pot, while she leaned against the trunk of the tree. Maxentius had tried to persuade her to take the makeshift seat but, as she rightly stated, there was no way a man of his stature could stand upright under the sprawling branches and she wasn't the one with all the injuries.

They began to talk about their lives. It was a very slow process as neither really understood the other, but by dint of gesticulations, actions and often, in Hannah's case, full-on theatrical productions, they managed to get a sense of what the other said. Hannah was surprised at how comfortable she was with this man, indeed with all three Romans. For a start, they were captives, and any perception of wrongdoing could result in their immediate death, but more than this, she had no fear that they would even try to hurt her, or use her in a bid to escape. Unable to explain it — even to herself — with these three, she felt safe.

One afternoon — and owing to unforeseen problems with a few of her other patients — much later than usual, Hannah helped Maxentius outside; this time to the stone bench rather than the pomegranate tree, as the daylight was fading and she did not expect that they would stay out for too long. Worried that the soldier might catch a chill, Hannah had brought a blanket with her, which she tucked around him. As they talked, darkness fell and Hannah, as ever, was mesmerised by the night sky. A myriad of stars, floating in an inky sea, waiting for the moon to begin its time-honoured journey across the heavens; illuminating the outcrop in their ethereal light.

"I could watch the stars all night," she breathed, pointing upwards so that her companion understood what she was saying. Maxentius nodded.

"I too find the night sky entrancing," he said. Then in tones so quiet, Hannah thought she had imagined it, he murmured "but not nearly as entrancing as you." She spun to face him, but he was looking at the stars, giving no indication that he had spoken at all. His words, however, stayed with her, making her feel strangely warm inside. Distracting herself, she asked him to tell her more about his life. He had told her about his comrades, but not much of himself and this tall, grave soldier remained an enigma, a puzzle she really wanted to solve. In the very short time that she had known him, Maxentius had become an important part of her world; although her head hadn't quite caught up with what her heart had already embraced, and she presumed it was just because he was a patient who relied on her to heal him.

He had shared something of his life, mentioning that he had travelled down from a county called Armenia, hundreds of miles north of Judaea, where he had been involved in a long campaign. He told her very little of his family, feeling the desire to keep that part of his life private for now and easily sidestepped Hannah's questions, simply by pretending that he didn't understand them. It wasn't that he didn't trust this beautiful physician who somehow invaded his every waking moment, it was that he feared for his future. He was nothing if not a realist and knew — despite Hannah's assurances to the contrary — it unlikely that he, or any of his comrades, would be allowed to live, and to share such intimate details with another was to give that person a little of your soul; he did not wish to burden Hannah with that.

Yawning, Hannah suggested that they return to his room, she wanted to check Sergius again, he was slipping away from her, despite everything she was doing and she didn't think he would survive many more days. She had attempted to tell both Maxentius and Marcus, but the young man's friends were not ready to face the inevitable.

Back in the soldiers' room, Hannah spent a long time with Sergius, trying to reduce his fever. Soaking cloths in a bowl of cool water to which she had added myrrh, known for its healing properties, she wiped his body down again and again until eventually he became settled. Getting him to drink a little more poppy juice, she quickly checked his worst wound, grimacing at the lack of healing. A couple of days previously she had needed to remove more dead and dying flesh, but could not suture it closed as there was still too much poison. She realised how desperately ill Sergius was when he had not come round at all during the operation, which although less traumatic for her patient, was of grave concern to his physician.

Satisfied that he would settle for a time, Hannah made sure the other two were comfortable and went to the adjacent room, which Aharon had set up as her bedchamber. A bedroll — folded out of the way during the day — lay on top of a very thick and comfortable rug; a cupboard where she stored her clothes, although as a general rule she couldn't be bothered to tidy them away, leaving them in a neat pile on the top; a shelf which held a flagon of water and several bowls; and a rather ornate chair — one Aharon had found in one of the finely furnished rooms of the palace. It was not much, but Hannah was not used to luxury and found the room perfectly adequate.

She stretched out and tried to sleep, weeks of disturbed nights meant that her brain was always on the alert for a call or a footstep, indicating that she was needed by one or more of her patients. Oh for one unbroken night she pleaded, closing her eyes.

Her dreams were convoluted and utterly incomprehensible. She kept seeing a woman she could not recall ever meeting, whose attire was so peculiar, that Hannah wondered, absently whether she had conjured her up because of something Maxentius had described about one of those distant lands. The woman, who didn't look much older than her, had long fair hair and eyes the same colour as her own. Curiously, she seemed to be here on Masada, but Hannah knew that was impossible — Raizel and she were the only two females between here and Engaddi.

The setting wasn't quite right though — some of the walls looked damaged, even ruined, so Hannah reckoned that it couldn't be Masada after all. At one point this woman was holding the oddest-looking jewel, a deep red stone in a very intricate setting; Hannah couldn't really make it out but she realised it was a costly gem.

Waking with a jolt, and presuming she had slept too long, Hannah was shocked to see that it was still dark. Pulling on her mantle, she tiptoed along to the next room, lifting the lamp to run her eyes over the three Romans. Sergius was tossing, so she gave him some more of the opiate, pondering over whether there were options she hadn't considered, acknowledging that she'd tried everything she knew. The other two were fast asleep, so once she was certain that Sergius had settled she walked quickly over to the larger palace and ran a cursory eye over the remainder of her patients there too. Thankfully all were resting peacefully, for which she was very grateful.

Traipsing back across the plateau, she placed her lamp on the cupboard and settled back into bed.

The dream came again, this time it was more vivid. The woman was working in a room — one that looked familiar but Hannah could not place it — with an older man. They were digging up pottery. Well that seemed a most peculiar activity. Who would want a pile of broken pots? The man was looking troubled and they talked for a moment. Suddenly the scene shifted and the woman was sitting on a wall; surrounded by lots of people smiling and laughing, all of whom were wearing the same strange clothing. Hannah had never seen anything like it, they must be from far, far away, but she had to admit that their attire looked comfortable.

A hand was shaking her, she tried to push it away, wanting to see what might happen, how it ended, but the hand was insistent and the image faded. Grumbling at whoever had woken her, Hannah prised her eyes open, her brain fogged with sleep and her head still lost in the dream.

"Hannah! I am sorry, but Sergius needs you." It was Maxentius. The fog was banished immediately. Hannah was on her feet and in the next room in an instant. Sergius was thrashing around on his pallet, crying out; his words unintelligible to the young physician, but she didn't need to understand him to know that he was in torment and that he would cause more damage to his wound if she couldn't calm him down.

Grabbing a bowl, she filled it with water, adding a healthy dash of salt and picked up a pile of cloths. Falling on her knees next to the young soldier, she peeled back the sheet, folding it over his lower abdomen before lifting his tunic. Groaning, Hannah saw that the bandages were soaked in blood and poison. How could this poor man still have so much infection? She could not comprehend how awful he must feel. He had barely eaten since she had found the three of them and his body was skeletal. He had no strength in his system to fight this. Still, she was determined to give him the best chance.

Cleaning his wound for the umpteenth time, Hannah decided to let it breathe for a little while; maybe the fresh air would be beneficial. At this stage, it certainly couldn't do any harm. Explaining to Maxentius what she was doing, Hannah continued to wipe away the gory matter that had congealed in the gash and rinsed it several times with more salty water. Marcus was still asleep, her movements hadn't woken him, which bothered her and Hannah hoped he wasn't succumbing to infection also. Biting her lip — she absolutely refused to cry — she told Maxentius that she would be back shortly and left the room. Returning to her own chamber, she washed and pulled on fresh clothes, a soft grey undershift and a pale pink tunic, caught at the waist with a belt into which she tucked a fresh cloth, then threw her mantle over her shoulders and went out onto the plateau.

Trudging over to the pomegranate tree, Hannah sat on the upturned pot and ran her mind over everything she had done for Sergius. In her heart of hearts, she knew that he was dying, but the thought that she would lose him, after trying so hard to hold him to this world, distressed her more than she expected it to. It brought the loss of her parents and Gideon, as well as poor Nachum into sharp focus, not to mention all those who had died on the night of the ambush; and the thought of just one more death was almost too hard to bear.

She didn't know Sergius, knew nothing of his hopes, his dreams, his family, she didn't even know what his military rank was, but in the few days she had been treating him, he had affected her in a way she could not have anticipated. He seemed to represent the futility of this stupid uprising, the countless and pointless deaths of so many young men, both Jewish and non-Jewish who had sacrificed their lives for what, to her, seemed very little gain. To Hannah, it was all such an appalling waste.

Exhausted, Hannah relaxed against the tree and shut her eyes.

Across the vast expanse of time, her soul touched another's, a young woman who, as she leaned against a ruined section of wall in an isolated citadel, also closed her eyes — just briefly — to enjoy the warmth of the sun.

In that split second, their worlds spun and collided and Hannah felt as though everything around her was dissolving. The fortress in front of her appeared to twist and bend — surely not — familiar sounds became garbled. The ground seemed to tremble and shift and, detachedly, Hannah wondered whether it was an earthquake. She tried to stand, but found her legs would not hold her; she couldn't even scream as her brain refused to cooperate with her mouth. Gripping the pomegranate tree as the only stable thing within reach, the young physician held on for dear life, terror roiling through her, for surely this must be an event of catastrophic portions.

As suddenly as it had begun it stopped. Slowly, Hannah opened her eyes and, as her world came back into focus, she experienced a flash of sheer unadulterated panic. Struggling to concentrate, she realised that her perception was distorted and, despite knowing it to be impossible, it seemed as though someone else's memories were overlapping hers. More alarming still, was that when she tried to recall anything of her life prior to this moment it was hazy; veiled by time and distance, fading away like stars ahead of the sunrise. Her head insisted that this was nonsensical and it came to her that she was probably still asleep, that this was simply a nightmare; the result of too many nights without a decent rest. Hoping, desperately, that this was the case, Hannah leaned back against the pomegranate tree and willed herself to wake up.

.......ooooo**OOO**ooooo.......

Chapter Twenty Five

When souls collide ~ bound across time

As the world around me reformed, I realised that I was leaning against a tree trunk and glancing up, I could see the familiar leaves of the pomegranate, struggling to endure in this harsh landscape. Although very pretty, they are scrubby trees and it was only because I was small that I was able to stand upright under its canopy. The plateau was covered in gardens and vegetable patches delineated by paths wide enough for a cart to be pulled along. Were they the same garden beds I had noticed in my dream?

I heard the sound of oxen to my left and as I turned I could see two walking along a bed of churned mud, pulling what looked like a plough. Nearby a couple of baby goats skittered about, their mewling calls attracting the attention of their mother who was chewing on the stubbly grass a few feet from them. A large stone trough brimming with water, stood at one end of the planted areas. As far as I could work out the trough seemed to have a hole near the base, half way along, which when unstoppered, would allow water to drain into narrow gullies, feeding the garden beds, although I had no idea how it was filled.

I looked down and saw that my outfit was unfamiliar. I was wearing a sort of tunic with holes for my head and arms, over the top of what felt like a thin under-dress with sleeves to my elbows. A belt made of twisted material cinched my waist. Running my hands across it, the tunic felt like linen and, scouring my memory regarding the clothing of Ancient Judaea, I recalled that this was of a higher quality than the coarser, woollen garments usually worn by rural or less wealthy people. The under-dress was soft grey and the tunic was pale pink in colour, my belt was in a darker shade. Sitting across my shoulders, I had a cream mantle with a fringed edge, clasped at my neck by a delicate pin, I felt that all these layers should make me hot, but I was quite comfortable. My feet were encased in soft sandals and I realised that my hair, rich, dark brown and quite curly, was lying over my shoulder in a loose plait. Then I looked at my hands, noticing that my skin was darker too, more olive.

Confused I stood a moment longer trying to get my bearings, the Northern Palace was to my left and I was in front of the Western Palace. The Byzantine church wasn't there, wouldn't be there for several hundred years. The sun was high and a light breeze was blowing up miniature dust devils. Over the high wall I could just see the sparkle of the Dead Sea off in the distance. The sounds of people going about their daily chores seemed normal, I almost forgot that I didn't belong here. What would happen if someone saw me?

"Hannah!" Startled I looked round, someone *had* seen me. How was that possible? "Hannah, quick we need you over here." I squinted in the direction from where the voice had come and saw a tall dark haired man with an air of quiet authority, approaching me from the Northern Palace. "Quickly!" The urgency in his voice compelled me to move and, without thought, I pushed myself off the tree and moved towards him, unconsciously lifting my tunic in case I tripped over its length.

"What is it, my brother?" Brother? I don't have a brother, I thought to myself, yet I knew his name was Aharon.

"The gravely injured one suffers, you wanted to save them, you need to help him, or we will have to finish him."

"No!" Sharply. "You cannot do this, it would be murder. I have fought for them for this long, please let me keep trying." What on earth was I doing? I'm not a nurse and I usually throw up at the sight of blood. He nodded cursorily and, assuming it to be a nod of agreement, I followed him into the cool of the palace, along a corridor and entered the room of my dreams.

It was quite large and spacious, something I hadn't noticed before, the floor was beautifully tiled and there were what looked to be rugs rolled up against one wall. Three men lay on wooden pallets, two of whom looked slightly less cadaverous than the one lying nearest the door. His skin was clammy and pale, his jaw clenched in agony. Shocked, I realised that these were the three men whom I'd seen when I stubbed my toe and that the critically injured man was the one the other two had been leaning over. How long they had been here I couldn't tell — they were all still alive, that was something — but it was obvious one of them was dying.

How could I help? I had no healing powers, no medicines. He needed surgery and clean sheets and intravenous antibiotics. Glancing round the room, I took in pitchers and bowls that looked as though they might hold water, a shelf lined with jars of ointments and herbs and a wooden cupboard-like piece of furniture with doors, which when I opened them, held sheets, blankets and smaller cloths. On the top of this, stood more jars as well as an array of dowels and strange looking instruments.

Not wanting to look too closely at them, I turned back to the other shelf. Okay, Hannah, get on with it. Finding a large bowl that held fresh water, I rinsed my hands, drying them on a towel I discovered was looped through my belt; I was prepared it seemed. Turning back to the sickest of the three, I felt his head with the back of my hand, he was burning up. I carefully peeled back the sheet and saw that his tunic was stained with blood and a yellowish substance I assumed was from an infection.

Holding his head in my hands, I looked him straight in the eye —

"This will hurt." I said, not knowing what language he spoke, he seemed to get my gist and nodded slightly, gritting his teeth.

Gently, oh so gently, I lifted his tunic, thankful to note that his lower half was covered with another sheet. His worst injury was confined to his abdomen; a gaping wound which might well have been inflicted by something like an axe. It was oozing blood and pus and he must have been in absolute agony. He had other wounds but they seemed less devastating and some looked as though they might be healing.

"Oh God." I whispered. "Help me help him." Not one for praying, I needed all the help I could get and it felt like the most natural thing to do; he looked too young to be getting injured in battle. Reaching into the basket I ripped up one of the sheets, soaking pieces in a bowl of water to which I'd added some salt, and dabbing carefully at the wound, washed out as much of the blood and pus as I dared. I didn't want to start it bleeding again, but the infection went deep and I knew it had to be cleaned properly. Moving to the shelf with all the jars, I removed the stopper from one of them — opium — it would dull the pain. How did I know it was in that jar? How did I know what opium smelled like? Was it even called opium? Dredging through my history, I recalled that it was called poppy tears, or poppy juice.

I mixed a small measure with some wine, poured from a flagon on the floor, into one of the little bowls. Going back to the man, I sat on the edge of the cot, lifted his head ever so slightly and held the bowl while he drank. He was familiar with my actions; I had done this before. Grunting with pain, he lay back on the lump of straw, covered with yet another sheet that was acting as a pillow and slowly, very slowly, the pained expression started to relax. His face began to lose some of the waxiness I had noticed when I entered the room and his breathing steadied.

Going back to his wound I worked on it for a while longer, making sure that it was as clean as it could be. The edges were neat and not jagged; either from whatever inflicted the wound, or someone — had it been me? — cutting it smooth. Without questioning my actions, I concocted another brew of herbs and oils, this time one that smelt rather pungent and, vaguely recalling that frankincense and myrrh were used widely for healing, I contemplated, briefly, whether this was what I was mixing up. The result was a sort of salve that I pressed into and around the wound, leaving the swatch of cloth with the remaining salve covering the gash. Ripping up yet another sheet, I would need more, where would I find them? I fashioned a long bandage, wrapping it round his body holding the swatch in place over his injury.

It must have been excruciating for him, but he barely made a sound, hopefully the opiate had taken the edge off his agony. Checking his other wounds, cleaning them all, then re-dressing any that needed it, noticing that one or two appeared to have been stitched up. Had I done that too? Finally and with infinite care, I changed all the sheets on his cot, piling the dirty ones into a basket at the doorway, which seemed suited to the purpose. Filling a larger bowl with fresh water, I washed his face and hands, removing any dust and sweat, cooling his skin. Not sure that I was doing anything other than making him comfortable while he waited for the inexorable call of death, my gentle movements lulled him off to sleep.

The room was so quiet, the other two men simply watched me work and I realised I was in a rhythm; I knew what I was doing. Whoever I was in this time, I was practised at healing. So I decided not to over think it, follow my instinct and continue what I had started. I turned to the other two, their injuries, while pretty gruesome were nothing like as bad as their comrade's. More deep lacerations than critical wounds, but they still needed to be bathed and dressed. I repeated my actions with the wine and opium, the second man lay quietly, while I cleaned his injuries and washed his face, many of his less serious wounds were almost healed. How long had I been looking after them? When I had finished he was covered in little bandages but he seemed relaxed, the fresh bedding was cool and dry and he nodded off to sleep. By the time I was ready to treat the third soldier, I was hot and dusty and my clothes reeked of blood.

"One minute." I whispered to him and leaving the room, ran further down the corridor into the next room along, suddenly registering that this was the room where I had sat down in my dream and that it was as spacious and cool as the one next door. The walls were painted and a large rug warmed the tiles. A small oil lamp burned, shedding soft light across the space. There was a bedroll in one corner and on a wooden cupboard, next to a bowl and a flask, lay a pile of neatly folded material that looked like clothes. Somehow I knew this was my sleeping quarters and, grabbing whatever garment was on the top of the pile, I changed more quickly than I thought possible, given that I had no clue how to dress myself in this fashion and then hurried back.

"Sorry." I muttered. "You have enough problems, you don't need your wounds to get more infected by me dressing them wearing dirty garments." Starting to pour out some of the pain numbing draft, I was startled when he put his hand on my arm and I looked at him, properly, for the first time since I'd entered the room.

"Max." I gasped, yet it wasn't Max, but so much like him they could have been brothers. This man was harder, rougher, his hair longer and unkempt from being sick and in captivity. His skin, although very pale, was swarthy, but his eyes, his eyes were that same deep green and right now they held my gaze.

"You finally use my name?" He questioned quietly. I realised that I understood his question. How was that possible? Surely I must have been speaking in Hebrew and if this were a Roman soldier he would likely have been speaking Greek or Latin. Yet we seemed able to make sense of the other's words. Pulling my arm out from under his grasp, I stared at him.

"Your name is Max?" Embarrassed, it seemed I should know this. I offered him the draft.

"Not Max really, Lucius Maxentius is my name, but that seems awkward for you; Maxentius is acceptable and I do not need this drink, my pain is not as bad as it was. Save it for them." Nodding at his comrades. His words were careful, stilted almost, as though searching for the right phrasing.

Not really knowing what else to say at this point, I busied myself mixing the saline solution and started to bathe his wounds. Like the second man he appeared less severely injured and luckily none of his wounds seemed to be infected, but massive bruising darkened his chest and back, which was a grave concern. Some of his wounds had begun healing and, again I mused over how long they had been in my care.

"You are lucky." I told him, "You will heal."

"How lucky? They will still kill me."

"Not if I can help it, I do not spend my days treating these wounds to have them kill you. Maybe they will use you to send a message to the Romans in Jerusalem, maybe they will allow you to go free." Not certain how much of this he understood, or how much I believed, I simply continued to clean and wrap his wounds and, as he was able to, got him to stand up, helping him over to the wall on which he leaned while I changed the sheets. Finished, I was about to help him back to bed when he motioned to the door.

"You want some fresh air?" Nodding, he slowly made his way out through the opening, stopping occasionally to catch his breath. I took his arm and although people were passing by, no one seemed to mind that I was helping this burly soldier, an enemy of our people, out onto the plateau. Well what could he do? One strong wind would blow him over, he was no threat and maybe we had done this before, maybe it was an everyday habit.

"Over there." He motioned to the pomegranate tree.

"You want to walk all the way over there?" It looked too far for the injured man to walk, as he seemed pitifully weak.

"Yes, the shade is…" again searching "…pleasant." We walked very slowly over to the shade of the tree and I spotted an upturned urn. Had I put it there? Helping him to sit I made sure he could lean against the trunk.

"Are you comfortable?" He looked at me unsure of my words. "This…" pointing at him and the tree, "…this is good?"

"Yes, this is good." He smiled at me, the same slow smile Max has and I felt at ease with this man, whom I should hate for what his country was doing to my country, but he was just one man and he did not appear to be a danger to me. We sat for a while in companionable silence, enjoying the air and the sounds of everyday life. As we sat, I realised that these actions were routine to me; I had been doing this for many days, maybe even weeks. I knew these men and their injuries, I knew a little about their lives and I knew, without a doubt that one of them would not survive. I also knew that this man and I must have conversed before, it seemed as though this had become a habit. I would help him out into the fresh air and we would talk.

"Thank you, Hannah," he said quietly. "Thank you for your care and your patience, you are a gifted healer. But how is it that you, a woman, are allowed to do this? This is a man's calling."

"I used to watch my uncle, he was a great physician and I asked him to teach me his skills. He was a kind man and thought he was humouring me, but I learned quickly and soon wanted more than he could teach me. He knew it should not be, but I was good at persuading him. I used to dress like a boy and help in his rooms when he operated on sick people. I learned that fresh air is better than closed rooms; that everything needs to be clean and never to touch a wound unless you have washed your hands. Then we fled the city, my brother said we needed to come here, that there were others also making their way to this outpost because they wanted your weapons. Even though I did not want to get caught up in a war, I didn't have much choice, Aharon refused to leave me to fend for myself back in Jerusalem. Then as I am the only one with the skills to treat wounds and sickness, I became their healer. It gives me a little status and I am allowed more freedom than many women. That's how…" I dried up, uncertain how much of my explanation he could comprehend.

"I understand, Hannah and I am grateful to you. Do you know why they decided to let us live when they found us in that room?"

"That was me." Blushing a little. "You were all so ill, it was three days before we found you and how you all, especially your gravely ill comrade, survived that long I do not know. After the ambush, the rest of your men were dead or had escaped and you three were the only Romans left. I asked Aharon whether I could try and heal you, I could not let them kill you too, it was not acceptable after so many days. It could not be called a battle death it would be murder. This I could not condone. They let you live, although…" hesitating, but needing to share my fears, "…I am afraid your comrade is seriously ill and may not survive. He needs better medicine than I can offer."

I spoke slowly and deliberately, hoping that he grasped what I meant. Looking around to make sure no one was close, he rested his hand on mine in a tentative gesture —

"You could not have done more. If he dies, it will be with honour and he will be among friends."

I knew I should pull my hand away, but I didn't want to. In this place, I was a Jewish girl talking to a Roman soldier, he could be killed for even so slight a physical contact and I should know better than to touch the skin of an enemy, but I liked the feel of his hand and I was still unsure how long I had been treating him — maybe he had done this before. Yet I knew that it couldn't be real, I was from another world, centuries after this time. I was sitting with my back against a rock drinking a cup of coffee.

"Your comrades, Marcus and Sergius is it not?" My tongue struggling a little over the unusual sounds. "How long have you known them?"

"We did not know each other until we were posted here, but we became strong friends. They have been loyal and hardworking, not shirkers like some of the scoundrels I have had charge of. I expect that many fled the rock, leaving their comrades to die, but their cowardice will find them and, what need do I have of them now? Marcus and I have been on this outpost for several years, Sergius joined us quite recently, and quickly became a trusted friend. He is still very young, maybe his youth and strength will work in his favour." He paused and took a breath, before continuing —

"We were to return to Rome as the year closes. I never thought this would…that this could…happen, that we would lose this fortress, it was thought to be unassailable and we should have been safe. Sergius saved my life, several men were attacking me and I was losing ground — he took them all down. I know he killed some of them, but before we could get the upper hand he was badly injured. Marcus and I dragged him away, ending up in the room where you found us." Half smiling. "I still don't know how they got up here without us seeing them."

"They are a desperate people, Sir and desperate people will go to any lengths to get back what they feel is theirs. Also, they knew you had weapons, they need those weapons for the fight they are sure will come."

"Still 'Sir'? When will you call me Maxentius," I looked at him. "You already call the others by their names why not me?" Feeling that this informality was overstepping the boundaries of propriety, I hesitated.

"You are their commanding officer. It is improper that I address you so casually."

"Please, Hannah; I would be honoured if you could and, you called me 'Max' earlier, I haven't been called that since I was a child." Looking back at him, I felt my qualms melt away.

196

"I will do as you ask." Still formal, yet we seemed to be almost comfortable, him sitting on an upturned jar and me leaning against the trunk of the pomegranate tree, shaded from the sun, which was beginning its downward journey. I had spent longer dealing with the three men than I realised and the day was waning. Presumably, there were other tasks to which I should be attending.

"Will you be comfortable here for a little while, or do you wish to return to your room?"

"I am fine, the air is refreshing. Where are you going?"

"I must put those sheets that can be cleaned into water to soak away the dirt and sickness and burn the rest. The wrappings I removed will also need to be washed, or I will have none to dress the wounds tomorrow. I will only be a moment." As I walked away I was sure I heard him whisper,

"Hurry back, my Hannah."

Odd, it made me feel warm inside, a warmth I was unfamiliar with. Confusion was running through my head, how could this be? Not wanting to deal with it, I hurried back to the sick room, where the other two men were sleeping almost peacefully. Sergius' face was red, and touching him gently, I realised his fever was spiking again; his skin was dry and hot. Quickly soaking a rag in cool water I laid it across his forehead, leaving it for a moment while I gathered the other sheets and bandages together and without knowing how I knew, took them across a courtyard to a room at the opposite side.

It looked like a laundry, there were large stone sinks, massive jars full of water and a huge wooden cupboard, which when I opened the doors found to be full of sheets, blankets, cloths and towels. A large fire crackled away in one of the biggest fireplaces I've ever seen and stacked along the walls were wooden racks on which I could drape things, it was well set up. Trying to orientate myself, I realised that I was in the administrative building at the top of the Northern Palace. Vast storerooms ran off to my left and somewhere among all the other rooms surrounding this courtyard, there would be a kitchen.

Filling one of the stone sinks with water I shoved everything in it. Did we have anything like soap, or something to sterilise the material. I needed it to be clean and then I remembered smelling something lemony in one of the jars in the sick room. Dashing back, I found what I was looking for and opening other jars I found a liquid that appeared to be vinegar. Pouring them together into a smaller flask, I went back across the courtyard and tipped the whole lot into the sink containing the sheets and pounded the water till it was all mixed in, crossing my fingers that it would do the trick.

I recalled from the depth of my brain that something called *quali* was used like soap. A grey mix created by burning vegetable matter and adding water until it formed lumps but, as I had absolutely no idea how to do that, my option would have to do. I would leave it overnight and let them soak. Tomorrow I would work out how to hang them outside to let the sun's heat kill any bacteria lurking in the material. If not, these drying racks would do the trick.

Satisfied that I had done all I could with the sheets and bandages, I went back to the sick room and changed the cloth on Sergius' head, he was burning up and I needed to stay with him. Brewing up another batch of opium and wine, I let it sit, while I went back outside to find Maxentius. He was standing now, his hand against the tree, it was at high point on the plateau and from here you could just see over the casemate wall across the desert towards the Dead Sea.

"It's a beautiful view isn't it?" I came up behind him, startling him out of his reverie. "Desolate but very beautiful." He turned.

"Yes, very beautiful." I had the strangest notion that he wasn't talking about the view.

"I must get you back. Sergius' fever is rising and I need to sit with him to keep him cool." Letting Maxentius lean on me, we slowly made our way back to his room. "I don't think you should sleep here." I worried. "You could become more sick. You are healing well and infection can be spread though the breath." Suiting my words to actions, I lifted his pallet, which was quite light and, carried it down the hall to my quarters, setting it near enough to the door for him to hear me call, but away from prying eyes. Picking up my bedroll, I went back along the hall.

"You can sleep in my room, I need to be in here. I will not move Marcus as he sleeps soundly, it will be worse if I rouse him, but my room is quiet and you can rest undisturbed."

"Hannah, I cannot expect you to leave your room. I will watch Sergius and call you should he get worse."

"Too late. I've moved your bed and how would you know what to give him? Go, I will come if he asks for you." I helped him along to my room, he was very tired now, the exertion was telling and he needed to sleep. Settling him onto his cot, I covered him with a fresh clean sheet and found a blanket in case he felt cold. Then, returning to the sick room, I mixed a draft of refreshing lemon, honey and water, with a drop or two of opium, he was going to have a proper sleep even if I had to trick him into it.

Back in my room, he was already drowsy.

"Drink this, it is cool and sweet and there is honey which is good for healing." He drank deeply and settled back. As I moved to the door he caught my fingers.

"You will get me won't you?"

"If there is time or need, I will get you."

'Thank you, my Hannah." Eyes drooping I watched as the opium worked its magic and sleep took him.

Chapter Twenty Six

In the sick room Sergius was not doing so well. He was muttering in his unconscious state, his skin was still burning up, but was becoming clammy as the fever took a tighter grip. I let my instinct take over again and ground more herbs together with diluted wine to see whether I could get him to drink it down. Tenderly lifting his head, I crooned a lullaby as I tried to get the liquid through his parched lips. I was losing him, but I wasn't going to let him go without a fight. I managed to get most of the mixture down his throat and he began to settle, his temperature dropping a little. Finding another sheet I soaked the whole thing in water, removed the dry sheet covering him and, wringing out most of the water, draped the cold wet sheet across the whole of his body.

I needed ice and knew there was no way that was available. Looking around I deliberated whether I could use small stones or pebbles dipped in cold water and would they stay cool long enough to have some effect? Without stopping to think, I ran outside, looking around for anything that might prove suitable. To my left lay a few small rocks. Was that enough? I could only hope and gathered them into my arms, using my mantle as a kind of sling as they were heavier than I anticipated — they might work.

Back in the room, I found a large bowl and placed the rocks into it, covering them with plenty of water, which was cold enough for me to think it must have been freshly drawn from the cisterns. Someone must be helping me — I had seen no one else enter this room, but all the water jars had been filled and the oil lamp trimmed. Grateful to whoever it was, I continued with what I was doing, making sure the rocks were clean and then emptying the dirty water out, I rinsed the bowl and refilled it with clean water, putting the rocks back in, realising that they were cooler — much cooler — to my touch.

Glancing at Sergius, I saw that his teeth were beginning to chatter; now he was cold. Whipping the wet sheet off, I dragged a blanket from the shelf, wrapping him in it and making sure his hands and feet were tucked underneath its warmth. Then, I wiped his face with a clean damp cloth, brushing his lank hair out of his eyes. I had done all I could for now. Checking that the stones were indeed cooling, I stepped back outside for just a moment.

Drinking in the fresh air, I stood looking across the top of the mighty rock thinking of all that had gone before and all that would come. This place should stand for ever, Herod's great citadel, for surely nothing could destroy it, surprised that I knew it actually would be and in the not too distant future. My present and future self struggled with this knowledge, as I watched the sun sink slowly towards the horizon. Too soon it would be gone and night would cover the land, hiding the tragedies I knew would come.

Walking back to where they lay, I checked my two patients. Marcus was resting quite comfortably and although his colour was higher than I would have liked, his skin was cool and his chest rose and fell steadily. He would heal this soldier, his spirit was robust and he would be able to fight any infection that might lurk deep within his body. I touched his wrist checking his pulse; it was strong and rhythmic, what I would give for my watch so I could be certain. I stood still and counted, guessing that his heart rate was within an acceptable range.

His comrade on the other hand was hot again, this fever was going through him too quickly, it would reach crisis this night. Did I wake Maxentius, so that he could sit with his friend or let him sleep? Lifting the rocks out of the water, I laid them along Sergius' body, making sure they touched his skin. I removed the blanket and let the night air waft over him, a small opening high in the wall, reminiscent of the slit windows in medieval castles, allowed enough air to enter the room without cooling it too much. I had no idea whether it was part of the original building or was made later, after the Roman garrison took over and right then I didn't care, it was a very welcome draft and helped to cool both my patient and me.

In the throes of delirium, Sergius was wracked with seizures that caused his wound to bleed again. I felt overwhelmed; whatever I did I wasn't able to help him. Had I been a fool to try to save him in the first place? Should I have let Aharon and the others kill him when they were first found? Would that have been the kindest thing to do? Had I just prolonged his agony for him to die anyway? Defeated, I slumped to the floor, feeling useless tears run down my cheeks. This is not helping, Hannah, I thought, pulling myself together and scrubbing my face on my sleeve. I wiped Sergius' face with a fresh cloth, dropping the warm ones back into the bowl of cool water.

Checking his body where the stones rested, I felt that he was cooling down again, his bout of delirium passed and his breathing settled. His skin seemed to regulate, not too hot, not too cold, but I knew it would not stay this way for long. Taking this opportunity to measure out another draught of the poppy juice, I decided also to try to rub some honey onto Sergius' poor sore lips hoping it might soothe them. Gently, I smoothed a small drop onto each lip, making sure it covered the chapped edges. Carefully unwrapping his bandages, I lifted the swatch of material coated with the salve and noticed that the infection was oozing again.

Tearing a small piece off the bandages I had just removed, making sure I used the clean end, I dipped the piece into the remaining salve and while that soaked in, I tore up the rest of the bandage to clean the wound again. Managing to wipe away excess blood and pus without disturbing Sergius, I placed the newly soaked swatch over the injury and tore another sheet up to bandage it in place. I would have to go and get more sheets; I was going through this pile like there was no tomorrow.

Job done for now, I sat on the floor, my back against the wall, just watching for any changes. Marcus slept peacefully on, blissfully unaware and I thanked God for it. I must have slept too for a short while, exhaustion creeping up on me. When I awoke it was completely dark outside and I had no idea of the time. Confused at my surroundings, I stayed where I was, struggling to get my bearings. Then it flooded back, I was not in my bed in the digs. I was in a sick room, hoping a stranger in my care didn't die.

After a few minutes I walked quietly to the other room to check on Maxentius. He was still fast asleep, looking so vulnerable in repose that I had to curb an unexpected desire to kiss his forehead and smooth my hand over his cheek. It was not acceptable behaviour in this time. I was not a twenty first century woman with freedom of choice and expression — here ancient laws and rules prevailed. Sighing, I went back along the corridor, but before re-entering the sick room, ran quickly over to the laundry and, intuitively searching the large store cupboard, found a stack of fresh bandages. Collecting them and another pile of sheets, I hauled them back across the courtyard. It was dark, but the moon had risen, giving enough light so that I didn't trip.

In the few minutes I had been gone, someone had placed a bowl of food and bread in the room, with a flagon of diluted wine. I hadn't even realised I was hungry until I saw it and devoured the whole lot gratefully. Sipping straight from the flagon, too tired to find a more suitable drinking cup, I thought about the day. This day that had started with the joy of knowing Max loved me and finished with me trying to keep a dying man alive. As I sat, I realised that although my day did sound completely preposterous, and nobody, in either era, would ever believe me, I wasn't totally freaked out. I was beginning to take this in my stride, but just as I accepted it, I was chilled by the thought that I might never see my Max again. How was I here? How was I able to think in two time periods, yet not be able to see any of my friends?

A bubble of panic started to build but just as I was about to have a full-blown anxiety attack, Sergius moaned, breaking through the hysteria threatening to swamp me. Getting up, I moved to his bedside, watching his features contort in pain and the inevitable seizures start shuddering through his skeletal frame. The crisis was close and I knew I needed to let Maxentius decide whether or not he wanted to be with Sergius, but I also preferred that he sleep as long as possible.

The fever intensified, throwing Sergius back into delirium; convulsions wracked his body and I knew I just had to let it run its course. It was severe and I was helpless. Giving up, I went to wake Maxentius. Shaking him gently, he came awake immediately; despite the sleeping draft I'd given him less than three hours earlier. He grabbed my hand and started to rise.

"Shhhhhh, it's just me. Sergius needs you, he is very sick. The crisis is on him."

He used the blanket as a wrap and was in the other room more quickly than his wounds should have allowed. I followed, waiting at the door to give them a little space. Sergius was unaware of Maxentius' presence; he was probably unaware of anything, descending deeper into unconsciousness, his body desperately fighting for survival and infection winning the battle. He tossed and muttered, spasms running through him like a freight train and his skin was on fire.

I was really scared. I had never seen anyone die and this man was in my care. I couldn't stand back and do nothing. Using another wet cloth, I cooled Sergius' forehead again, handing Maxentius a couple more cloths asking him to do the same to his friend's hands. I lifted the sheet soaking in the bowl and without waiting to wring it out, laid it over the soldier's body, water dripping all over the floor. Maxentius held Sergius' hand, talking to him all the while — talking to him about garrison life on Masada, recalling conversations they had shared about places each had seen and battles each had fought.

Sitting by my patient's head, I smoothed his hair crooning the same lullaby I had sung to him earlier, trying to reach something inside him that could hear and respond. Maxentius studied me while he was talking, listening to my voice calling to his friend. The crisis was taking Sergius and all we could do was watch. I felt utterly powerless and the expression on the face of the man sitting alongside threatened to undo me completely. I needed to be strong for him, as a feeling of foreboding was creeping up on me. I knew Sergius would die tonight, the fever was too strong and the subtle changes, indicating that I was losing him, were beginning to manifest.

I studied his features for what felt like a very long time, singing quietly and hoping against hope that I was mistaken. Eventually, breaking off my lullaby, I looked across the bed.

"Maxentius," I whispered, "I cannot save him. He is slipping away. I think you need to let him go."

"No." Voice cracking. "I can't, he saved my life."

"You have to tell him its time to leave; that he protected you and that you and Marcus are safe. I think he's fighting it because he fears for you."

"He's my friend." Helplessly.

"Yes, I know and I hate this too, but I can't save him, I can't save him." Sobbing uncontrollably now. "You have to let him go."

Maxentius looked at me reading in my face what he didn't want to believe. Turning back to Sergius, he spoke in undertones telling his friend how the battle was over, that they were all safe and that he could let go. His voice was breaking, but he fought to keep it steady and strong. He talked and talked, it seemed to me that he talked for hours and all the while I stroked his friend's face, soothing his fiery skin with my cool hands.

I removed the bandages that were restricting his movement and let the air touch his broken skin. What did it matter now? Dropping the pieces onto the floor next to me, I told myself I would deal with them later, my patient was more important than some bloodied bits of cloth. After what, to my weary mind, felt like an age, Sergius began to calm down, his seizures slowed and he stopped muttering. Slowly, oh so slowly but surely, his body stilled and cooled and all became quiet. Controlling my features, I moved down the side of the bed and held Sergius' wrist. His heart rate was dropping and I knew he was leaving us. I nodded to Maxentius,

"Time to say goodbye." His expression broke my heart.

"Goodbye Sergius. Honoured comrade and faithful friend, you will be missed."

The beat against my fingers faltered, slowed and stopped. It was very peaceful at the end; Sergius slipped quietly away. I checked his heart just to be absolutely certain, but he was gone. No longer wracked with pain, he had gone to whichever heaven he believed in. Unable to vent my distress and anger, I balled up the bandages lying next to me on the floor and, uncaring that I was getting blood and puss on my hands, pummelled the cloth, twisting the pieces together trying to rip them into shreds. They stubbornly refused to tear and in my frustration I hurled the lump towards the cabinet, hearing a light thud as they landed against the wooden frame and rolled underneath. It didn't help.

Maxentius' head drooped; his devastation was palpable and I couldn't bear to witness it. Touching his shoulder, I started to walk out of the room leaving him to his grief. Grasping my hand, he stopped me and slowly stood up. Turning me to face him, he started to speak, gave up and kissed me hard on the mouth — my heart missed a beat. Okay, well that was a completely unexpected and rather interesting response to grief — my own body responding in a way I could never have anticipated. Without thinking, I leaned into him, kissing him back and then pulling free, ran out of the room, along the corridor, out into the fresh air. The night sky was besprinkled with millions of stars and at any other time I would have been awed by their exquisite radiance, but not this night. This night all I could see was Maxentius as he watched his friend depart this world.

Unable to stop myself, I let out a primal scream —
"Nooooooooooooooooooooooo." Bending over and keening, the stress of the last few hours took their toll as, exhausted, I dropped to the floor. The world started to spin and as though from a great distance I saw Maxentius come out onto the plateau. He reached out his hand and just before the darkness claimed me, I heard his voice, calling my name,

"Hannah, Hannah, Hannah!"

Hannah's Journey

Hannah's journey both starts and continues in The Pomegranate Tree.

An intricate ruby clasp connects two women across millennia and as their souls collide, so their lives entwine.

In AD 66 Hannah, a young Hebrew physician discovers and begins to treat, three badly wounded soldiers following the Zealot ambush of Herod's fortress at Masada.

Two millennia in the future, another young woman — drawn to Masada in an attempt to trace the origins of a ruby clasp, and also called Hannah — is assisting on an archaeological dig at the same site. Haunted by visions of the ambush, she struggles to understand what is happening to her until, following an accident, she finds herself caring for the three soldiers. Not knowing whether she will ever return to the modern world and the man who loves her, Hannah realises that she is witnessing life on Masada, through the eyes of her ancestor — the young Hebrew physician.

Uncertain that she will ever return to her own world, Hannah somehow finds the strength within herself to adapt to life in the ancient world, and aware of what will happen at this desert fortress, must find a way to save those she loves without changing history. She knows that, eventually, an avenging Roman army, determined to quash every vestige of dissent, will lay siege to the citadel and that all, save a very few, will die by their own hand before the Romans breach the defences.

This is just the first in a multitude of challenges faced by Hannah and Maxentius — the Roman soldier with whom she falls in love — as their lives unfold. Challenges that take them from Masada to Pompeii — a vibrant port city in the bay of Naples, arriving not long before devastating eruption of Vesuvius, and then onto a fort along the harsh northern frontier of Roman Britain — a land conquered but not yet pacified.

A tale that spans two thousand years and connects the lives of two women and the two men who love them. Lives that become inextricably, bound across time.

The Pomegranate Tree
Hannah's Heirloom ~ Book One

After receiving an ancient ruby clasp from her long dead grandmother, Hannah Wilson decides to visit Masada, supposedly the place where this gift was given to one of her ancestors. Travelling with her is Max Vallier, her best friend, who was already going to Herod's fortress in the desert, as part of an archaeological excavation team.

Once there, Hannah is disturbed by strange visions. Visions, which seem to revolve around the AD66 attack by Zealot rebels, on the Roman garrison based at the fortress.

As her two worlds begin to entwine, Hannah realises that she is experiencing the events of the past as they unfold, events that so far she has only dreamed about. Pulled into the ancient world, she tends to three Roman soldiers who survived the attack, but who are now captives. Back in the modern world, she finds artefacts that tie her to her ancient counterpart. Meanwhile, her relationship with Max takes an interesting turn, but just as they admit their feelings for each other, a tragic accident tears them apart.

Fate intervenes and Hannah slips into the world of Ancient Masada. There, away from all modern trappings, she must rely on her wits and instincts to deal with the demands of her alternate life. A life in which she, an unmarried Hebrew woman, is a healer — a trained physician, fighting to keep alive the men under her care. This life becomes more complicated as she realises she is falling in love with one of the Roman soldiers, a love that could have deadly consequences.

Unsure whether she will ever be able to return to the modern world, Hannah accepts her destiny, rising to the challenges of life on an isolated fortress and, believing that she has a chance to save those she loves by using the knowledge she has brought with her from two thousand years in the future. The knowledge that, eventually, Jerusalem will fall and, that those escaping the city will make their way to this outpost, followed by an avenging Roman army intent on destruction.

Will Hannah escape? Will she ever see Max again, or is she doomed to die along with hundreds of others as Masada falls - and what does any of this have to do with an ancient ruby clasp?

Echoes of Stone and Fire
Hannah's Heirloom ~ Book Two

Pompeii was once a bustling port nestling under a forbidding mountain. Then in AD79, the mountain erupted, smothering the town under a thick blanket of ash and volcanic debris, leaving it lost for centuries. Now, rediscovered and a world-renowned heritage site, archaeologists from across the globe yearn for an opportunity to uncover the town's past. Some things though, are best left alone - revealing the secrets hidden beneath the stones could prove perilous.

Eighteen months have passed since Hannah and Max left Masada, Herod's isolated fortress in the Judaean desert. The place where just as they admitted their feelings for each other, they were wrenched apart. Hannah slipped into an ancient world, discovering how her ancestor had received the ruby clasp - her talisman. Somehow she survived the ensuing tragedy and Max's love was strong enough to bring her home. Since then, Hannah has had no awareness of her ancient counterpart and wonders whether the slender thread that united them had been broken, lost beyond time, leaving only a memory.

On a spur of the moment trip to Rome, familiar dreams recur. Unable to recognise where her ancestor is, but realising that she is not on Masada, Hannah struggles to understand the reason behind her visions. Then, a chance meeting with two friends sees Hannah and Max invited to join an excavation team, one whose goal is to determine what lies beneath the ruins of Pompeii. Although excited to be a part of such an investigation, Hannah experiences a growing sense of unease, an unnamed fear circling at the edges of her consciousness.

Her worlds begin to converge and Hannah realises to her horror, that her fear, this reconnection of minds, must be related to Vesuvius and that the woman she is bound to was actually in Pompeii before the eruption. Hoping she can somehow warn her ancestor without being drawn back into her other life, Hannah tries to convey her knowledge through her dreams.

As before however, fate intervenes. After entering a house, which bears a Hebrew inscription, Hannah falls back through time. Although familiar with this fusion of souls, she still has to rely on her instincts to adjust to life in ancient Pompeii. A world where her ancestor is a physician to gladiators engaged in mortal combat, where riotous mobs run amok and where a ghost from the past returns to haunt her. All the while knowing she needs to save her family from the devastation that will befall this town.

Will Hannah escape the cataclysmic eruption? Can she persuade her loved ones to flee before burning debris engulfs the town? Will she ever find her way back to Max the love of her life waiting, not so patiently, millennia away? Or will echoes be all that remain?

Embers of Destiny
Hannah's Heirloom ~ Book Three

AD80 ~ It is a year since Hannah and Maxentius escaped from the cataclysmic eruption of Mt Vesuvius and, after a pleasant interlude in Rome, they must now embark on a new journey. This time to the troubled frontier of Northern Britannia, recently subjugated, yet maybe not quite pacified.

This harsh borderland is a far cry from the luxuries and relative security of Rome, and danger lurks where least expected. A garrison of soldiers, some rather disgruntled with their isolated posting and it's new commander; local tribes people, although outwardly accepting of their erstwhile enemy, may still harbour a burning resentment that their lands have been occupied.

Meanwhile, in the modern world and now married to Max, Hannah Vallier is working in the archives department of a museum on Hadrian's Wall; cataloguing artefacts from some of the original wooden forts, recently discovered following a series of aerial surveys. While most of the finds are mundane, Hannah is shocked when she comes across an all too familiar item. It is her, or rather her ancestor's pomegranate; the one carved by Maxentius in the aftermath of the massacre at Masada, carried from there to Pompeii and then on to Rome.

Confused as to how it could be here in Northumberland, Hannah searches a new database for answers, finding a fragmented inscription indicating that Maxentius and Hannah had indeed been posted to Northern Britannia; that Maxentius had been commander of a garrison, the fort for which, coincidentally, had been almost exactly where she was now sitting. Realising what this might mean, Hannah needs to talk to Max, who is away on business.

Before they get the chance, disaster strikes! Believing the love of her life to have been killed and unable to deal with her grief, Hannah retreats into the past, re-connecting with her ancient family. Unfortunately, scant historical evidence for this period means that Hannah is unaware of what might be looming, instead she must trust that any information she holds will be enough to save them once again.

Adjusting to a world on the frontier of Empire, Hannah meets the local wise woman and, as they share their love and knowledge of healing, a tentative friendship blossoms. The burgeoning cordiality between the garrison and the locals is jeopardised however, as a multitude of challenges conspire to undermine the fragile peace. Hannah realises that the threat might come from a most unexpected quarter, for there is one within the fort whose enmity will have dire consequences.

At the same time, Hannah's heart whispers that maybe, just maybe Max is still alive and that he is calling her home.

Will Maxentius be able to preserve the hard won trust of the locals, or will everything descend into madness? Is there any hope of discovering who is inciting such hostility before it's too late? Can Hannah learn to trust her heart, or will she remain forever caught out of time, her destiny floating away like embers on a breeze.

www.ingramcontent.com/pod-product-compliance
Lightning Source LLC
Chambersburg PA
CBHW051503170626
46811CB00002B/628